WHEN THINGS WERE

WERE

BLACK AND

WHITE

A Story from Detroit

Dan David

Thanks to the many pre-publication readers
who contributed provided invaluable
feedback as the book was being
written and revised.

CHAPTER 1

To hear it now, the Detroiters of 1963 spent their days building cars and their nights swingin' to Motown Music, but at that time I was only five, and I was a pretty uninformed five-year-old at that. I hadn't heard of Barry Gordy or Stevie Wonder or Smokey Robinson. And, long before I became aware of its existence, Hitsville went splitsville and left the Motor City for Los Angeles.

I was equally uninformed about Detroit being the automobile manufacturing capital of the world. I didn't know where cars came from and I didn't particularly care to know. I never thought about where light bulbs came from either, or shoelaces, or Purina dog chow. Nobody I knew ever talked about building cars or working for a car company. The guy next door to us worked for the gas company, the neighbor behind us was a furrier, and my dad was a policeman.

Sometimes I think people from other states must think that Detroiters spent those days sitting around the campfire singing songs about how Henry Ford invented the Model T, but the only relationship our family had with the automobile was that we owned one, a 1956 black and white Chevy Bel Air, which we never thought of as a "classic car of the future," but just as something my dad settled for because it was all he could afford.

One sad Saturday in August of 1963 my father told my brother and me to get into the car because we were going to the supermarket. My brother gave me an angry look, as if it was somehow my fault, but he hated going to the supermarket because he was three years older and actually had to go into the store, while I was allowed to remain in the car with my father because I was only five and slowed my mother down.

My father generally took a hands-off approach to child rearing, and not knowing what else to do just went about his usual business as if I wasn't there. As soon as he dropped my mother and brother off at the front door of Wrigley's supermarket I'd move to the front seat, where my mother never let me sit because she was sure I'd crash through the windshield, and then we'd ride off to Ray's Hardware or Chick's party store, just a couple of guys riding in the front seat of the car, come what may.

That was until the wretched day when, on the way to the store, my mother unexpectedly announced that I was too old to stay in the car. I don't know what brought this about, but I've always suspected that she felt I was having too much fun. My mother was against fun in general, but ever so much more so if it happened to occur while she was doing a chore that she hated.

When we got to the store I tried to move to the front seat, hoping that my mother was so preoccupied with her shopping list that she wouldn't realize what had happened until after Dad and I drove off, but as soon as I turned back toward the car she grabbed my wrist and yanked me toward the store.

I looked to my dad for help, but he just shrugged his shoulders.

"Meet me back here at four o'clock," he called to my mom.

I wondered how my mom would know when four o' clock came around since she wasn't wearing a watch, but I figured it was one of those things I'd understand when I was older.

I should have stumbled along and grabbed at every item I could reach so she'd regret bringing me into the store in the first place, but I wasn't that clever. Luckily I have a short attention span, which resulted in a lesser-but-almost-as-effective degree of stumbling and grabbing, and by the time we reached the cereal aisle she had enough.

"I'm never going to finish on time. I need you boys to stay here."

"I promise we'll stay right here," my brother lied, and then he drew a cross on his heart. I was pretty sure anything involving a cross had something to do with God, and certainly my brother's insincere gesture must have offended Him, but even though my mother must have known my brother was lying she was willing to look past it because she was in a hurry and it was probably easier for her to lie to herself than to expect the truth from my brother.

There was a small display of toys in the cereal aisle, and I hoped the toys would hold my brother's interest until my mom got back so we wouldn't get in trouble, but his attention span wasn't any longer than mine and after a few minutes he was restless.

"Let's get out of here," he said.

"Where are we going?"

"To get some free cheese."

I panicked, a skill which I had mastered thanks to the outstanding example provided by my mom. And, though I was given to spells of unwarranted panic, in this case my fears were well-grounded. The dairy aisle was the domain of Elsie the Cow. I hadn't seen Elsie since the days when I was riding in the shopping cart, but it's not the kind of thing you forget.

Unlike the cartoon version of Elsie on the Borden's milk carton, the supermarket Elsie was a larger-

3

than-life rubber head that hung on the wall above the milk cooler. If she had just been hanging on the wall like a stuffed moose I'd have been okay, but her mouth had been motorized so it was constantly moving, as if chewing cud, except there was no cud and her mouth was empty. I took that to mean that she was hungry and looking for something to eat, most likely me.

This was not the sort of thing I could explain to my brother. In the first place, he wouldn't have been able to understand how I could be afraid of something as harmless as a disembodied-yet-somehow-still-animated cow head. I had a limited understanding of robotics, plus she looked pretty real, and so I assumed that it was an actual cow head. Once, while we were fishing, I had seen fish heads still gasping for water even after they had been cut off, and I was sure this must be the same thing.

"Mom said we should stay here," I protested, as if that were the real issue.

My brother grabbed me by the wrist and pulled. "Come on!"

"No!" I shouted.

He made a fist. His fist wasn't as disturbing as Elsie's mouth, but it had the advantage of proximity, and so I let him drag me along.

When we got there a crabby lady with cat-eye glasses was giving away little cubes of cheese. Elise was at least fifteen feet away, which seemed like a safe distance, but I kept an eye on her just in case she had unwholesome powers which I had not yet discovered.

The Cheese Lady held the plate of cheese out of our reach.

"One per customer. No seconds, and don't think you can fool me, because I've got a terrific memory for faces."

"Can we keep the toothpicks?" I asked.

"What do I want with them?" she said, and grudgingly held out the plate.

4

I thought to myself that, on the unholy day when Elsie's headless body burst into the store and reunited itself with its head, the Cheese Lady would be the first to be trampled.

My brother popped his cheese in his mouth and swallowed it without hardly chewing at all, but I bit mine in half to try and make it last.

"Pretty good cheese, isn't it?"

I didn't recognize the voice, and when I looked up I saw a guy, maybe fifty years old, who acted like he knew me. He was wearing work boots and a plaid shirt, and his hair was neatly parted and slicked back with Brylcreem, and even though it looked like his head was on its way to church, his body looked like it was ready to dig a ditch.

"Are you talking to me?" I asked.

"Yes I am, young man. Pretty good cheese, isn't it?"

"I guess so." I didn't know why, but I wanted to leave.

"Do you know where cheese comes from? It comes from cows."

"Cheese comes from cows?" I couldn't imagine how that could be possible, but he sounded confident.

"Well, it comes from milk, and that comes from cows. And the cows eat grass, don't they?" He smiled at me, but I didn't like the way he looked, like maybe he had too many teeth or something.

"I guess," I answered, trying not to say anything that would encourage him. I looked around for my brother, but he was gone. Maybe they were giving away little bits of sausage in another aisle.

"And do you know who makes the grass grow, and who makes the sun shine so the grass can grow?" he said, with a mysterious tone.

"God?" I answered.

"That's right. God makes the grass grow and He makes the sun shine. Do you know God?"

5

It seemed like a stupid question, because everybody knew about God, but I answered it just to get him off my back. "I know who He is."

"But do you know God? Do you know Jesus?"

I was trapped. I really couldn't say I knew Jesus, because then he might ask questions like, "What did Jesus have for dinner last night?" Then again, I didn't want to say that I did not know Jesus because I could tell the old guy was just itching to tell me all about Him.

I tried to wait him out, hoping that he would get bored and walk away or die of a heart attack or climb on a step ladder and stick his head in Elsie's mouth, but instead he leaned in close, like he was getting ready to share a big secret.

"I know Jesus. I talk to Him every day. And he talks to me."

"Say, Pal, can I help you with something?" another voice boomed.

I recognized that voice. It was my dad, and he looked mad. At first I thought I was in trouble for leaving the toy aisle, but he brushed past me and squared off against the old man.

"I was just telling the boy about the Lord."

"I'm the boy's father. If he needs to know about the Lord I'll take him to church."

The old guy sized up my dad. My dad was a strappin' six footer, but he was lanky and slump-shouldered and his clothes looked as if they were going to fall off his boney frame. The old guy was broad bodied, barrel-chested, and emboldened with the Word of God, and was not about to back down.

"Have you found Jesus?" he said to my father.

My dad cracked a smile. "I didn't know He was lost."

"Sir, I am trying to be serious."

My dad reached into his back pocket and took out his wallet, taking care to push his jacket back far enough to reveal the butt of his handgun, and then he slowly opened his wallet and showed his badge.

"Do we need to go Downtown?" my dad asked.

The old guy pulled up his shirt sleeve and started scratching his arm, real fast. The place where he was scratching was already red and raw, like he scratched there a lot. His smile was gone, and his flinty voice was now a whimper.

"Am I in trouble?

"Not if you can take things down a notch or two. Listen, fella, uh, what's your name?"

"Joseph Sawinsky."

"Yeah, Mr. Sawinsky--"

"You can call me Joe—"

"Yeah, Joe, you can't buttonhole little kids in the dairy aisle. Some people might take it the wrong way. Now why don't you finish your shopping and head on home, and it'll be like none of this ever happened."

Mr. Sawinksy shook my dad's hand, thanked him again, and left.

My dad looked at the toothpick hanging from my mouth, and, being a trained detective, realized that there must be free samples nearby. He spotted the Cheese Lady, who had backed herself out of my father's field of vision during the confrontation. She politely held out her plate.

"Hey, can I have an extra one? It's for my boy," he asked, and then, without waiting for a reply, took three.

"Sure," she answered, forcing a smile.

My dad handed me the cheese and then got serious. "I have been in every corner of this store looking for—"

I knew I was in trouble, and that I was finally going to get it for leaving the toy aisle.

"—your mother," he continued. "She was supposed to meet me by the check out lanes at four

7

o'clock. You wouldn't by any chance know where she is?"

"No. I even lost—"

"Your brother? He's playing with the electric door. Well, let's go get him and then wait for your mom in the car."

Sure enough, my brother was at the front of the store, stepping on the rubber pad and watching the door swing open. My dad grabbed him by the shirt collar and kept walking without even slowing down.

My mom was walking in the store just as we were walking out. She was carrying a small paper bag and didn't seem to notice us.

"Dorothy! Where have you been?"

"I just ran next door to the drug store to see if they had any—"

"You left the boys alone in the store?"

"They didn't even know I was gone," she snapped.

"Do you know what time it is?"

My mom dropped her head in defeat. "I was running behind."

"Then why did you think you had time to…Ah, forget it." My dad massaged his forehead like he was running his fingers through the hair that was longer there.

"Boys, let's go back in the store. I guess we're shopping for groceries." He laughed. "I'm ready for more cheese. How about you?"

"But dad, the lady said only one per customer," I said, being careful not to use a voice that would set him off.

"So what? It's not like she memorizes everybody's face. No wandering off," he said, placing the palm of his hand on my brother's head. "And keep an eye out for Jesus. I hear he's missing."

8

CHAPTER 2

Our house was in a corner of Detroit that was just barely within the city limits, a neighborhood that was home to so many police officers and firefighters that it eventually became known as "Copper Canyon." It was an orderly neighborhood made of story-and-a-half houses that were arranged in perfect rows on streets that ran exactly north and south. My dad never said so, but I think he chose our house because it was only two blocks away from Warren, where he wasn't required to carry a gun during his off-duty hours.

Home was a safe and orderly place where Elsie was a friendly cartoon cow. She even appeared in television commercials where she helped distraught housewives solve their everyday problems with the aid of Borden milk products. Unlike the realistic rubber Elsie in the store or the cartoon Elsie on the milk carton, the televised Elsie was a quasi-human who wore a short sleeved dress with a white apron, walked upright, and, if you could get past the fact that she was only six inches tall and had the head of a cow, seemed to be the typical American housewife. She was even kind of pretty and sort of reminded me of Lucille Ball, except that Elsie was a little more composed in the face of an emergency.

My mother had none of Elsie's composure, which was unfortunate because she lived in a constant state of emergency. Rather than make plans and avoid emergencies, my mother thought it best to prepare for all emergencies and then deal with life as it happened. For instance, she didn't plan for meals. She opened the cupboards, surveyed the goods, and tried to figure out a way to cobble a meal out of whatever she happened to have on hand. That was kind of tricky because she only bought what was on sale, which was not necessarily what we needed, and she might discover that she had five boxes of pancake mix but no syrup. She always managed to pull it off, but life was pretty unpredictable. And so, on that crisp January morning, I woke up not knowing what the new day would bring, but not in a good way.

My mom had been up for a while and was already busy in the kitchen by the time I dragged myself out of bed. She was wearing a nice blue dress and a white apron, and I wondered if she shopped at the same store as Lucille Ball and Elsie the Cow.

She didn't say "good morning" or ask if I had slept well, but instead gave me an update of the current crisis. "The Women's Society is coming over to sew cancer pads and we need to get ready."

I had no idea what she was talking about. She was all dressed and dolled up, my brother was at school, I had already changed out of my pajamas, and the house itself was in a constant state of readiness.

My mom ushered me through a tidy breakfast of Frosted Flakes and milk. She put the milk and cereal away while I was eating, cleaned up spills as I made them, and as soon as I had finished she washed the bowl and spoon and it was as if no breakfast had occurred.

"Now, go keep yourself busy until the ladies come," she said, and began brewing a pot of coffee.

I decided that the best way to keep myself busy and out of trouble was to work on a puzzle of the United States. I would do it right in the middle of the living room floor so that when the ladies came over and saw what I had done they'd be very impressed and my mother would be proud. Unfortunately, my mother did not share my vision.

"What have you done?" The way she said it, you'd think I'd taken a crap on the carpet. She picked up the puzzle board and dumped the pieces into a shoe box.

"You messed up all my work!"

"The Women's Society is coming over and we need room to work. We're sewing cancer pads."

She could tell that I was getting upset and decided to calm me down by telling me about cancer.

"Cancer patients need our help. Cancer is a horrible disease that grows inside of you. You get lumps, called tumors, and they keep growing and spreading until they take over your whole body."

I lifted up my shirt. "Do I have any tumors?"

My mom pulled my shirt back down. "You don't have cancer."

"You didn't even look!"

"People your age hardly ever get cancer. It's not like polio."

People who are panicked by the thought of one disease are rarely comforted by the thought of two diseases. "Polio? What's polio?"

"Polio is a disease that crippled and killed a lot of people, but mostly children."

Polio? Cancer? Tumor? Where was she getting these words? How come no one had ever told me about them before?

"Now I'll bet you feel pretty silly worried about your little puzzle when children are dying of polio."

"Am I going to get polio?"

"Nobody gets polio anymore. They found a vaccine—"

"A vaccine?"

"It's a shot that they give you. It keeps you from getting polio."

11

"Is there a vaccine for cancer?"

"Not yet, but now that the doctors are done with polio they're working on a cancer vaccine, and I'm sure they'll have one within a year or two."

"Are you sure?"

"I am sure."

"Do you promise?"

"I promise that within a few years the doctors will have found a vaccine or a cure for cancer, and it will be gone forever, just like polio." She handed me the box and the board. "Go put this in your room."

"Are you sure I don't have cancer?"

"I'm sure.   Now, run up to your room and put your puzzle away."

I went to my room and dumped the puzzle pieces on my bed.   There was an order to things, but I couldn't see it.   Somehow, all of this junk had to fit together and make a country.   Maybe, when I got older, things would make more sense.

I rubbed my belly.   There were lots of lumpy things that I hadn't noticed before, and with that many lumps it seemed that at least a couple of them had to be tumors.

"Honey, put on your shoes and socks.   And stop looking for tumors.   The ladies are going to be here any minute."

I didn't know how my mother knew that I was looking for tumors, but it actually gave me some comfort. If she was right about that, then maybe she was right about finding a cancer vaccine.

"I can't find my socks."

"Your socks are where they always are, in your top drawer."

That was the rule.   The top drawer is for socks. Socks always go in the top drawer.

Always.   That was my mother's favorite word. We always had applesauce and sour cream with potato pancakes. My socks always went in the top drawer of my dresser. We always wound the alarm clock at bedtime. Someday, I would grow up, get married, and have my own home. I would eat potato pancakes with sour cream and applesauce, keep my socks in the top drawer of my dresser, and wind my alarm clock at bedtime.

The ladies began to arrive, knocking gently as they reached the door. I could recognize their voices: Mrs. Ballenger, who lived a few houses away, arrived first. She probably walked. Mrs. Conger, Mrs. Ford, and Mrs. Albin all came in the same car. Mrs. McDonough always came in her own car, and she was always the last one to arrive.

I thumped down the stairs making as much noise as I could so the ladies would know I was coming, but the only person who noticed me was Mrs. Ballenger. She was the oldest lady in the group, and never had any children of her own, but was the only person in the Women's Society who seemed to understand kids.

"Oh my!" she exclaimed, fanning herself with her hand. "Who is that handsome gentleman coming down the stairs?"

"Mrs. Ballenger!" I protested, pretending that her adulation annoyed me. To my horror she actually stopped praising me, and I told myself that in the future I should accept her remarks more graciously.

I must have looked a little droopy because she asked me what was wrong.

"I think I have cancer."

"Come here and let me check you over."

I took her hand and held it against a particularly unwholesome lump in my belly. "Do you think that's a tumor?"

"Probably," she calmly stated. "Dorothy, I'm taking your son the basement. I've got to cut out this tumor, and I don't want to spill any blood on your rug."

"Wait a minute! Are you sure I have cancer?"

13

"Maybe not. Let me check again." She rubbed my belly. "No, I think that's the usual stuff you find in all little boys."

I felt a little better.

"Is there something else?" she asked.

"I have a puzzle, but I'm too stupid to put it together."

"That doesn't seem like a crisis. Why don't you get it and we can do it together?"

I ran upstairs and got my puzzle. Mrs. Ballenger picked up a few of the pieces and dropped them back in the box.

"I think I see what's going on here. This puzzle is pretty challenging. I don't suppose I could have done it when I was your age."

"No, you don't understand. I'm starting Kindergarten tomorrow, and I don't want everybody to think I'm stupid."

"Well, we couldn't have that now, could we? Let's see. You can find Michigan, can't you?"

"Now what do I do with it?"

"It goes here," Mrs. Ballenger said, pointing to a spot in the board. "You can always find Michigan's place because it's surrounded by lakes."

Mrs. McDonough chimed in. "How can the boy start Kindergarten tomorrow? It's January. Who starts Kindergarten in January?"

"Oh, that's right. You grew up in Indiana. In Detroit, we start school twice a year, either in September or January," my mother explained, using the same voice she used on me when I asked too many questions.

Mrs. Ballenger held up a puzzle piece. "See if you can find a state that's jagged and would fit next to this one."

I dug through the box, but it seemed hopeless. "I had all of the states sorted by shape, but then I had to put

14

the puzzle away and they got mixed together." I glared at my mother.

"Perhaps you should have separated them by color," Mrs. McDonough said. "It's not such a popular idea nowadays, but it's always made sense to me."

It was Mrs. Ballenger's turn to glare, and then nobody said anything for a couple of minutes. I couldn't understand why she was so upset with Mrs. McDonough.

. I had to make a few trips up to my bedroom to retrieve some missing pieces, but by the time the meeting was winding down, the whole puzzle was complete.

"There! That's all of the states," I announced.

"Not really. This puzzle doesn't have Alaska or Hawaii," said Mrs. Ballenger, with a curious smile. When Mrs. Ballenger smiled like that, it either meant that she was telling me something I really needed to know or that she was pulling my leg.

"Alaska? Hawaii? What are you talking about?" I could hear the panic in my voice. I had already learned enough new words for one day.

"We've added two states since this puzzle was made," she stated flatly. There wasn't the slightest hint of humor in her voice.

"When did that happen?" I demanded.

"Oh, about four years ago, I suppose."

I looked at the puzzle. It didn't seem possible. There were big oceans on two sides and big countries on the other two. Where would you put two more states? They couldn't just haul in dirt and make the country bigger.

"They can't add states. Things like that don't change." I said, and I waited for her to break into a smile and tell me how clever I was for seeing through her little joke.

"Everything changes." Mrs. Ballenger said, gently rubbing her eyes.

15

"What do you mean?" I asked, trying not to sound scared.

Mrs. McDonough leaned over and put her hand on my shoulder. "Honey, you better get used to change. Just when you think you're winning the game, somebody changes the rules."   She was smiling, but there was something mean about her smile, and my stomach began to hurt.

"How am I going to figure anything out if everything keeps changing?" I shouted.

"It's just a puzzle," Mrs. Albin offered.

"It's not just a puzzle. It's the United States. You can't change…" I couldn't finish. Nobody seemed to understand, not even Mrs. Ballenger.

"Kiddo, change isn't bad. Most changes make things better." Mrs. Ballenger was too understanding and too calm, and that worried me.

"Like what?" I asked.

"Well, when I first moved to this neighborhood the side street wasn't paved. It was just a dirt road. But that was a long time ago, before you were born. Lots of things were different before you were born," Mrs. Ballenger explained.

Mrs. Ford spoke up. "Before you were born, there was no television. We used to listen to the radio."

"I can remember when we got our first radio. Before that we read books and magazines, or we played outside," Mrs. Ballenger added.

"And there was a big war, World War II, and most of our husbands fought in that war," Mrs. Albin remarked. I liked to hear Mrs. Albin talk because her dentures whistled whenever she said an s.

"My husband fought in World War I," announced Mrs. Ballenger.

"And before you were born there were diseases—" whistled Mrs. Albin.

"Like polio!" I shouted.

16

Mrs. Albin nodded her head. "Yes, polio, and diphtheria, and whooping cough, but we don't have to worry about those diseases any more. "

Mrs. Ballenger kissed me on the top of the head. "Well, aren't you the clever young man, being born at just the right moment?"

I wasn't sure how that happened. In fact, it didn't sound right. I figured that I was the kind of guy who would be born at just the wrong moment.

"Change makes things better?" I asked, just to make sure.

"Well, usually," Mrs. McDonough said.

I bolted up. "What do you mean?"

"Oh, like my old neighborhood. It's changed, but not for the better. Now it gets dark awfully early down there."

"Eleanor McDonough, we are the Women's Society for Christian Service!" Mrs. Ballenger gripped my shoulder as she talked, and I got a little scared, especially since I had never heard her use that tone of voice.

"What's wrong? Are things getting bad?" I asked.

"Not in this neighborhood," said Mrs. McDonough. "It's just that there are still a few problems we haven't resolved."

"But not in Detroit, right? Not here?" My stomach started to hurt all over again.

The room got very quiet, and finally Mrs. Albin spoke out. "I think Mrs. McDonough was talking about starving children in Africa and things like that. Isn't that right, Eleanor?"

"Oh, it seems to me that there were some Africans involved." She smiled again, but Mrs. Ballenger glared at her and the smile was gone. Mrs. McDonough sniffed and made one final comment. "Yes, dear, everything is fine."

I didn't believe her.   I remembered my dad saying, "Even a blind man can smell the shit wagon when it's coming down the street," and I figured this must be the sort of the thing he was talking about.   Sometimes you don't get the whole truth, but you can tell that what you're getting is a load of crap.

Maybe I wasn't getting the whole story from the ladies, but when my dad got home from work I'd try to get the truth out of him.

CHAPTER 3

About an hour before dinner, my mother told me that my brother would be eating dinner with Mark Hedgecock and, because there was an empty place at the table, I could invite a friend. I wasn't sure who to invite, but I knew if I went for a walk around the block I'd probably run into somebody.

When I got to the other side of the block, on Waltham Street, I saw a kid playing in his front yard. At least, it kind of looked like he was playing. I had to wear dungarees and a tee shirt when I played outside, but he had on a button down shirt and tan pants.

With no introduction of any kind I just called to him from the sidewalk. "Do you want to come over to my house for dinner?"

"Let me ask my mom!"

He went into the house, and came back out with his mom, who was carrying a pencil and a pad of paper. She asked a bunch of questions and glared at me like I had my shirt on inside-out, asked my address and phone number, wrote something on her pad, and finally said it would be okay, except she said it in a way like she really didn't think it was okay. The only good thing that came from that conversation was that I learned my new friend's name was John.

I got back just before my dad came home from work. He hung his hat and coat in the closet, emptied the bullets from his revolver, and then put it on the top shelf of the closet. I wasn't allowed to touch the gun, but that rule didn't matter much because my dad never left it around where I could get my hands on it. Maybe he was practicing for the day when I'd be tall enough to reach the top shelf.

"Put this in the refrigerator," he said, handing me a package wrapped in white paper.

"What is it?" I asked.

"Just some hamburger."

"Are we having hamburgers for dinner?" I hoped that we were, because hamburgers would make a good impression on my friend.

"No, it smells like your mother is cooking up a pot of Bohnensuppe." I figured that was okay, because it was one of my favorite meals and I was pretty sure that John would like it. As far as I knew, everybody liked it. I ran to the kitchen, put the meat in the refrigerator, and then ran back.

"So, what's new?" I casually asked.

"Nothin'," my dad answered.

"Really?" I said, trying to conceal my concern. "I mean, there aren't any new states or diseases and we didn't start a war or anything?"

"Dorothy, what have you been saying to this boy?" my dad shouted to the kitchen. "He's acting like the world is going to end."

"It's nothing," she shouted back. "I'll tell you about it after dinner."

My dad scooped me up and held me by one arm. I looked down at the floor, and it seemed like a long way off. My mom warned me that I shouldn't leave my toys on the floor because my dad was an oaf and would step on them, and now I could see what she was talking about. No wonder he stepped on toys. He could hardly see them.

I knew I wasn't going to get any answers with my mom around, so I changed the subject. "My friend John is coming over for dinner."

"Does his mother drive a blue Chrysler?"

"I don't know."

"I'll bet that she does, because it looks like she's here right now."

"Oh my God, I'm still wearing my apron!" my mother shouted.

My mom made John and me wash our hands, and then we all sat down at the table.

"Can I say grace?" I asked.

"All right," my mother answered. I think she expected me to recite the familiar "God is great, Good is good" prayer that we said every night, but I wanted to impress my friend with a snappy number I picked up from one of my friends at church.

"Rub-a-dub-dub, thanks for the grub, yay God!"

My mother did not approve of my new appreciation for humorous verse. "Young man, where did you learn that awful prayer?" she snapped.

"From Jeff Conger."

"Well, that sort of behavior might be acceptable in April Conger's home, but in this house we say a respectable Christian prayer. Now start again."

I looked at my dad, just to see if I was in trouble, but there seemed to be a little smile at the corner of his mouth. I took a deep breath and started our usual prayer.

"God is great, God is good..."

My parents said the prayer with me, but John whispered something I couldn't understand, and touched his shoulders and forehead before and after the prayer. John's prayer was more complicated, and I was pretty sure that made it better. I hadn't quite figured out the whole routine of church, but there was a lot of standing up and sitting down and turning to various pages in the hymnal or the Bible, so it seemed to be that God liked things that were complicated. We were probably making God angry with our crappy little prayer, and I decided to let John teach me his prayer when my parents weren't around.

"Oh, I see you're Catholic," my mother said.

"Yes, ma'am."

"We're having Bohnensuppe," I proudly announced.

John's face turned into an ugly little knot. "Bohnensuppe? What's that?"

"It's a German dish," my mother said, trying to be calm.

"But I'm Irish!"

My dad took over. "You eat potato soup don't you?"

"Sure," John answered.

"Bohnensuppe is pretty much the same thing."

"Except it has peppercorns and wax beans," my mother added.

"Wax beans!" John exclaimed.

"They're not made of wax. It's just what they're called," my mother tried to explain.

"Dorothy, why did you have to bring up wax beans? I just about had the boy straightened out, and now he's acting like we've offered him a bowl of reconstituted horse blood."

"May I be excused, please?" he asked, as polite as ever.

"Sure."

John quietly walked to the closet, got his hat and coat, walked home, and never talked to me again. My mother turned white, and my father broke out in laughter.

"I guess the boy doesn't like Bohnensuppe," my father managed to say between laughs.

"Not again!" I moaned, and I ran from the table. I went into the living room, picked up a pillow from the couch, and buried my face.

"What on earth is all that about?" my father asked.

"He's starting school tomorrow and he's worried."

"About what?"

"About the whole world actually," she sighed.

"What do you women do at those quilting sessions?" my father asked.

"They're not quilting sessions. We're sewing cancer pads!"

I could hear my father's chair slide across the floor, and then I heard him thunder into the living room. He grabbed me up from the couch, pulled the pillow from my face, and tossed it down.

"Well, if we're not going to eat we might as well get something done," he said.

"Not going to eat!" my mother huffed. "I've got a whole pot of—"

"Keep it on the stove. We'll eat when we get back."

My dad lurched into the kitchen and retrieved the white paper package from the fridge, still carrying me with his other hand. Then he tossed me over his shoulder and we bounced down the stairs into the basement.

With a great air of mystery he unfolded the paper on his workbench. "For once I'm going to get a good night's sleep."

"What's that supposed to mean?" I asked.

"Let's just say that the Andersons' dog won't be keeping me up tonight."

He took a little bottle from the shelf where he kept his paint. He unscrewed the lid, and spilled a little white powder onto the palm of his hand.

"What's that?"

"Sometimes, when we've got to raid a gambling joint, there's a dog out front. Not for attacking, just to make a lot of noise so they know if somebody's coming. So we give him a little present. I get about half a pound of hamburger and mix it with a little something I get from the pharmacist. A few hours before we're going to raid the place we swing by, I toss it over the fence, the dog eats it, and he—"

"Dies!"

"No, it's not poison. I'm not allowed to kill dogs."

"Not even if they have rabies?"

"Not if I can help it. I'm supposed to catch it with a dog stick so they can observe it for a few days."

"But what if it's attacking somebody?"

"Then I can shoot it, but not in the head. We have to send the head to Lansing so they can see if it has rabies."

"But what if…"

"Son, will you please let me tell my story?"

"Okay."

"So, about an hour later the dog gets the shits—"

"Walter!" my mother scolded. She must have been listening from the top of the stairs. My dad lowered his voice and spoke in a hoarse half-whisper.

"The dog gets diarrhea, real bad, so bad that he can't even bark. The best he can manage is a little woof."

"And that's what you're giving the Andersons' dog?"

"Yep."

I could hear my mother's shoes clack-clack down the stairs while my father mixed the white powder into the meat. "Walter, you can't do that. It's cruel!" Apparently my father hadn't lowered his voice quite enough. He rolled his eyes. "I don't remember you having that much sympathy for me when I had diarrhea."

"The Andersons just got new carpeting. What if he goes inside of the house?"

"Then I'll know that God was listening to my prayers last night."

My mother muttered something I couldn't understand, and my dad chuckled quietly a couple more times.

"Dad?"

"What?"

"When I go to school, maybe I shouldn't tell anybody that I'm German."

"Why not?"

"I don't know. It just seems like a lot of people don't like Germans."

"Believe me, a lot of people have it worse than Germans."

"Like who?"

He thought for a second. "The Polish, for instance. They have to put up with Polack jokes."

"I guess. I just don't want everybody to think that I'm stupid."

"Why would they think that?" he asked, with an uncharacteristic tone of concern.

"Walter, do you think he's ready for Kindergarten? Maybe we should hold him back." She looked worried, and I took that to mean that there was something about Kindergarten for which I was not prepared.

My father didn't seem worried, just a little annoyed. "What are we supposed to do? He's already been registered. We can't send him to school with a note pinned to his shirt saying that we've decided he's not ready!"

By this point my dad had finished mixing the powder into the hamburger, and he began rolling it into a ball.

"Son, let's go for a walk to Chick's. I'll buy you a comic book."

"Okay," I said, and I ran upstairs to put on my hat and coat.

It had snowed the night before, but all of the sidewalks were shoveled, and I didn't see any ice, but my father made me hold his hand. His other hand held the ball of hamburger, but my father kept his hand cupped around it and if you didn't know to look you wouldn't even notice he was holding something.

"So what's the problem with school?" he asked.

"I don't know anything. Everybody is going to think that I'm stupid."

"Geez, son, nobody knows much of anything before they go to school."

"But the other kids—"

"The other kids don't know any more than you do."

The Andersons' dog, which was pretty big and very black, ran over to the fence and growled as we walked past their house. My dad flipped the hamburger over the fence with a gentle overhand toss. The dog made one last bark, sniffed the meat, and began to eat.

"Good night, Fido," my dad whispered.

"His name is Max," I corrected. I wanted to feel superior, but I just felt stupid. Everybody else was learning the names of states, but I was wasting my time learning the names of dogs. "Mrs. Ballenger said we added two new states."

"That's right. Alaska and Hawaii."

"How can I learn anything if everything keeps changing?"

My dad broke into laughter. "Is that what all the fuss is about?"

"It's not funny!" I shouted, and I stopped walking.

"Son, the world changes, but not all at once. Besides, I doubt if there are going to be any real changes any time soon."

"Are you sure about that?"

"Pretty sure. "

"Now do you want a comic book, or don't you? Your mother is going to be pretty upset if we're gone too long, so we can either go to Chick's or you just stand there thinking until it's time to go back home."

For the rest of the evening I tried to think of everything that might let people know that I was German. Other people had a Grandma, but I had an Oma. I never liked the sound of that word. It sounded like something my dad made up, and I wondered if people in Germany actually called their grandmother "Oma." That didn't bother me too much, though, because it wasn't likely the kids at Kindergarten would be talking about their grandmas. Other people said "God bless you" after a sneeze, but we said "Gesundheit." I'd have to be on my guard, but I thought I could control that, too. If I could fake my way through the first few weeks, they'd probably teach me how to act American, and I'd finally be like everybody else.

CHAPTER 4

The next morning, when I arrived at the school, I noticed that most of the classrooms looked the same. They had wooden floors and wooden desks with wrought iron frames that were screwed down in perfect rows. The kids looked very serious and were getting ready for class to begin. They had their books and their loose-leaf binders with little plastic pockets to carry their pencils. All down the hallway, in room after room, things were the same. There were rows of desks filled with industrious little learners. I couldn't imagine myself sitting so still, or being so quiet, or remembering to bring my binder to class. My mother was right. I wasn't ready for school. I wondered if it was too late to ask to be held back.

Then I saw what I hoped was my classroom. It was colorful and fun, with large hanging decorations and a big playhouse right in the middle of the room. Children were laughing and crawling on top of each other. One boy put a cardboard building block on another boy's head, it fell off, and then they both laughed. It was the happiest, most colorful place I had ever seen, and, somehow, I knew that was where I belonged.

My brother, who was helping me find my classroom, whacked me in the back of the head, and pulled on my arm to drag me away.

"I want to go to that room!" I protested.

"No you don't. That's the retard room."

I didn't know what a retard was, but I was pretty sure that I must be one, because I knew I belonged in that room. I could tell by the way my brother said "retard" that it was supposed to be a bad thing, but I didn't care. Those kids were having more fun than anybody else.

My brother kept rushing me down the hallway, further and further away from the wonderful classroom. I kept looking back over my shoulder, waiting for my brother to say "April fool," but it didn't happen.

"Where are you taking me?"

"Room 113. Geez, I'm beginning to think you are retarded."

He eventually coaxed me down the hall and into the Kindergarten room. It didn't have desks or rows, but there were round tables and tiny chairs and you could tell that it was way too orderly to have any kind of real fun. Some of the kids were crying, and I thought that they must have wanted to go to the retard room, too.

I was one of the last to arrive, so just after I got there the teacher sat us in a circle. She asked us to recite our names, beginning with me.

"What's your first name, dear?"

"Detlef."

"I said your first name." Some of the mean kids laughed, as if I were so stupid that I didn't know my own name.

"Detlef."

"What's your whole name?" she asked, trying to be patient.

"Detlef Niebaum." That time everybody laughed. Did they know that it was a German name? I had hoped that my blond hair and blue eyes made me look like the All-American boy and no one would suspect that I was German. The teacher looked at her list, then made a check mark. Why did she make that mark? Did it mean that I was German? Or retarded? It was one thing to be a retard if you're in the retard room, but I didn't want any of these kids to think I was a retard.

I thought about asking the teacher what a retard was, but I had already endured enough ridicule. Just asking that kind of question would place me under suspicion. This was the kind of thing I needed to ask my mom. She liked to deliver bad news, and yet she was also good at hiding things from the neighbors.

When the teacher dismissed us I was in a hurry to get home, but I had trouble with my galoshes and I ended up being the last person to leave the classroom. The walk home seemed to take forever, and by the time I arrived at our doorstep I was in a state of near panic.

"Detlef, how was your first day of school?" my mom asked cheerily.

"I don't know. What's a retard?"

"Did somebody call you retarded?"

"No. There was a room called the retard room and I wonder what that means."

"A retard is somebody who's a little slow."

Slow? I was the last person getting my boots on. Maybe I was a retard. I needed more details.

"What do you mean?" I asked, and I could feel the color draining form my face.

"Oh, you know, they just have trouble keeping up with the other kids, so they put them in a room where they learn at their own pace."

"You mean, they might have trouble putting on their galoshes?" I asked, almost hoping that I was retarded so I could play with the other kids and do my work at my own pace. Maybe in the retard room I wouldn't be the last person to put on his galoshes. Maybe I'd be somewhere in the middle of the pack, and I would blend in with the crowd.

"Oh, I suppose they'd have trouble with their galoshes. But mostly they have trouble with reading and writing." Her voice lowered to a whisper. "It's a mental condition."

From that point on, the question of whether or not I was retarded was never far from my thoughts. I discovered I wasn't merely slow; I was the slowest. I was always the last person to finish his work, always the last person to put his scissors away, and always the last person picked when we played kickball. My mother tried to say that I was just taking my time and I was probably doing better work than the other kids, but I figured that was because she didn't want to own up to the fact that she'd given birth to a retard. When I tried to write, the letters were crooked and sloppy, even by Kindergarten standards. When we had to trace our hands to make a map of Michigan, I got mixed up and traced the wrong hand. I felt something must be wrong with me, that deep inside of my brain there was some kind of a defect.

My classmates did not share my doubts. They knew I was retarded. I was never called a "lunkhead" or a "klutz" or a "slowpoke." Whenever I did something stupid, they called me a "retard." They called me a retard when I dropped my scissors in the pot of paste, they called me a retard when I put my drawing in the wrong pile, and they called me a retard when I didn't understand Albert Cotto's great joke.

"What did Hitler say when he saw a baby?" Albert asked, and for a moment there was absolute silence.

"I don't know," I answered.

"Hotsy totsy, newborn Nazi!" he shouted.

Everybody else laughed, but I was confused.

"What's a Nazi?" I stupidly asked.

"The Nazis are the people we fought against during World War Two," Albert moaned. "Didn't your parents teach you anything?"

"I thought we fought against the Germans," I said.

"The Nazis are Germans, you retard!"

31

Everybody laughed, and then the teacher came over to rescue me.

"You boys stop your laughing! You shouldn't tease Detlef this way. You know he's—"

My throat got so tight that I almost couldn't breathe. The dreaded moment had come. Mrs. Tilden was about to announce to the whole class that I was retarded. I tried to think of a way to stop her, but it was too late.

"—German," she said. "Detlef is from a German family."

Albert looked at me. "I always knew you were a retard, but I didn't know that you were a Nazi, too. I guess that explains everything."

"Albert! Go sit in the corner!" Mrs. Tilden demanded.

"Stupid Nazi retard!" he muttered as he walked away.

"Shut up!" I yelled. "Or my dad will come over to your house and step on your toys!"

Everybody laughed all over again, and I tried to explain the gravity of my threat.

"I'm not kidding. He's an oaf. He doesn't even look where he's going!"

Even Mrs. Tilden laughed at that.

Kindergarten is supposed to be a place where kids learn to work and play together, but by the time summer break came around the only thing I had learned is that I was certainly German, probably retarded, and possibly a Nazi.

When school resumed in the fall, nothing had changed. I was still in Kindergarten, of course, since I had started school in January. I had hoped that over the summer the other kids would have forgotten that I was a Nazi retard, but they just picked things up right where they left off.

In November I got a bad case of the mumps and had to stay at home for a couple of days. I slept through the morning and part of the afternoon, and when I woke up my mom was ironing clothes in the living room and watching a movie on television.

I missed the first part of the film, but it seemed to be about an old lady who was trying to save her house. She was standing in front, pleading, while a wrecking ball crew was getting ready to demolish her house. Just as the ball was heading for her house, the show was interrupted. My mother looked concerned, but the movie was the only thing that was keeping me awake, and I drifted back to sleep.

For the next couple of hours I drifted in and out of sleep, and I was only somewhat aware of what was happening. It wasn't until my father came home that I was finally alert enough to ask questions.

"What happened?" I managed to ask.

"You were pretty sick," my mother answered. "I thought we might have to take you to Dr. Stein."

"No, I mean, what happened? I think I dreamed the president was shot."

My parents looked at each other.

"It was a dream, wasn't it?"

"No, it wasn't," my father answered.

"I thought you said the world wasn't going to change!" I said in my most accusatory voice.

"Sorry, son, I didn't see this one coming."

"What if everything is changing?"

"It's not. This is a once-in-a-lifetime thing, like when they shot Lincoln or McKinley."

"But—"

"But nuthin'. 1964 isn't a whole lot different from 1954, and when 1974 comes around you're going to be surprised how little has changed."

Over the next few days I learned new words, like "assassination" and "Lee Harvey Oswald." Like all good

33

Americans, I hated Oswald. I wished that somebody would assassinate him.

Two days later I was well enough to go to my Oma's house, and we were all gathered around her 19-inch black-and-white Admiral television to catch a glimpse of Oswald as he was being transferred from one jail to another. Unexpectedly, a man shot Oswald in the gut.

"Oh my God, Oswald's been shot!" my father shouted.

"Good. I hope he dies!" I replied.

"Detlef, you take that back," my mother said. Mom was nice, maybe a little too nice. I'd been watching a lot of movies, and I noticed that a lot of the womenfolk got a bit weak when blood was shed.

"No! I hope he dies!"

My father put his hand on my shoulder. "Son, the suspect is supposed to go to trial, not get shot in the gut by some crazed gunman. For all we know the guy who shot Oswald is as bad as he is."

My father seemed just as confused as my mother.

"No, Dad, it isn't like that at all. It's like a cowboy movie. When a bad guy shoots somebody, the good guy has to shoot the bad guy." I explained.

"Maybe the guy who shot Oswald is in cahoots with him, and maybe he plugged Oswald just to shut him up. We can't have these assholes shooting at each other or it will be like the Wild West."

The way my dad said "like the Wild West" I could tell he meant it in a bad way. Sure, maybe that guy shouldn't have killed Oswald. Maybe Roy Rogers should have shot Oswald, and then Dale Evans could have sung a ballad about how he heroically gunned down the man who killed President Kennedy. I thought about explaining it to my dad, but he didn't seem to be in a listening mood.

I waited a couple of days to see if chaos erupted in the streets, but everything seemed the same as it always had been. President Johnson seemed to have things in control. There weren't going to be riots or wars, and our neighborhood was going to be just as it always was. The immutable Order of Things was greater than any one man, even the President of the United States.

In January I advanced to the first grade, but my situation only got worse. When the teacher put big stars on the best papers and little stars on the good ones, my papers had no stars. I was still the last person to get on his coat and boots. I was still the last person to turn in his work, and even then it was sloppy and incomplete. Kickball had given way to softball, but I was still last pick. Not only was I was unable to hit, run, catch, or throw, I couldn't even find my position in the outfield, and another student had to shout directions to tell me where to stand.

"That way, you retard! Now keep walking! No, not that far!"

One day near the end of the school year, my first grade teacher, Mrs. Langlois, said she had a surprise for us. She read a list of words, and we had to write them down and spell them correctly. For some reason, they were easy words from the beginning of the semester. Mrs. Langlois was not a kind woman, and I suspected that it was a trick, but then I looked around and the other kids were happily writing. Maybe it wasn't a trick. Maybe it was pity. Maybe she was giving us easy words so everybody could get a gold star. The idea of getting a gold star which I did not deserve filled me with joy. Yes! A gold star just because she feels sorry for me!

"Children, today you don't have to turn your papers in."

Just my luck. The one time I got everything right, and she didn't want to see it.

"I'm going to pass back some papers. You did these way back in January."

35

The old papers had the same easy words in the same order.

"Now, compare the two papers and you can see how much you've improved!"

The other students were laughing. I couldn't see why. It was just an old paper. Maybe I'd understand when I got my paper back, but I didn't want to wait that long, so I glanced over at Lynn Spiro. The crooked letters of her first paper had given way to neat, orderly printing. I could hardly wait to see mine so I, too, could laugh at myself.

A few seconds later my old paper landed on my desk. It looked exactly like the one I had just written. Merciful Mother of God! I hadn't learned anything! Did this mean that I couldn't learn at all? Or was I just very, very slow? In either case, my question had been answered. I was retarded.

No adult had ever told me I was I retarded, but that was no comfort. "He's a retard," adults would politely whisper when a retarded person was in the room. It seemed to be a secret, one that was shared with everybody except the retard himself. Perhaps retarded people didn't even know they were retarded. That must have been what was happening with me. I was retarded, but no one told me. Mrs. Langlois knew it, the other kids knew it, my parents knew it, but, out of pity, no one told me. I didn't want this kind of pity. I wanted the kind of pity where I got a gold star that I didn't deserve.

By that point I'd had some contact with some of the students in the special ed room, and from what I could tell some were more retarded than others. Perhaps, among retards, I was near the top. Maybe I was on the cusp, between retarded and regular, and through some act of kindness I had been given a chance to be with the regular kids. Well, it didn't work out, and I thought I'd better get into the retard room before I flunked first grade. Maybe it wouldn't be so bad. Maybe, if I were with my own kind, they wouldn't tease me. Maybe I'd be the smartest person in the room for a change. Maybe I'd be happy.

That was the way it seemed to work. People were happiest when they were with their own kind. Sailors lived in ships, firemen lived at the firehouse, farmers lived on farms, Canadians lived in Canada, Indians lived in teepees, Eskimos lived in igloos, and Negroes lived, well, I wasn't sure where Negroes lived, but they must have lived with their own kind. In fact, I was pretty sure I had heard that Negroes were happiest with their own kind. That's why retards, like me, belonged in the retard room.

It was time to take matters into my own hands. I couldn't talk to Mrs. Langlois. She was a white-haired war horse, a veteran teacher who did not listen to children. But who else could I ask? Mom? No, her love and sympathy would keep her from revealing the truth. This was a job for Dad. He was a straight shooter. If anybody would tell me the truth, he would.

When I found my father, he was in the basement, working on a leaking water pipe. He was holding a hacksaw with a broken blade, and it was clear his project was not going well. I knew I should wait for a better time to talk to him, but I was too tense and couldn't wait any longer. With no explanation of any kind, I blurted out my concern.

"Dad, am I retarded?"

He was fishing through his toolbox, looking for an extra hacksaw blade that he did not have.

"No, of course not."

His answer was terse and unsympathetic. Perfect. If I had been retarded, he would have stopped what he was doing and had a long talk with me. I could tell by his tone of voice that he didn't want to be bothered with such an asinine question.

"Detlef, do me a favor. Run to Ray's Hardware and get me a hacksaw blade."

"Okay."

"Do you know where Ray's is? Can you find it by yourself?"

"Uh-huh."

"Now, when you get there, you'll see a big counter. Go to that counter and tell the guy behind it that you need a hacksaw blade."

He gave me a handful of change. "That's more than enough."

I started to run to the store.

"Detlef!"

I turned back.

"Keep the change."

Yes! I would have enough for a comic book.

"Just don't stop at Chick's on the way back to buy yourself a comic book. Come home first—then you can go to Chick's."

Would a retard be trusted to buy a hacksaw blade? No, sir. Maybe I was the slowest person in class, maybe I was the last pick when choosing sides, maybe I couldn't print legibly, but I wasn't a retard, and today that was enough.

That was our neighborhood. There was an order, a time and place for everything. Aces were higher than kings, and kings were higher than queens. When choosing sides, some kids were always picked first, and some were always picked last. The order didn't seem to change. No matter which game was being played, kings were always higher than queens. The kids who were picked last in kickball were also picked last in softball. They'd grow up to be privates in the army or dishwashers or maybe even end up as bums.

And so, for the next few years, it was my mission to find my place, and maybe move up a notch or two, if such a thing were possible. I knew I wasn't an ace or a king, but maybe, if I worked hard, I wouldn't have to spend the rest of my life as the Two of Clubs.

CHAPTER 5

By the time we got to Chandler Park, the game had already started.

I was still trying to piece things together. I had never heard of Chandler Park, and I couldn't imagine what kind of a game would be so important that my mother would actually drive the car to get us there, but I didn't ask questions because driving made her nervous, not just in the regular sense like most people get nervous, but a special kind of nervous that only my mother seemed to possess.

"What did that sign say? Did that say Chandler Park?" she snapped.

Nobody said anything. There was no telling which sign she was talking about or what the right answer should be. My brother and I were in the back seat, but I was on the passenger side, so when she turned her head around she made eye contact with me. "Well? What did it say?"

"I don't know. I can't read big words so well."

My mother knitted her brow, not like she was thinking, but like she was Satan. "I wasn't asking you. I was asking your brother," she explained, but still kept glaring at me. So, by the time we got there, I knew nothing of our destination, and had only learned that it's best to sit out of my mother's line of sight when she's driving.

The game, as it turned out, was baseball, and my father was playing second base. This surprised me, not because he was playing second base, but rather that he was playing at all. Nobody had ever mentioned it, and I never noticed a hat or glove around the house, but there he was in the infield, in a white uniform, hunched over and pounding his fist into his mitt.

I recognized the other players on my dad's team as men from our church, and most of them seemed too old or too fat to be good at anything. Mr. Ed Lorraine, who lived just one block away, was the only person on the team who looked like a real athlete. He wasn't quite as tall as my dad, but he moved more gracefully and his arms were ropy and round, and the sinews flexed even when he made a small movement like adjusting his hat.

Reverend Hotchkiss, the church pastor, was pitching and seemed to be doing a decent job, despite his boney frame and slight pot belly. His pitches whizzed past the batter and slapped into the catcher's mitt with a satisfying sound of leather-on-leather. The only other person who looked like he might have any talent at all was my father. He was lanky and lean with big hands that looked like they might be able to handle a bat, but he was hunched over and swaying his arms in a strange apelike fashion and didn't seem particularly athletic.

Mr. Woodcock, the frail superintendent of the Sunday school, was playing third base. Mr. Dick Dennison, who looked almost small and round enough to be one of Santa's elves, was in the outfield, and I was despairing over his pathetic condition when I saw the ball heading right to him. He charged the ball, snapped it up, and gunned it to second base to end the inning.

"Sit on the blanket," my mother ordered.

While I was watching the game, my mother had spread out a red plaid blanket. She was sitting in a folding lawn chair that we brought from home. My brother, who was three years older, was allowed to go off by himself, but I had already found a comfortable spot on the grass and I wanted to stay there, and I reasoned that I was old enough to have earned that privilege.

"Can't I just—" I tried to suggest.

"No. You need to sit on the blanket."

I couldn't imagine what was wrong with sitting on the grass. I played on the grass all time at home. I looked around. Other kids were sitting on the grass, and one boy was even chewing on a piece of grass.

"I want to sit on the grass," I protested.

"Absolutely not. People walk their dogs in this park, and we all know what dogs do."

I pulled myself halfway up and dragged myself onto the blanket.

"And no knuckle walking. Do you want people to think you were raised by apes?" I took another gander at my dad and wondered how they could think anything else.

By now the teams had switched sides, and my dad was sitting on the bench. He threw his hat off, propped his feet on a cooler, and with his bare head and white uniform he looked more like Milky the Clown than a ball player.

I tried to watch the game, but nothing much seemed to be happening. There was a lot of pitching but not much swinging, and although the other mothers were shouting things like, "You can do it, Honey," or "Strike this bum out," all my mother managed to say was, "Stay on the blanket."

Eventually I lost interest in the game, and began tracing the plaid pattern of the blanket with my finger.

"Hey, Detlef, how's it going?" The voice sounded familiar, and I turned to see that Mr. Lorraine, our athletic neighbor, had come over to talk to me.

"Hi, Ed," my mother groaned.

Mr. Lorraine looked a little too uninvolved. He had his hat pulled back and was drinking a bottle of pop.

"Don't you have to bat?" I asked.

"I batted last inning."

"Didn't you strike out?" my mother asked. She smiled, but it wasn't her usual smile. It was more like the smile a cartoon fox makes before it steals the farmer's chickens.

"Nope. Sacrifice fly. I drove in a run."

"That's still an out, isn't it?" she asked, still smiling. I decided it was time to choose sides, and I scooted away from her and moved toward Mr. Lorraine.

"How many times do I need to tell you to stay on the blanket?" she scolded.

"Geez, Dottie, you're doing the same thing to him that your mother did to you."

"You know my grandma?" I asked.

"Ed and I grew up in the same neighborhood," my mother snipped.

Mr. Lorraine put the palm of his hand on top of my head and gently turned my head so I was facing the game. "Your dad is coming to the plate."

My father was pulling at the waistband of his uniform, and then he swung the bat around a few times, and then he took off his hat and scratched his head like he didn't even know where he was. He looked less like someone from a baseball card and more like something that was drawn by Disney.

He loped over to the plate, hunched over, and waited for the first pitch. The pitcher gunned one right past him, and he didn't even seem to notice it.

"He didn't even swing," I moaned.

"That's okay. That one was out of the strike zone," Mr. Lorraine explained.

When the next pitch came it looked like my dad was going to just stand there again, but when it seemed like it was too late he snapped to life. He didn't take a big step and a mighty swing like the players, but quickly and smoothly brought the bat around.

"Good one, Wally!" Mr. Lorraine shouted. "I think that might be a double."

Sure enough, my dad ran past first and tore toward second. His arms and legs were flapping wildly, as if he had been dropped from an airplane without a parachute.

"I don't believe it," Mr. Lorraine complained. "Don't get greedy, Wally!"

"What's happening?" I asked.

"I think he's going to try and stretch it into a triple."

That was just my luck. My dad had a chance to get a good hit, and I could have told all the kids at school about it, but he was going to be called out.

Mr. Lorraine set his pop bottle on the arm of my mother's lawn chair so he could wave his arms at my father. "What were you thinking? You had it beat by a mile!" Then he stopped moving entirely and just stared. "Holy crap. I think he's going to make it."

Just as he got near the base, my dad's feet went out from under him in what looked like a comical movement, but once he hit the ground he began a smooth slide toward third.

"Detlef!"

I spun my head around to see my mother's angry face. "What?"

"Look at your foot! It's hanging over the edge of the blanket."

Sure enough, my foot was dangling over the grass. I quickly pulled it back, but by the time I looked up again, my father was standing and dusting himself off with his apey arms.

"What happened?"

"You dad just got a triple!" Mr. Lorraine exclaimed.

"Mom! You made me miss Dad's triple!"

43

I expected my mother to look apologetic, but she just turned red. "Don't embarrass me in front of Mr. Lorraine!"

Mr. Lorraine furrowed his brow, then quickly stepped in my direction and swung his arm at my head. I tucked my head under my arms and waited for him to hit me. I heard a smack, and winced, but I didn't feel anything.

Mr. Lorraine tapped me on the shoulder. "It's okay," he said. He was holding a ball.

"Hey, you kids need to be more careful!" he shouted. An older boy with a ratty red hat and a mitt waved for Mr. Lorraine to throw the ball, but Mr. Lorraine just stood there. The boy motioned again, but Mr. Lorraine tightened his jaw and the boy ran over.

"Now, I've got half a mind to keep this, but if you promise to play over there where it's safe I'll let you have it. But if I see you playing catch near little kids again, I don't care if it's the middle of the game, I'll walk right on the field and take it away. Understand?"

"Okay, Mister."

Mr. Lorraine handed the ball back to the kid and even gave him a rough pat on the shoulder to show that there weren't any hard feelings.

"Dang it," he said. "Inning's over. They left your dad stranded." He picked up his pop bottle and handed it to me. "Here, you can finish drinking this, and when you're done you can have the deposit."

I was pretty sure my mom would make me pour it out as soon as Mr. Lorraine was out of sight, so I took a big drink while he was still there. That way I had already contaminated myself with any germs he might have had and she would probably let me finish it.

That night, when I was taking a bath, I noticed that my ankle was swollen. My mother said it was because I had been bitten by a spider and that I should have stayed on the blanket. I guess that was the difference between me and my dad. He could play a whole game without a scratch, and I got hurt just watching.

The next morning, which was a Saturday, I asked my dad if he could teach me to play baseball. I knew that I wouldn't be able to catch or throw because I was afraid of the ball, but I thought maybe I could learn to hit. I had never heard of any "batting only" kind of position, but I was pretty sure that if I stood far enough in the outfield no one would be able to hit the ball to me and then I wouldn't have to catch or throw, so maybe batting would be enough.

My dad found a hunk of old wood to use as home plate, and he plopped that on the grass.

"Okay, I'm going to pitch and your brother will catch. Pick up your bat and stand at the plate."

I did just what he said, and planted both feet on home plate and faced him.

"Son, you can't stand like that. You'll get hit by the ball."

I was confused.

"I'm going to be throwing the ball right at home plate. Are you sure you want to stand there?"

I thought about it for a few seconds. "Yes!"

"Okay, but you're going to get hit by the ball."

"What?" I couldn't understand why my father wanted to hit me with the ball.

"You don't stand on the plate. You stand next to it," he instructed.

"I thought you had to stay on the base."

"Only when you're running."

When you're running? What was he talking about? You don't stay on the base when you're running. When you ran you went between the bases.

I thought about it for a while, and then stepped off the plate.

45

"Okay, now you're behind the plate." He pinched the bridge of his nose with his thumb and forefinger. "It's like you want to get hit."

He walked over to the trash can, which was on the side street by the garage, and fished out an old wooden shingle. He cracked it in half and put the pieces next to home plate.

"Put your right foot on this piece, and your left on the other. There you go. Now you look like a ballplayer. Okay, now swing when I throw the ball. No, you gotta swing sideways. You're chopping wood!"

It went on like that for about half an hour. My dad had lots of advice, all of which was good, but I was unable to accomplish anything he suggested. Words like "keep your eye on the ball" and "step into it" were for athletic guys, like my dad and my brother. Maybe I was more of a "stay on the blanket" kind of guy.

I wondered if you could do that. Could you go through life staying on the blanket, or was there a point where you had to get into the game? I was afraid of the ball, so staying on the blanket was an alluring concept. Of course, I almost got hit by a baseball when I was sitting on the blanket, so even that seemed a little risky.

Maybe I wasn't supposed to sit on the blanket, either. Maybe I was in a special category of people who are supposed to wait in the car

CHAPTER 6

Getting into the game of life wasn't as easy as I thought. After I learned that I was not retarded, I decided that my problem was that I was not cool, which all of a sudden seemed to be a very important quality. I had not even heard of this concept a month before, and yet now it was the single quality by which all elementary students judged each other.

I had no special talents or abilities. I had no possessions that were especially desirable. I had never met anybody who was famous. The few kids who were cool kept their distance, so there was no chance of becoming cool-by-association.

My mother told me not to worry about it. She said that I should act like myself and people would accept me for who I was. This was the same woman who said that if I ignored bullies they would leave me alone. As it turns out, bullies become angry if you ignore them, and then they beat you all the harder.

I decided that what would really make me cool was a pair of D batteries. If I had showed up at the home of any student in my elementary school and said that I had a pair of D batteries, we'd have become instant friends. That is because everybody in my neighborhood had a toy that was starved for batteries. If you were very lucky, your parents gave you a set of batteries when they bought you a toy, but unless you lived in Grosse Pointe or Farmington Hills you had better make those batteries last, because parents in Detroit did not rush to the store when batteries wore out. My mother made promises, which I am sure she intended to keep.

"Don't worry, honey; I'll pick up some batteries the next time I'm at the grocery store."

By the time she visited the store, batteries were the furthest thing from her mind. She was trying to find the bargain bin where she could get a great deal on a can of dented creamed corn. She cast herself in the role of the devoted mother who was on a quest to find the best nutrition on her limited budget. When you look at it that way, and she did, batteries don't seem that important.

When you've spent three days building a helicopter with your Gilbert Erector Set, and you've hooked up the motor to the rotors with two gears and a drive chain, and it's the only cool thing you've ever done, two size D batteries are everything. If I got my helicopter working, and if the other kids saw it, then, just maybe, I would be cool.

So I waited day after day for my batteries, but they did not come. All I got were moments of false hope. One day, with great excitement, my mother called me down from my room.

"Detlef! Come here! I've got something for you!"

The batteries! Yes! I thundered down the stairs just the way she told me not to, and I ran into the kitchen to see her leaning over a large cardboard box.

It was filled with hand-me-down clothes. I looked through the box, hoping that the clothes were actually for my brother and that in their midst were the batteries that were intended for me. However, once I got over my disappointment and actually looked at the clothes, they weren't half bad. I saw a cowboy shirt that looked pretty good, a couple of pairs of almost-new jeans, and a striped shirt that would probably make me look like a pirate. These clothes were definitely a step in a cool direction.

48

My brother couldn't stand it. The clothes were too nice, and none of them were his size. He waited until my mother left and spoke to me in conspiratorial tones.

"Do you know why you got these clothes?"

"I don't know. Because some boy outgrew them, I guess."

"The reason you got these clothes is because the kid who used to have them died of smallpox. They washed the clothes, you know, to try and kill the germs, but they probably should have boiled them."

"You're lying!" I shouted, not really believing what I was saying.

"You can wear them if you want, but stay away from me."

He pointed at the cowboy shirt.

"I'm not sure, but I think that's the shirt he was wearing when he died."

It made too much sense. No kid would willingly give up such good clothes. That was the end of the cool clothes.

My brother wasn't cool, but he did his best to fake it. He had a telescope, which was almost cool in its own right. He liked to brag about how he used it to look into other houses and watch teenage girls undress, but I spent a lot of time checking out his story and I found that the teenage girls in our neighborhood didn't spend a lot of time walking around stark naked in front of undraped windows. Eventually, out of boredom, I used the telescope for its intended purpose and pointed it at the sky. It was actually pretty neat, and I began looking more often.

And so, one cold Saturday night when everybody else was asleep, I slipped out of bed and looked into the sky. I had barely focused on my first star when my brother heard me.

"I hope you're not using my telescope!"

He crept over and pushed me out of the way.

49

"Let me see!"

He looked for a few seconds, then was angry.

"What were you looking at?"

"Just a star."

He moved the telescope around, looking for something more interesting.

"Uh-oh," he gulped.

"What?"

"Nothing. You're too young. It would only upset you."

"No, it wouldn't. Let me see."

"Okay, but don't say I didn't warn you."

I looked into the telescope and saw a blob of red light.

"What's that? The ball on top of the Penebscot building?"

"No, the Penebscot building's too far away. If we're lucky it's just an airplane."

Just an airplane? That did not sound good.

"But you know, it's not like any airplane I've ever seen. It's round, and it has red lights all over it."

I began to worry. I knew that there were no round airplanes. What could he mean? I hoped it wasn't a...

"It's a flying saucer!" he whispered.

I knew it! Round airplane! What was he thinking?

"And it's headed this way!"

That was just my luck! There I was, trying to enjoy a quiet night looking at the stars, and some moron from another planet had to wreck it. It wasn't bad enough that I got beat up at school, now guys were coming from a whole 'nother planet.

"Do you want another look?"

I didn't want to look, but I didn't want to miss it, so I peered through the telescope yet again. It looked like the same red blob I'd seen a minute before.

"I don't know. It just looks like a red ball."

50

"You have to focus."

I turned the knob, and it just got blurrier.

"It doesn't help," I said.

"Let me see."

He looked for a moment, and then gulped.

"What?" I asked.

"It's getting bigger. It's almost here!"

That was it. I couldn't take any more. "Mom! Dad!"

My parents needed to be told. Maybe Dad could get on the roof with a rifle. Maybe we could call the Air Force. Maybe it was time for an Air Raid Drill. That's it! Dad could take us to the school, and we could hide in the gym!

My brother's fake panic turned into actual fright. Alien invasions were one thing, but you didn't want to face my father when he had been awakened in the middle of the night.

I don't remember what frantic gibberish came forth from my mouth, but my parents picked up on the idea that I was afraid of aliens and that my brother had something to do with it.

From my perspective, it seemed as if my parents had lost their minds. Here I was, trying to save our family, perhaps the entire planet, and they stood there in disbelief. It was just like when Jor El tried to warn the citizens of Krypton that the planet was about to explode. We had indisputable proof, the ever-growing red ball of doom heading straight for our house, and they were wasting time talking!

Load the guns! Hide in the basement! Let's go on vacation! Do something, for crying out loud! And yet, they just talked. Finally, I had no choice but to listen.

Nothing they said made sense. They were living in denial, and I was inconsolable. They held me by the shoulders, speaking with hot breath.

My mother said aliens didn't exist, but there was the issue of her credibility. This was the same lady who hadn't come though with the batteries. If aliens teleported into our living room she'd probably tell me that if I ignored them they'd leave me alone.

And then my dad said the one thing I needed to hear.

"Look out the window. See all of those houses? Even if a spaceship was coming, what makes you think it would land in our back yard?"

Of course. Nothing that cool could ever happen to me. Heck, nothing really special ever seemed to happen to anybody in our family. Lightning never struck our tree, nobody was going to find dinosaur bones or a treasure chest buried in our yard, famous people were always from someplace else, and that's just the way it was. In that single moment I was relieved to be safe, and disappointed, knowing that nothing cool would ever happen in our family, our neighborhood, or even our city.

But Fate has a wicked sense of humor, and something big did happen, and it started right in our neighborhood. Some day, invaders would come, and the adults would be scared. Brave men who had fought Nazis and Japs would be upset, and mothers would cry, and there would be predictions of doom. But it wouldn't be the Russians, or the Red Chinese, or the aliens. Disaster would not arrive in a glowing red ball.

When terror would come to the hearts and minds of our friends and neighbors, it would arrive in a yellow school bus.

CHAPTER 7

I wish I could say that was the only time I woke my parents in the middle of the night, but over the next few months there were more episodes. One time I woke everybody up because I thought electricity was leaking out of the light fixtures. Then I had nightmares about howler monkeys, Paul Bunyan, and finally the one-armed veteran who sold pencils outside of the Downtown Hudson's Department Store.

By this point I had perfected my technique, and even while I was screaming I planned how I would evoke my parents' sympathy. I would describe in detail how the one-armed veteran was going to gut me alive with his hook, and then my mother would pet my head and coo me and comfort me until I fell asleep.

But eventually my mother did not show up. My father came alone, and he did not pet me, nor did his words bring me comfort.

"I don't care if Hitler shows up with a tomahawk in one hand and a rattlesnake in the other, you just stick your head under the covers and keep quiet!"

After that I was able to sleep on my own.

The next morning my father told me that if I was so easily scared that perhaps I wasn't mature enough to participate in the field day. Once a year, the Detroit Police Department had a Field Day in Tiger Stadium to raise money for the families of officers who had been killed in the line of duty. There were a few actual field events like a tug of war between the police and fire departments, but in order to make things more exciting the police department hired a few second tier circus acts and created their own clown brigade, staffed by members of the police force.

The well-meaning officers who made up the clown brigade generally had no previous performing experience, nor did they possess any special skills. Not one of them could twist balloons into animals or juggle or do acrobatics or much of anything that you would expect from a regular circus clown. However, the police clowns had one ingredient which made their shows spectacular.

What they lacked in talent they made up for in gunpowder. They discovered that no matter how flimsy the sketch, a good explosion always brought a reaction from the crowd, and what began as the occasional use of starter pistols and firecrackers soon evolved, or perhaps descended, into a barrage of percussive blasts from cherry bombs, shotguns, overloaded flash pots, small artillery, and poorly constructed bombs.

Sons of police clowns, once they had reached the age of five, were allowed to be part of the act, and I had finally come of age. Not only did that mean I'd be out on the field in the midst of the mayhem, but it also meant that, like the rest of the clowns, I'd dress in the Tiger locker room and be able to walk down the tunnel to the dugout to watch the other acts. After much consideration and many promises from me, my parents decided that I could participate on the condition that I would never again wake them in the middle of the night. And, for the most part, I kept that promise, breaking it only once, years later, when I was visited by the ghost of Walt Disney. In my own defense I have to point out that it was my mother who told me that his body had been frozen so he could be brought back to life at a later date.

Before any props were built, before the costumes were sewn, and even before the creation of the threadbare plot that would tie it all together, my father and Howard Howse, the rotund leader of the clown brigade, sat at our kitchen table and dreamed up ways to make explosions.

"What if I took a bunch of flash powder, wrapped it up in flash paper, and set it off with a flash bulb from a camera?" my father suggested.

"Yeah, that might work. But you'd better add some gunpowder—just to be safe," Howard replied.

Even at that age, I knew that there was something terribly wrong with the idea of adding gunpowder "just to be safe."

Really good explosives, like cherry bombs and Roman candles, were illegal in Michigan, so once a year several sworn officers of the law drove to Ohio to illegally purchase fireworks. Because it was my first year with the field day, my father pulled me out of school for a day so I could make the trip with them, perhaps because he thought it was a rite of passage, or maybe he wanted me to see how my old man could broker a good deal, but listening to him talk to the clerk did nothing more than convince me that he should not be allowed to talk about fireworks, much less use them.

"Let's see, I'll need some Roman candles. Give me five—no, make that eight boxes of those. No, the big box. You got any cherry bombs? How many come in a box? A half gross? You'd better give me four boxes. We can use those for anything."

My father exhausted his knowledge of fireworks long before his curiosity and dollars ran out, and the conversation soon degraded to "what does that do" and "go ahead and give me a dozen of those red whatchamathings." So, in addition to the cherry bombs and Roman candles, there were a couple of boxes of miscellaneous fireworks that, by the time we got back to Detroit, nobody could positively identify. This, of course, did not keep them from being used. It just kept us from knowing what was going to happen when the fuse was lit.

Despite the large number of explosives, safety was not an overwhelming concern, which explained the great number of injuries and accidents. My father had more caution than most, but not enough to suggest that we stop using fireworks. He salved his conscience by giving me a good talkin' to while we were loading the fireworks into the car.

"See that guy over there? Don't stare, just glance at him. Did you notice that one of his eyes looks funny?"

Did I notice? Hell yes! The guy looked like something from a Sir Graves Ghastly movie. One of his eyes had a milky white cast and wandered in all directions.

"About ten years ago, that guy was pretending to fix a washing machine. It was a great sketch. He'd throw in clothes, they'd come back out, water shot out, and then he got this giant wrench and whacked it on the side, which made a Roman candle shoot fireballs into the air. Do you know how a Roman candle works?"

"Not really."

"A Roman candle shoots exactly ten fireballs into the air. Well, that guy was really hamming it up for the crowd, got caught up in the moment, and lost count. He leaned over the Roman candle and it fired directly into his eye."

It sounded horrible, even gruesome, and I was sorry that I hadn't been there to see it.

"So, let that be a lesson to you…"

I knew what he was going to say. "Don't play with fireworks." My mind drifted as I waited for the typical lecture.

"Hey, listen, this is important. Let that be a lesson to you—always make sure you count carefully before you lean over a Roman candle."

What was that? That was no stern lecture. It wasn't even a harsh warning. I wanted to hear that if a Roman candle ever hit me in the face I should pray that it killed me, because whatever the fireworks did to me wouldn't be half as bad as what my dad would do when I got home. I wasn't even allowed to use matches, for crying out loud—why was my dad telling me how to light Roman candles? I needed a life lesson. I needed to hear that kids shouldn't touch matches, fireworks, or blasting caps.

But there was no such moral, because this was the Field Day. It was a strange world, one that smelled of gunpowder and greasepaint, and it came with its own set of distorted and dangerous rules.

Some of the clowns had their own specialty items. One guy had a slapstick that fired .22 caliber blanks, but that only produced a moderate bang. Another clown had split the barrel of a twelve-gauge shotgun into four parts and peeled it back like a banana skin. The fact that the gun had been mangled and was in an unknown degree of safety did not stop him from firing it several times during each show. The biggest boom, which came only once every show because it took so long to reload, came from a small cannon that somehow found its way into every sketch.

The best skit ever was a hillbilly sketch that had been performed the previous year, and it set a new record for shotgun blasts and explosions. A group of hillbilly clowns were raided by Federal Revenue Agent clowns that, for some reason, were dressed as Keystone Kops. There was lots of shooting back and forth, and it climaxed when the hillbillies' still exploded with a percussive blast that could be felt all the way to the bleachers. For some reason the blast blew off the pants of all of the hillbillies and none of the Feds, and then the hillbillies were carried off in a makeshift paddy wagon that was constructed from corrugated cardboard and a stripped down Volkswagen Beetle.

Howard and my dad weren't sure how to top the hillbilly sketch, and in one of those regrettable "wouldn't-it-be-great- if-we" moments, they decided to perform a magic trick. I knew this was a bad idea. A lot of kids don't like clowns to begin with, and the combination of clowns and magic seemed like a particularly unholy alliance.

Howard had a dabbling interest in magic, but neither he nor my father possessed any real skill or knowledge, and it was clear that their enthusiasm was based only on the fact that they had simply run out of ideas. However, Howard knew a doctor who was an amateur magician, and suggested that they borrow some props from him.

So, a few nights later, my dad, Howard, and I drove to Grosse Pointe to meet the magician at his home. He was waiting for us in his garage, and he didn't seem like a much of a magician at all. He was round-shouldered and pot-bellied, and had a hard time unlocking the door that led to his basement.

"Welcome to the Inner Sanctum," he said. He tried to be dramatic, but he sucked air between his teeth after he spoke, and I began to realize that he was not really a magician but just some guy who owned some magic equipment.

Except for the furnace and a small laundry area, the doctor's entire basement was devoted to magic. There were posters of Thurston and Blackstone, three-legged tables draped in black velvet, and colorful boxes decorated with dragons, but before I could take even one step toward them my father told me to sit on the stairs and keep my mouth shut.

"How about a floating lady?" the doctor offered. "I need a volunteer. You gentlemen are a little too heavy, but maybe…"

The doctor looked in my direction, and I thought I might get my chance to be part of a real magic trick and maybe even find out the secret, but his eyes moved past me and landed on a cardboard box, and he used that instead.

My dad and Howard weren't too impressed, and asked if he had something with a little more bite.

"I have an illusion where a person is cut in half."

"With a buzz saw?" Howard asked.

"No, with a hand saw."

"What does that thing do?" my father asked, pointing to a coffin in the corner.   It wasn't a brightly painted magician's prop, but a very realistic black and brass coffin.

"Oh, I don't think you'd want that.   That's the Cremation."

My father and Howard smiled at each other, and I felt sick to my stomach.   The doctor went into full dramatic mode, which meant that he tried not to hunch over quite as much, and he waved his hands over the coffin.

"First, the coffin is brought onto the stage.   Your assistant is put into the box, and the lid is closed."

The doctor opened a musty suitcase and removed a large wooden-handled torch, like the ones angry villagers carry in horror films.   He doused the rag at the end of the torch with lighter fluid and lit it with a kitchen match.

"There's a load of flash powder inside of the coffin, which you set off with the torch.   This makes a very satisfying explosion which forces open the front panel, and then the audience sees this!"

He pulled the front of the coffin down with his finger, revealing a very realistic skeleton.

"Then, the door is closed, you wave your arms, and the assistant is restored back to her lovely former self."

Coffin. Fire. Skeleton. Even I knew it was a bad idea yet, somehow, only I knew it was a bad idea. Even if everything went right, and I was pretty sure that it wouldn't, it was going to scare the hell out of most of the kids.

"You know Dad, with the coffin and the fire and skeleton…"

"Yeah, it's going to be great, isn't it?"

By now the doctor was trying to find a way to douse the burning torch. He shook it like a matchstick a couple of times but that didn't do anything, and then it looked like he was just going to hold onto it until it went out, but Howard snatched it away and dropped it into the laundry tub and ran the water. The torch hissed and there was an awful smell, but eventually the flame went out.

Although thousands of man-hours were spent buying fireworks and building props, there was no time set aside for rehearsal. To actually rehearse a skit was considered cowardly because any real clown should be able to perform with only the vaguest of instructions. A few minutes before the performance there would be some talk of "you do this while Howard does that" followed by exclamations of "Howard can't do that because he's wearing the gorilla suit." Then, with a hazy mental image of what was supposed to happen, an image that varied greatly from one clown to the next, the cops would go out and stumble through five minutes of slapstick, seltzer bottles, and explosions.

With such sparse planning, it is understandable that it wasn't until the day of the show that they discovered their omission.

"Hey, Wally, why don't you put the flash powder in the coffin?" Howard called to my dad.

"Sure. Where is it?" my dad answered.

"Didn't you get it when you went to Ohio?"

"No, that wasn't on the list," my father said, as if there had been a list.

Their voices dropped to low tones.

"Well, we'd better find something that burns," Howard said.

My dad brightened. "I'll talk to the groundskeeper. I'll bet he's got some gasoline."

Gasoline! Mom had warned me about gasoline. Of course, Mom was afraid of lots of screwy things, like the deep end of the pool and the stuff inside of golf balls, so maybe her judgment was suspect, but, even so... gasoline?

A little while later my dad came back with a red metal can.

"Hey, Howard, how much should I use?"

"Oh, about a cup."

"Is that going to be enough?"

"Make it a good cup."

My dad grabbed a ceramic coffee mug, filled it with gasoline, and then poured the gas in the coffin, kind of spreading it around. Then, without rinsing it out or warning its owner that it had contained gasoline, he put the cup right back on the table where he found it.

"Okay, now keep that lid closed so the fumes build up real good," Howard advised.

"Good idea," my father said.

About an hour later it was time to go on. The apparatus was on wheels, so a bunch of us pushed it out. I was wearing an Arabian costume--a vest with no shirt, a turban, and I had a big sword in my belt. I don't know what a sword had to do with the magic trick, but I thought I looked pretty cool.

Jay Howse, Howard's grown son, was the clown who was to be cremated. To add drama to the trick, Jay pretended like he didn't want to go in the coffin and three big clowns physically forced him into the box.

"Stand back," my father said, as Howard came out with the torch. I stepped back a few paces, but he shouted, "Way back!" I didn't like his tone. It did not have a "just in case" quality.

While Howard was coming out, the clown inside of the coffin slipped through a trap door and hid in the wheeled base that supported the box. He closed the trap door, which protected him from the blast that was to follow. In order to give Jay enough time to slip through the trap door, Howard whooshed the torch about, making figure eights in the air.

It wasn't until I reached high school that I learned that a cup of gasoline, properly mixed with air, can propel the average automobile a distance of one mile. However, I immediately learned what a cup of gasoline can do when it is put in a large box and allowed to vaporize for about an hour. When Howard lifted the lid and gingerly brought the torch near the box, there was an explosion of apocalyptic proportion. The biggest part of the blast went straight up in the air, but a pretty good splash of fire leapt from the front of the box, and it barely missed Howard, who was standing a bit off to the side.

The front panel, which was supposed to be blown open, was blown clean off, along with the top, the sides, and the end panels. The skeleton, which had absorbed some of the gasoline and was now on fire, was propelled a dozen feet into the air. Only the base, which contained a very scared clown, remained intact.

To the audience, it was the greatest spectacle in the history of live entertainment. There was an instant burst of applause, followed by cheers and whistles.

That did not last long. Terrorized clowns were ducking for cover as bits of flaming coffin fell down from the sky. They were running this way and that, but not in a humorous, clown-like fashion. No, this was more like fleeing, and the cheers from the audience turned to a prolonged gasp.

The skeleton had remained more-or-less intact, and it landed, still burning, in the infield grass, which also began to burn. Several clowns ran toward the skeleton and began stomping out the burning grass with their big, floppy shoes. Others stomped on the skeleton itself which, as far as the kids in the audience knew, was the burning remains of a recently killed clown.

Stomping out a gasoline fueled fire is no small task, and soon the heat of the flames began working its way through the clowns' shoes and burning their feet. I could hear them shouting obscenities, even from where I was standing.

By this point the kids in the audience believed they had witnessed a murder, and a particularly gruesome one at that. From their perspective it appeared that three clowns had forced a very unwilling clown into a box, reduced him to a flaming skeleton, and then danced on his fiery remains while chanting obscenities. Panicky parents insisted that it was just a trick, but the evidence was so graphic that no amount of consolation could change the children's minds.

My father was standing beside me. He must have run over, but I had been too busy watching the real action to notice.

"Are you okay?"

"Yes."

"Okay, go back to the same gate where we came in. I'll meet you there."

Some of the clowns had taken off their funny jackets and were using them to beat out the flames, which, by now, were nearly extinguished.

I moved to the gate, and I could hear little kids crying, and mothers trying to reassure them.

"Where's the clown?" one kid asked.

Jay was safely hidden in the base of the magic prop. I wondered why he didn't pop out to show everybody that he was okay. Maybe he felt bound by the Magician's Code, the promise that a trick could never be revealed. Or maybe it hadn't occurred to him.

Some children cried softly and others wailed in horror as the clowns gathered up as many pieces of the skeleton as they could find.

The announcer finally figured that he should do something, and he said, "Let's hear it for your Detroit Police Clowns!"

There was some polite applause. By now most of the remains of the coffin and the skeleton had been piled on the base, and with great solemnity the clowns wheeled the whole thing away.

As soon as they were out of sight, Jay leapt out of the base, and Howard sprayed everything with a fire extinguisher. Jay was unharmed, but while crawling back through the trap door and out of the base he picked up a lot of soot and he looked like he'd been dragged though a campfire.

Back in the locker room, it was very quiet, like we had just lost the big game. Nobody said anything, but I still had an unanswered question.

"Dad, how come you didn't let the clown out of the trap door so everybody could see that he was okay?"

Eyes popped. With everything else going on, it just hadn't occurred to anybody. I heard a voice say, "Oh, there are going to be some kids with nightmares tonight!"

With that, everybody burst into uncontrollable laughter. One guy began coughing up his pop, and it came out through his nose as he leaned over the trash can. Others had to lean on tables or locker doors to support themselves and keep from doubling over.

The clowns began to imagine what would happen when the spectators tried to explain what they had seen, what they would say when people asked if they enjoyed the show.

There was a knock at the door, and it was one of the stadium guys who wore the green suits, ushers or whatever they were. He said a lady was there with her kid and she wanted him to see that the clown was okay.

Howard said sure, let him in, then shouted for everybody to be quiet.

A pretty woman, dressed a little too nicely for a Field Day, came into the locker room. The clowns tried to calm down, but overshot it a little and acted somber, even to the point of being grim. The woman looked a little confused. Most of the clowns had taken off part of their costumes, and they were sitting around like regular people, drinking pop and dealing cards. Howard pointed at Jay.

"There's the guy you're looking for."

She escorted her child toward Jay, who was hanging his soot-covered shirt in his locker. He turned around to greet the shaken child.

Like all white-faced clowns, Jay's teeth looked yellow, and his tongue and gums were exceptionally red. Maybe the kid could've handled that, but Jay was still covered with soot, and had just removed his skull cap, exposing his unruly, sweaty hair, and although he was animated, he looked more undead than alive.

"Look honey, it's the clown from the coffin," his mother said, trying to reassure her child.

"Hiya, kid," Jay said, extending his hand.

The kid turned around, buried his face in his mother's dress, and screamed.

"Maybe we'd better leave," she said.

As soon as they left, there was another round of laughter.

That night, after the second show, we scoured the infield for any remaining pieces of the coffin. My father and Howard, in very secret meetings in our garage, repaired and rebuilt the prop as best they could. Partway through the process I had to go to the paint store on Eight Mile to get some plaster of Paris, which they used to repair the skeleton. Although I had helped them, I was not allowed in the garage and I had to stand at a distance when they loaded the coffin in the back of Howard's truck.

Even from where I was standing, I could see that it didn't look the same.

Later, when my father returned, I asked him how it went. He laughed in a sad way and said, "We won't be borrowing any more magic tricks from that guy."

CHAPTER 8

The Field Day had turned out much better than I expected. I had a story to end all stories, the kind of thing that never happened to anybody, but it did happen, and it had happened to me. Every day, Mrs. Langlois let one person tell a story at the beginning of class. I had to wait a couple of weeks, but my turn finally came.

Today would be the first time I made up my mind to show those bastards. I was just learning to swear, and I did not feel comfortable with all of the words, but I had picked up the word "bastard" and grown fond of it. So I was not just going to show those guys, I was going to show those bastards. Who those bastards were and what I was going to show them would change as the years passed, but those details didn't matter. I had a "you've-shown-one-bastard-you've-shown-'em-all" attitude. As long as I showed any bastard anything, I was making progress.

I was careful not to drop any hints about the Field Day. I preciously guarded all details, saving everything for my big day. No one knew that I had been in the Field Day or even that there was such a thing as the Field Day, much less the events that had transpired.

I had practiced the story many times, so when my turn came, I was ready. I told it with great detail, using wild gestures, and I raised my voice and paused for emphasis. As the story began, when I told how I hung my clothes in one of the very same lockers that the Tigers used, I saw them look at me with admiration—no, not mere admiration—they looked at me with awe. By the end of the tale I was no longer Detlef Niebaum, pathetic German kid. I was the famous Detlef Niebaum, entertainer extraordinaire. I imagined myself standing on the sidewalk next to President Johnson as passersby whispered, "Who is that man standing next to the famous Detlef Niebaum?"

It didn't last long.

"Mr. Niebaum, do you really expect me to believe any of that?" Mrs. Langlois frowned.

"Sure. It all happened, just like I told it."

"You were a clown. At age five?"

"Uh huh."

"And you performed at Tiger Stadium and dressed in the locker room?"

"Uh huh."

I could feel the crowd turning against me.

"And there were explosions and fireworks, just like you said."

"Yes, Mrs. Langlois."

"How many people in this class believe what Detlef is trying to tell us?"

Not one hand went up.

"Call my mom!"

"Excuse me, Mr. Niebaum. What did you say?"

"You can call my mom. Ask her."

Yes, that would solve everything. My mom was there, and she saw it all.

"Good idea, Mr. Niebaum. And while I'm talking to her, I've got a few other matters I'd like to discuss with her. Like, for instance, why you're getting a D in handwriting."

That was low. I had crappy handwriting, but she didn't need to tell the whole class.

"Now, do you still want me to call her?"

"No, Mrs. Langlois."

A hand went up. It was Jimmy Korman.

"Yes, James."

"Mrs. Langlois, I live down the street from Detlef, and I don't even think his father is a policeman."

What? Of course he was a policeman. Everybody knew that. Mrs. Langlois probably knew, and she would straighten him out.

"Oh, really, James. Why do you say that?"

That's what Mrs. Langlois said when she was setting you up for the fall. She was going to get him but good.

"Well, I see him going to work in the morning, and he doesn't wear a uniform or carry a gun. He just wears a suit and tie."

Everybody laughed, then Jimmy added a little more.

"He doesn't even drive to work. He takes the bus."

What did that have to do with anything? Everybody laughed again. Those bastards.

And so it began, my quest to show those bastards. I needed to do something so big, so impressive, that it would show them all.

I knew better than to try a stunt like jumping off the garage roof wearing a pair of homemade wings. I wasn't too good at sports, so I was pretty sure I did not have what it took to be a daredevil. I could do something heroic, like pull a little kid out of a burning building, but it was unlikely that the opportunity for such an event would present itself in the next couple of days. Besides, with my luck, nobody would see me.

That weekend, my family went up to our cabin to close it down for the winter. My father and my Uncle John had pooled their money and bought twenty wooded acres near Rose City, about three or four hours north of Detroit.

The trip was not half the fun. I tried to pass the time reading comic books, but it made me carsick. My father was preoccupied with the traffic, so I tried to converse with my mom.

"Mom, how come there's always a bad guy in the comic books?"

"Well, honey, without a bad guy there wouldn't be a story."

"You don't need a story. Superman could just fly around and do cool stuff."

"What kind of stuff?"

"You know, like bending iron bars with his bare hands, or he could throw up a handful of corn and make it pop before it hit the ground."

"How would he do that?"

Jeez. Didn't she know anything?

"With his heat vision. Or maybe they could show him feeding the animals in his intergalactic zoo in his Fortress of Solitude. Or maybe he could take a vacation to the bottle city of Kandor, but he'd have to be careful because he doesn't have any powers there, but still, don't you think he'd want to see some of his Kryptonian…"

"Walter! Talk to your son. I think you've been feeding him too many comic books."

"What?" Dad sounded like he was ready to laugh.

"Walter, do you know what kind of nonsense comes out of your son's mouth?"

"Detlef, what is your mother talking about?" he asked.

"I don't know. I was just telling her that it would be cool if Superman used his heat vision to make popcorn. Stuff like that."

"Jeez, Dorothy, what's wrong with that?"

"I just think he reads too many comic books. Don't you think he should be reading something more substantial?"

"What does it matter what he reads, so long as he reads? Besides, they're only twelve cents!"

"Except for the eighty page giants, Dad. Those are a quarter."

My mother scowled at me. "Detlef, you keep out of this! This has nothing to do with you!"

"Dorothy, the kid wasn't that crazy about reading until we bought him comic books. Now we can't stop him. Isn't that good enough?"

Just then I spotted a sign for the Call of the Wild Museum.

"Hey Dad! Can we go to the Call of the Wild Museum? It's coming right up!"

"We're a little pressed for time. We'll go sometime when we're not in such a rush."

This conversation was repeated every time we went to the cabin. We were always "pressed for time."

Some of my other friends' families had cottages, cute little Hansel and Gretel places with lots of gingerbread trim, but we had a cabin. My dad and Uncle John built it themselves, using salvaged materials of varying quality. There was only one main room, which had bunk beds that had been cobbled together from two-by-fours and old box springs, an old gas cooking stove that had to be lit with a match, and a big round table with four chairs that had saw marks from when my dad used them as sawhorses while building the cabin. There was an enclosed entryway, part of which had been sectioned off to house a toilet and sink, and I liked the fact that I had to leave the cabin itself to go to the bathroom. It made me feel like Daniel Boone or Davy Crockett or one of those coonskin cap guys.

Unlike the other cabins in the area, which were made of logs, ours was sided with rolled shingles that were supposed to give the appearance of bricks but looked quite a bit like roofing shingles, so our place looked less like a hunting lodge and more like a shack for distilling moonshine.

I found that comforting, because it implied a carefree hillbilly lifestyle that came with its own set of rustic rules. At home I wasn't allowed to play with matches, but at the cabin I was allowed to light the kitchen stove. I was only allowed to have toy guns at home, but at the cabin I had a BB gun, and sometimes my dad let me shoot his .22. At home I couldn't cross the street without permission, but at the cabin I could take a spoon and dig in the dirt road. At home I wasn't allowed to drive in nails except in scrap wood because I bent the nail over or missed it entirely. At the cabin I could drive nails into the cabin itself, and nobody cared if left behind a trail of bent nails and hammer rings.

This was just an overnight trip and there would be no time for shooting guns or hammering nails. It was too cold to go swimming, which we only did at the neighbor's cabin since the bottom of the lake by our cabin was covered with muck and leaves, but I did manage to drop a line in the water and try to catch some fish. I didn't have any live bait so I tried to make do with little hunks of American cheese that my mother brought for sandwiches, but the fish were not interested and, after a while, neither was I.

Late Saturday afternoon my father announced that we would be leaving, and he asked if I wanted to help him drain the pump. I followed him down the hill, and watched as he lifted the lid off the pump hole, and then climbed inside. I stood on the ground nearby, hoping that he'd need me to run up to the cabin to get something.

There was a loud metallic clang, which I took to be a good sign, because it was only when things went wrong that I was called to duty.

"What happened?" I asked.

"Will you look at this?" My dad held up his pipe wrench, or at least, what was left of it. The top jaw had broken off, leaving only a jagged prong at the end of the wrench.

"What happened?" I asked again.

"This son-of-a-bitching thing never was worth a crap."

I liked working with my dad, and I liked it even better when he used foul language.

"Maybe we can fix it." I saw the broken piece of wrench lying in the hole, and I thought we could try to put it back on with Elmer's glue or masking tape.

"Fix it? I'll show you how to fix it!" Without even looking, he tossed the wrench out of the pump hole. It spun end over end, high in the air, over the dock, and splooshed into the lake.

Why couldn't he ever do anything cool like that when the kids from school were around?

"Detlef, do not tell your mother about that," he commanded.

"Why not?"

"Because she bought me that wrench, and it would hurt her feelings. Now, let's go up to the car and see if I have another one in the trunk."

With one graceful motion Dad pulled himself out of the pump hole.

"So Mom doesn't buy good tools?"

"She's given me plenty of good tools, like the Shopsmith and the band saw. She just can't be trusted to pick them out on her own."

We headed up the hill. Dad wasn't in any kind of a hurry, and I suspected he really didn't want to leave. Maybe that was the answer to everything.

"Dad, do we have to go back? Maybe we could live at the cabin."

"We can't live here. I've got to go to work and you've got to go to school."

By now we were back at the car, and he popped open the trunk and unrolled some tools that were wrapped in a rag.

"I could go to school here. They've got schools in Rose City, don't they?"

He pawed through his tools for a little while, and I wondered if he had even heard me. He found another pipe wrench, which I thought looked a lot like the one he broke, and slammed the trunk shut.

"Okay. What's going on at school?"

"How did you know that something was going on at school?"

"Did you think you could fool me? I'm a policeman, for crying out loud!"

He laughed pretty hard, and I got angry.

"Then why don't you wear a uniform?"

I grabbed the wrench and ran down the hill. He laughed all the harder. When I got near the pump, I threw the wrench as hard as I could. It did not spin end-over-end. It did not sail over the dock. It landed in the water about two inches from shore, and it was only fully submerged when the occasional wave splashed over it.

With no other options left, I sat on the ground and cried.

My father was not upset. He didn't run down to catch up with me. He just walked along like nothing had happened and made no mention of the wrench. He glanced at it, decided it wasn't going anywhere, and left it where it was.

"Hey, Sport, what's going on?"

I told him everything. I told him that the kids at school said I wasn't a clown and that he wasn't a policeman. I told him that Mrs. Langlois was in on it, too. I even told him that I was getting a D in penmanship.

He took it all in, and did his best not to laugh, although he couldn't help himself a couple of times.

When it was all over, he just dropped himself back into the pump hole.

"Detlef, I need my wrench. Why don't you get it for me?"

He said it with the same "hey-Pal-can-you-give-me-a-hand" voice he used to send me to Ray's Hardware. I scooted the rest of the way down the hill to the shoreline. The wrench was wet and very cold, but Dad said he wanted it so I brought it to him.

"Thanks," he said. He shook off most of the water, then dried it on his shirt. He went back to work, talking all the while.

"Maybe next time there's show-and-tell, instead of telling a story, you can show them something," he suggested.

Show them? Yes, that's the mission. Show those bastards. Dad was right on track.

"But I don't have anything to show."

"I don't know. You could show them a magic trick or something."

Magic trick? What was he talking about? Sure, the kids would like a magic trick, but I wasn't a magician.

"You mean, like the trick we did at the Field Day?"

"I keep telling your Uncle John that he doesn't have to tighten the cap so hard. No wonder the wrench broke!" He took a second to compose himself. "I mean, no, not like the Field Day. That was a disaster. You know, a card trick or something."

"But I don't know any card tricks."

"You can probably find some magic books at the library. The bookmobile is coming next week, isn't it?"

"Yeah."

"Well, ask the librarian if she has any magic books for kids. Now, let's get the lid back on this pump so we can go home," he said, and then he swung himself out of the hole in an athletic yet apelike manner that he displayed only when no one else was around.

We got the lid back on the pump and walked back up the hill. I headed toward the car.

"Where do you think you're going?" he asked.

"I'm going to put the wrench back in the car."

"Not yet."

He went into the back porch of the cabin and emerged with an oil can and a rag.

"We've got to clean up the wrench before we put it away."

He threw the rag at me. I tried to catch it, but it just hit my hand and fell on the ground. While I was picking it up, he took the wrench from me and walked over to the picnic table and sat down. In just a second or two he had taken it apart.

"Now, dry it off real good."

"Will that keep it from rusting?"

"Probably not. That's why we're going to give it a light coat of oil. Hand me that rag."

He tore the rag in half, gave me a piece, and kept the other for himself.

"Is that how you became a policeman? By reading a book in the library?"

"No, I never thought about being a policeman."

"What happened?"

"After I got out of the Navy, I went to the Wolverine school to be an auto mechanic." He took the upper jaw of the wrench, smeared it with a light coat of oil, then wiped it off. He pushed the oil can at me, and I rubbed some oil onto the body of the wrench. I wasn't very good at it, but he wasn't in a hurry. "I heard that the police department was hiring mechanics to fix the cars in the motor pool. So I went down to apply for a job, but there wasn't an opening. I was getting ready to leave when the guy behind the counter asked me if I ever thought about being a policeman."

"That's all there was to it?"

"No, there was a lot more. I had to take a bunch of tests, and climb a rope, and all kinds of stuff."

"I hate tests."

"Me, too. In fact, I just flunked one about a month ago."

"Really?"

"Yeah. The sergeant's exam."

"Were you mad?"

"Well, I kind of flunked it on purpose," he muttered.

"Why?"

"Because if I get promoted they'll move me out of the Liquor License Bureau. When I was first hired I wore a uniform and walked a beat, and that was pretty dangerous. Then I worked on the Vice Squad, and that was dangerous, too."

"Did guys shoot at you?"

"Sometimes. Anyhow, after I was promoted to detective they transferred me to Liquor License, and that's not very dangerous at all. Now your mom doesn't have to worry about me, and I don't have to deal with guys shooting at me."

"But why did you flunk the test?"

"Because if I get promoted to sergeant they might move me back to the Vice Squad. Or worse."

"What could be worse than that?"

"I don't know, but I'm sure they'd find something."

"So you're going to be a detective for the rest of your life?"

"I'm not sure. I signed up for some college classes. Maybe something else will work out for me."

Why was he trying to improve himself? He seemed fine the way he was. Besides, how was I ever going to be like him if he kept changing? I couldn't hit a moving target. The only chance I had to be like him was if he screwed up and lost a lot of ground, and then maybe I could meet him halfway.

"You know, Dad, instead of doing a magic trick, maybe I could be a superhero."

"I don't think they have superhero books in the library."

"I guess not. If you want to be a superhero you usually have to be born on another planet or have a million dollars to buy a bunch of gadgets."

"Well, if you ever do get a million dollars to buy some gadgets, don't let your mother pick them out, or they'll break in half just when you need them the most."

"Dad, did you ever send Mom to Ray's Hardware to buy hacksaw blades?"

"No, I never did."

"Good."

"I'll tell you what. Get a couple of magic books from the bookmobile, and if you read them and like them, I'll take you to Hudson's to buy a magic book that you can keep."

"Thanks. And sorry about your wrench."

When the bookmobile came to our neighborhood, I checked out three magic books. The best one was 101 Best Magic Tricks by Guy Frederick, and I decided that was the one my dad could buy for me. Before I had to take the books back to the library, I learned a few good tricks. I could make a penny disappear by rubbing it into my elbow, shuffle four kings into the deck and make them come to the top, and make a rubber band jump between my fingers.

When I returned the books, the librarian said I might like reading Ventriloquism for Fun and Profit by Paul Winchell. I knew him from television, and he was pretty funny. His book had everything—how to talk without moving your lips, some comedy routines for you and your dummy, and instructions on how to make your own dummy out of paper mâché. I was pretty sure we had most of the materials around the house.

I didn't tell my dad about the ventriloquism book. My plan was to secretly become a ventriloquist, construct my own dummy, and then surprise everybody. I didn't get very far. My mother found me rooting through the kitchen cabinets.

"What are you looking for?"

I looked at my list.

"A piece of broom or mop handle, two rolls of good thick paper towel, and some shellac. I think that's in the basement."

"Anything else?"

"I'll need five to ten pounds of non-hardening clay, half a pound of paperhanger's paste, and a pound of plastic wood. But I can get that at Ray's hardware."

"Really? And who is going to pay for this?"

"I will."

"Hmmm. What do you need it for?"

"Nothing."

I could tell by my mother's skeptical tone that I wasn't going to be building a dummy any time in the near future. I secretly worked on my ventriloquism whenever I could, reading the book over and over. Paul Winchell was very encouraging, saying that you didn't need any special gift or talent, which I thought described me pretty well, and that anybody could be a ventriloquist. He told of how he had spent nearly a year in bed suffering from the crippling effects of polio, and how he studied ventriloquism during that time. The book concluded with a philosophical chapter that explained how ventriloquism changed his life. Working with the dummy gave him almost superhuman abilities, allowing him to think and speak for two people at once, and enhancing his physical coordination to the point that he shot a 96 the first time he ever tried to golf.

That convinced me that I was on the right track. If ventriloquism could get him through polio, then magic, or ventriloquism, or maybe both together, would help me show those bastards once and for all.

It was many weeks before it was my turn again to tell a story in Mrs. Langlois' class. I was pretty sure that some of the other kids had gone twice since my last turn, but Mrs. Langlois insisted that she kept track on some list that none of us ever saw.

Finally, on the last day before Christmas vacation, I got my chance.

"Who would like to share a story?" she asked, and hands went up all around the room. Some students moaned, and other ones made pathetic facial expressions, but I went for the "lift-my-butt-out-of-the-seat-while-reaching-for-the-ceiling" approach.

"Mr. Niebaum, why don't you tell us a story?"

I sprang from my seat and stood in front of the class.

"My friends, I am going to make this penny disappear by rubbing it into my elbow."

Technically this was not a story, but Mrs. Langlois did not object. I rubbed the penny into my elbow, then I dropped it onto the floor. Everybody laughed, but I didn't mind because it was part of the trick. When I picked up the penny, I secretly dropped it into my shoe. I held my hand as if it still contained the penny, and began to rub it against my elbow. Everybody was still laughing, but in just a second…

"Excuse me, Mrs. Langlois…"

It was Jimmy Korman.

"Yes, Mr. Korman."

"Didn't Detlef just have a turn a few days ago?"

"No, I didn't! I haven't had a turn since-"

"Since when, Mr. Niebaum?"

She had me. I didn't want to bring up what had happened last time.

80

"That's what I thought. Why don't you take your seat? Well, this is enough of story telling. You're going to be moving up a grade in January, and you're getting too old."

On the way home, Tom Carlotti ran to catch up with me. That was odd. He never talked to me.

"Detlef, can you really do it?"

"Do what?"

"Make a penny disappear."

"Sure."

"Let me see."

It was a little difficult. I had to remove my mittens, it was hard to bend my elbow while wearing a heavy coat, and my winter boots made it a little harder to get rid of the penny, but I managed to get through the trick. A couple of kids I didn't know stopped to watch, and when it was over they said it was a pretty good trick.

It wasn't a perfect victory. By the time we got back from Christmas break it was old news, and everybody talked about what they got for Christmas and how sad they were to be back in school. But, for a couple of minutes, I impressed Tom Carlotti and a couple of kids I didn't know. I guess that was something.

CHAPTER 9

Like a lot of other boys in my neighborhood, I got a gun for Christmas. Not a real gun, of course, but a toy gun. You could always count on a gun or two for Christmas or your birthday, but this gun was special. It was the Johnny Seven O.M.A.

If you went by what they said on television, boys liked to play games like "Cowboys and Indians" or "Cops and Robbers," but in my neighborhood the name of the "bang you're dead" game was "War."

"Hey, Mom, we're going outside to play War," we'd shout as we ran to the back yard.

Everybody knew what that meant. It didn't mean that we were going to play with little green army guys, and it didn't mean that we were going to play Capture the Flag. It meant that we were going to re-enact World War II as if it had been fought by eight-year-old boys who were afraid to cross the street because their mothers might give them a spanking.

What we lacked in guts we made up for in guns and gear. Our supply of musty backpacks, ridiculously large helmets that refused to stay on our heads, and plastic canteens that made the water taste funny came from Silverstein's, an army navy surplus of such proportion that it looked like it could have supplied the entire D-Day invasion with gear left over. Silverstein's was easy to find, because it was the only business on McNichols Road that had a Sherman tank parked out front.

Although Silverstein's had all manner of uniforms and canteens and backpacks, they did not have suitable guns. They had a rack of rifles that looked very real but were built to actual size and were too big to be handled by kids. Had that been the only flaw we might have looked past it. Unfortunately, the guns were bolt-action weapons that only fired a single shot without reloading, and even though all other laws of science and logic were negotiable in our ersatz war, only toys that looked like machine guns could be fired like machine guns, so the weapon of choice for the well-armed eight-year-old came from the toy department of the department store.

The first wave of weapons to hit our neighborhood were realistic copies of actual military rifles and hand guns. The really good ones were scaled-down versions of Lugers or Thompson sub-machine guns or M1 rifles, especially if they were equipped with devices that made machine gun noises or fired caps.

However, the best gun of all, the gun by which all others were measured, was not a copy of a military weapon, but something created especially for eight-year-old boys. It was the Johnny Seven O.M.A. It was called the O.M.A. because it made you a One Man Army, and the "seven" referred to the fact that it was actually seven weapons. It shot missiles, launched grenades, fired bullets, set off caps, made machine gun noises, and even had a detachable pistol. The pistol was essential because the actual weapon was too large and cumbersome to carry around for any length of time. It had a couple of fold-out legs and could be set up like a tripod and fired from a prone position, and in that state it was the ultimate weapon for destroying any enemy who voluntarily stood directly in front of it at a distance no greater than six feet.

The actual game of War was pretty chaotic, and rarely made it beyond the point of choosing sides and passing out weapons, but this is mostly conjecture on my part because I was often the first casualty. My brother

83

would send me inside of the house to get an extra gun for a kid who didn't have one, and while rummaging through the toy box I'd find Tinker Toys or a comic book and I'd forget about playing War. My brother was probably tricking me, but I was happy to be tricked because I wanted to be excluded before it came time to choose sides.

My fear was not that I would be picked last, like I was in baseball or hockey, but that I'd be picked first. When it came time to choose sides, it was often suggested that I should be a Nazi. Although my father had served with the Navy in World War II, we had distant relatives in Germany who fought on the other side, and although I never mentioned it the other kids seemed to know.

I never actually had to be a Nazi, not because my friends cared about my feelings, but because we needed two roughly equal sides and none of the other kids wanted to be on my Nazi team. So, in our bizarre re-telling of the Second World War, everybody was American.

Still, it was a reminder that, with the exception of my father, all of the other Niebaums since the beginning of time had served in the German army. My dad's father had even been a soldier in the German Army in World War I.

I was faced with an uncomfortable truth. Germans were evil, and yet we were Germans. Did that mean that we were evil? I didn't think so. The only person in our family who came close to being evil was my brother, and he was adopted. I went to my dad for an explanation. I found him in the basement, burning wrapping paper in the incinerator.

"Dad, we're German, right?"

"Of course."

"But didn't America fight the Germans?"

"Yes, we did."

"Does that mean that our family is bad?"

"Not all Germans are bad. You see, Germany is divided in half. One side of the country is filled with good Germans, and the other side has bad Germans."

"And our family is from the good side."

"Yes. Our family comes from Essen, which is West Germany, and that's the good side."

"Are you sure?"

"Check it out for yourself. The Ruhr Valley is so far west that it's almost part of the Netherlands."

"No, I mean, are you sure that Germany is divided like that?"

"Yes. There's East Germany and West Germany."

"You mean there are two Germanys?"

"Yes, there are two Germanys."

For a moment I actually believed what he was saying, but then I realized how ridiculous it sounded. Two Germanys—what was he thinking? Maybe in some theoretical sense Germany was divided, but surely there wasn't some border or wall dividing the country into two parts. My father had obviously talked himself into believing something that wasn't true. He'd done it before, and it must have been his way of dealing with situations he couldn't change.

I thought back to the last time we visited our cabin and my dad said we didn't have time to go to the Call of the Wild Museum. Sure, he told himself that we'd go someday when we had more time, but I knew it would never happen. It was another one of his delusions. He talked himself into believing there were two Germanys just like he talked himself into believing we would go to the Call of the Wild Museum.

Of course, I wanted him to be right, so when school resumed in January I decided to run his notion past Miss Houk, my second grade teacher. Miss Houk was a font of disturbing information. She was the one who told us that Michigan and Ohio had once been at war with each other, and it turned out that she was right. If anybody knew about two Germanys it would be her.

Standing up in class and asking if there were two Germanys would be social suicide, so on the first school day after Christmas break I waited by my locker until everybody else had gone home, and then I headed back to her room.

She was hunched over a stack of papers, whisking through the pile and shaking her head from side to side as she slashed out red marks with her pen.

"Miss Houk?"

She glared at me as if to say, "This had better be important."

"My father says that there are two different Germanys, a good one and a bad one. Is he right?"

Her glare turned to a scowl. She spun her chair, grabbed the globe from her shelf, and set it on the desk. Her finger pointed to a mass of land.

"Do you see two Germanys?"

I was ready to say "no," and slink away in humiliation, but I gave the globe an obligatory glance.

And there, next to her finger, were two small blobs. East Germany, and West Germany. Dad was right. There were two Germanys. There was hope. Maybe, someday, we would go to the Call of the Wild Museum.

Miss Houk went on to explain that West Germany was good, like America. East Germany was evil, like Russia. And in that instant, the world made sense. America must have conquered evil Germany, and freed the good Germans. I was also happy to see that good Germany was bigger than bad Germany. I walked home, thinking it through. West Germany was full of woodcarvers and cuckoo clocks, and the people wore Alpine hats and yodeled. East Germany was populated by former Nazis who smoked cigarettes and wore black leather jackets.

There was one final test. I went home and dug through the top drawer of my dresser. Somewhere, in with the bottle caps and little plastic army guys, was my harmonica. A Hohner harmonica. And there, on the back, were the words of comfort. "Made in West Germany." Of course.

Perhaps by coincidence, or perhaps because of our conversation, Miss Houk soon began talking about Russia. Russia was our enemy, worse than Germany, because Russia had The Bomb. In Russia, they didn't have televisions or telephones or even indoor toilets, but they wanted them, and they were going to come to America to take ours. They were plotting, building Sputniks and atomic bombs, and one of these days they'd put an atomic bomb on a Sputnik, and then we'd really be in trouble. That's why we had to get to the moon before they did.

She went on to explain that our twice-a-year air raid drills were to prepare us for the inevitable Russian attack. I didn't pretend to understand. During air raid drills we all went down to the gym. I couldn't imagine why the school administration felt that the gym was impervious to atomic attack; it sometimes leaked during a bad rainstorm.

I thought it would have been prudent to put us on a cross-town bus and send us to Silverstein's where we could all gear up for the invasion that would occur in the aftermath of the initial bomb blast. Maybe there was some secret room in the back where Mr. Silverstein kept the real weapons, working versions of the Johnny Seven O.M.A. Maybe the reason the toy manufacturers put the Johnny Seven in our hands was so that we'd be ready to use the real thing when the time came.

Miss Houk leaned forward, with her hands pressed against the top of her desk. She looked around, perhaps to check for Russian spies, and in a half whisper spoke to the class.

"When they ring that air raid siren, remember that it might just be a drill, or maybe it will be the real thing. You never know until it's too late. You might be in the gym for ten minutes, or you might be there for ten days."

I was getting more jittery by the minute. What if Russian spies learned that we assembled in the gym? The air raid instructions were posted on the bulletin board where anybody could see them. Wouldn't this make it easy for them to wipe us all out with a single bomb?

A few weeks after her speech about the Russians, Miss Houk once again spoke to us in the hushed tone of a conspirator.

"Russia is not our biggest problem. Yes, they're bad, and yes, they have the atomic bomb, but we've got bigger concerns."

Bigger concerns? What bigger concerns? Aliens? Robots?

"Our biggest problem is Red China. They have a problem with overpopulation. Does anybody know what that is?

Gerald O'Bannion raised his hand. "Is that when a country has too many people?"

"That's right. Look at Red China—see how big it is?"

By this time I was really getting to hate that globe.

"All of that land, and it isn't enough. They want more. And how can we stop them?"

I knew the answer! I raised my hand with such exuberance that she actually called on me.

"Can't we just drop a bomb on them?"

"Detlef, you didn't give your idea much thought, did you?"

Give it much thought? I didn't even know about this problem until a couple of minutes before. It didn't matter. I could tell by her tone of voice that I was going to get ridiculed yet again.

"The Red Chinese have too many people. They don't care how many we kill. It just helps them solve their problem. They can send ten times as many soldiers as we can, and even if we kill them all they can still send more. And..."

I hoped she wasn't going to say what I knew she was going to say.

"And," she continued, "they have the atomic bomb."

Right after that the dismissal bell rang. I think she planned it that way, so we'd have plenty to think about as we left. Well, this time I would think things through, and I'd come up with an answer so brilliant that she'd have to acknowledge my genius. On my way home from school, I came up with an idea. We could repaint an American plane with Russian symbols and drop a bomb on China. This would start a war between our enemies, the two evil forces would cancel each other out, and America would win by default. It was perfect, no it was beyond perfect; it was brilliant. That evening, as my father walked through the living room, newspaper in hand, I stopped him and told him the details of my scheme. His reaction was quick and powerful.

"No war is no good for nobody!"

And with those words, both he and his newspaper vanished into the bathroom. I felt cheated. I knew the only reason he didn't give my idea the proper consideration was that he was in a hurry to get to the toilet. If I had caught him on the way out of the bathroom he might have had a very different opinion. Even taking that into consideration, I thought it might be wise to keep my plan from Miss Houk.

But even as we grew to fear the Russians, and the Chinese, and the aliens, they never made it into our game of War. It was still the Germans, the bad Germans, who received our hot lead.

"Budda-dow, budda-dow, I got you."

"No you didn't."

"Yes I did."

"You missed."

"Shut up, you're dead."

"No I'm not."

"I can't hear you, because you're dead."

That was the great thing about Germans. We had already defeated them, and the end of the story was scripted. Before I was born, my dad, and Mr. Hedgecock from next door, and Mr. Frasier who went to our church, and a bunch of other guys who were just like them had already conquered the Germans.

And so we fought our imaginary battles against the Germans, and Miss Houk fought her imaginary battles against the Russians and the Red Chinese.

Through all of this, there was one country which was never mentioned. Ever. My friends and I didn't even know it existed. None of us had heard of Viet Nam.

CHAPTER 10

To my surprise, I found out that some people did not like Negroes. I could understand why people were upset with the Japanese and the Germans, because of Pearl Harbor and Hitler and all that, but I was pretty sure that we had never fought a war against the Negroes.

I knew that Negroes had been slaves, but heck, if anything they should have been mad at us. Of course, that was a long time ago, and Michigan was a Northern state and we fought against slavery in the Civil War. I took that to mean that people from Michigan liked Negroes. Even if some people didn't like Negroes, I expected that they would live Down South. Just as there were good Germans and bad Germans, there had been good Americans and bad Americans. Good Americans lived in the North, were conductors on the Underground Railroad, and built cars; bad Americans lived Down South, owned slaves, and grew tobacco.

My understanding was that Abraham Lincoln had taken care of all of that slavery nonsense long before I was born. A Southerner named John Wilkes Booth killed Mr. Lincoln, but they eventually trapped Booth in a barn and set it on fire, at which point a Union soldier named Boston Corbett shot Booth in the neck and killed him. I could tell from the way Miss Houk told the story that she wanted us to believe that everything had worked out in the end because Booth didn't get away with his crime, but I had a hard time believing her. What about poor Mr. Lincoln?

Things didn't work out for him, and he was the guy who did all of the right things. What about Mr. Lincoln's family? I was beginning to have my doubts about "shoot-'em-up" cowboy logic.

Decent people, like Mrs. Ballenger and my dad, said "Negro" or "colored person," but racists said "nigger." Since I had never heard anybody actually use the word "nigger," I figured that most everybody was okay with colored people.

In our house, "nigger" was the one word which was never used. I learned that suddenly while reciting a rhyme I'd learned at school.

"Eeny, meeny, miney, moe,
Catch a nigger..."

Whap! I felt something clobber me on the back of my head. Not the usual slap from mom, but a solid thud that must have come from my father.

"Don't use that word!" he admonished.

I wondered what word he could be talking about. The kid who taught me the rhyme shouted it shamelessly, without a hint of naughtiness in his voice, so I was shocked to find that one of the words was bad. I slumped over and began to feel sorry for myself. The previous summer I was rhyming things with William Tell, and I got hit in the head that time, too. I wished my father would give me a list of words I wasn't supposed to say instead of using his painful "trial and error" method.

"What word?"

My father didn't want to say it. That stunned me. My dad tried not to swear in front of us, but he wasn't always successful, especially if he was frustrated or caught in traffic. Then he'd yell out obscenities with reckless abandon.

"Holy shit, every asshole and his brother are on the road."

I loved it when my dad used obscenities, not only because he was swearing, but because he did it so well.

Some of the kids at school used the occasional swear word, but it was always whispered and never as part of a sentence. My dad had vivid phrases which he bellowed out of his unrolled car window.

But this new word was different. It was a word that even Dad wouldn't say, not even indoors. Which word was it? What did it mean?

"We don't say," and his voice quieted to a whisper, "nigger."

With unprecedented eloquence, my father explained that it was a bad word, and that bad people used it to describe colored people. It took a couple minutes for things to sink in, but I finally got it. His lecture wasn't about bad words. It was about bad people, and he didn't want me to act like a bad person.

Dad made two suggestions. First, I shouldn't use a word unless I knew what it meant. Second, from now on, I should recite the verse differently.

"Eeny, meeny, miney, moe,
Catch a tiger by the toe."

I changed the way I recited my chant, but I didn't take his suggestion about knowing words before I used them. After all, I didn't know what "eeny" or "meeny" meant. Did he mean that I was never to sing "Ta-ra-ra-boom-de-ay" again? No, that wasn't it. He meant that "nigger" was a word used by bad people, and I should never use it.

That could have been the end of it, but I still had one lingering question.

"Dad, have you ever met anybody who doesn't like Negroes?"

"Sure. Plenty of times."

"Like Down South, or when you were in the Navy?"

"Some. But mostly around here."

"In Detroit?"

"Sure."

93

"But I thought that all of the people who didn't like Negroes lived in the South."

"Where did you get, that idea? Detlef, even at the time the Civil War broke out, most Southerners didn't own slaves."

I felt sorry for my dad. Miss Houk had been pretty clear in her description of life in the South, and if most Southerners didn't even own slaves I'm sure she would have mentioned it.

"And there are plenty of people in Detroit who aren't too fond of Negroes."

"Like who?"

My father paused. For a second I thought he wasn't going to answer, but then he spoke.

"If you ever have a colored friend, make sure you keep him away from Mr. Lorraine."

"Mr. Lorraine? Are you sure?"

"Yeah, I'm sure."

"Does he think we should bring back slavery?"

"Of course not. He's not violent, and he's not in the Klan. He doesn't even tell racist jokes. He's not going to go out of his way to hurt or hate colored people. I'm sure that he hopes that they all lead happy and productive lives, just so long as they're happy and productive in another part of town."

I couldn't make sense of it. Mr. Lorraine worked for the Gerber baby food company and, whenever he'd hear of a young couple struggling with expenses, he'd drop by with a few cases of baby food. No thanks necessary, and after his first visit he'd return every so often, not even bothering to stay and talk. He'd just drop the food off by the back door and ring the bell.

Mr. Lorraine was good to the neighborhood kids, too. He'd pump up your flat tire or help you perfect your curve ball. If your flashlight needed batteries he always seemed to have a couple that he really didn't need. If a big kid picked on a little kid, he'd take the big kid into his garage for a good talkin' to.

Other than being a racist, Mr. Lorraine was a great guy.

"Dad, are you sure we're talking about the same Mr. Lorraine? The same one that goes to our church?"

"Yup. The same guy."

"But he helped lay the tile in the church basement, and he plays third base for the church baseball team. He served me pancakes at Sunrise Service!" I could tell that my voice was growing higher in pitch and I was talking a lot faster, but I couldn't help myself.

My dad shrugged his shoulders.

"Maybe he's not a racist at church. Maybe he's only a racist when he's at home or at work," I suggested.

My dad shook his head. "A couple of years ago we were square dancing at church, you know, like we do every Thursday. Sometimes we have guests, and on this evening a nice young colored couple showed up. There's a lot of switching partners and moving around in square dancing, and we kept an eye on things to make sure that the colored woman never ended up as Mr. Lorraine's partner. We managed to keep them apart, and I thought there wasn't going to be any trouble, but then Ed refused to dance with a white woman. It took me a few minutes to figure it out, but she had been dancing with the colored man, and Ed didn't want to touch her. He considered her unclean."

"But she was white!" I protested.

"Yeah, but she'd touched a Negro, and Mr. Lorraine... Well, he must have kept track of all of the women who had danced with the black man. You know, if this was the only thing I knew about Mr. Lorraine I would probably say something like, 'That racist bastard. I hate his guts.' But it's not that simple."

After that, I paid more attention and I began to see the signs of racism. Mr. Lorraine never voiced his opinions in front of children, but he spoke pretty freely to some of the adults. They thought he was somewhat of a sage, and repeated his comments to each other, and then to their children, and the children repeated them to me.

Mr. Lorraine had many wild and fear-filled predictions. According to him, it would begin when a few blacks moved into our neighborhood, and things wouldn't seem much different. Others would follow, and soon the changes would be more obvious. Crime would increase a little. Things would get a little shabby. Lawns would be left unmowed, and houses would go unpainted. The White people would leave in droves as crime reached epidemic proportions. It would be unsafe to walk the streets, the public schools would decline to the point that no real learning took place, and the Whites would set up new residences in better houses with better schools in another location.

I didn't believe any of it, and I figured that it was just a stupid thing that Mr. Lorraine said just to get the other people stirred up.

I still couldn't understand why Mr. Lorraine had a problem with Negroes, so once again I approached my father. He was reading a book, which he seemed to do more often than he had before. That was another thing I didn't understand. He used to spend more time hunting and fishing and working on his car, but lately all he seemed to do was read.

"Dad, why doesn't Mr. Lorraine like colored people?"

He didn't even look up from his book. "Because he's a jackass."

Of course! That was the perfect explanation. He was a jackass. Considering all of the decent things he'd done I really couldn't hate him, but if he was a jackass I could disrespect him, and that was close enough. Not a bad guy, but a jackass. "Jackass" was a harsh and appropriate word. I tried it out in my mind, pretending what I would say to my friends if the subject came up.

"Mr. Lorraine? Yeah, he means well, but he's a jackass."

I didn't have much time to imagine, because my father interrupted my thoughts. He had set his book down and was looking me in the eye.

"Detlef, you and I can call him a jackass, but you know you can't say that to your friends. Or your mother. This conversation has to stay between the two of us."

Well, even if I couldn't say "jackass" to my friends, my dad and I had a secret, a pretty big one, and it involved a swear word. Besides, even if I couldn't call Mr. Lorraine a jackass I could still use the word every now and then, if the situation merited its use.

It wasn't long before I got my chance. Some of the guys at school were making some remarks about colored people. Michael Colson was the loudest.

"Hah! Let me tell you what colored people are like!" he proclaimed.

"How would you know what they're like? Have you ever talked to one?"

I couldn't believe what I had said. I hadn't planned it, and I was surprised by my own logic. I figured that would shut him up, but it didn't.

"Detlef, what makes you such an expert?"

"Nothing. That's why I have the sense to keep my mouth shut."

"You know what I think?

"What?"

"I think you're a nigger lover."

"That's because you're a jackass."

Michael squinted his eyes and tried to look mean. I thought he might punch me, but then he shouted, "I'm going to tell!"

Michael ran back to the building. The other students, who had not been on my side from the start, taunted me.

"You're going to get it!"

When I got back to the building I was told I had to see Miss Klingenschmidt, the principal. She was sitting behind her desk.

"Michael tells me that you called him a bad name. Is this true?"

"Yes," I confessed.

"I must admit that I'm surprised and disappointed. What gave you the idea to use such a word?"

"I don't know. It's just the way he was acting."

I thought I detected a smile starting to form in the corner of her mouth, but then she became very stern. "Young man, I think you owe Michael an apology. Now, why don't we call him down here so you can apologize and we can put this whole thing behind us?"

I didn't know what to say, so I didn't say anything.

"Young man, would you prefer it if I called your parents?"

"Yeah, that would be a lot better!"

She was surprised by my enthusiasm, and only then did I realize that she was trying to threaten me.

"Detlef, I know your father pretty well, and considering his studies, I don't think he'd approve of this kind of language."

My father's studies? What was she talking about?

"My father isn't home right now," I blurted out, and I could hear the panic in my voice.

"Fine. I'll talk to your mother."

"Can't you wait until my father comes home?" I begged.

She didn't answer, but pulled a yellow card out of a box on her desk and began dialing.

"Hello. Mrs. Niebaum? This is Miss Klingenschmidt at Pulaski. What? You were going to call me?"

After that she spoke quietly, and I couldn't hear anything. She looked very serious, but when she hung up the phone she forced a smile.

"Detlef, why don't you make yourself comfortable? Your mother will be here in a few minutes."

I didn't like where this was headed.

"Miss Klingenschmidt, what do you think about colored people?"

"Oh, the same as most people. They're just like everybody else, except their skin is a different color."

"If they're the same as us, how come they don't live in our neighborhood?"

She knitted her brow. "I don't have an answer for that."

At least she didn't tell me that "Negroes are happiest with their own kind." I was beginning to recognize baloney, the things adults said but didn't really mean. "We'll go to the Call of the Wild Museum when we have more time." "I'll pick up some batteries on my way home from work." "Negroes are happiest with their own kind."

I appreciated her honesty, but I really did want to know why no Negroes lived in our neighborhood. Was it because they were uncomfortable living around people like Mr. Lorraine, or was it something else?

I never finished my thought, because just then my mom rushed into the office.
Her head was covered with a babushka, but you could see that her hair was still in rollers. She had no gloves, her coat was unbuttoned, and she was wearing slacks. She always dressed up when she visited school. I must have done something very terrible for her to come to school dressed this way.

And she was crying. I made my mother mad lots of times, but I had never made her cry. I was drowning in guilt. My father had told me not to use that word, but I didn't listen, and now my mother was crying.

My mother didn't say anything. She just grabbed me by the hand and pulled me out of my chair, down the hallway, toward the outside door.

"Mom! I have to go to my locker and get my jacket!"

She didn't even slow down. She just let go of my hand and kept scurrying toward the door.

"I'll wait for you in the car," she said in a voice that did not sound like her own.

I ran to my locker, threw on my jacket without zipping it up, and ran down to the stairs. Miss Thurm, a sixth grade teacher, opened the door of her classroom and stuck out her head.

"Slow down, young man."

I kept running, out the door, to the car. I opened the door and sat in the front seat. My mother's crossed arms were on the steering wheel, and her forehead was pressed against her wrists. I wasn't sure, but I thought she was crying. She didn't seem to notice me, but just sat there with her head bowed forward.

"Mom?"

"Detlef, I have some bad news. "

She was sobbing pretty hard I wasn't sure what she had said, but it seemed to have something to do with my grandmother having a heart attack in her sleep.

"Oma is dead?"

"No, she's alive."

"Oh, good," I stupidly said. I had temporarily forgotten that I had another grandmother, my mother's mother. My mom always felt her own mother got short shrift, and that might have been true because we didn't visit her nearly as often.

I was hit by a double horror. First was the realization that my Grandma was dead, and second, my mother was angry with me because she thought that I wasn't all that upset about it

"Detlef, how could you say such a thing?"

"No, I didn't mean that way—it just came out wrong."

"I had no idea you were such a mean-spirited, selfish—"

Just then, my brother came out of the building and trotted over to the car. "Detlef, get in the back seat!"

That must have been a new rule. "People who don't show the proper grief aren't allowed to ride in the front seat." I got out of the front seat, left the door open, and crawled into the back. I slid all the way across the back seat, positioning myself directly behind my mother so she wouldn't be able to see me. When my brother and I had situated ourselves in the car, my mom spoke.

"I have some bad news. Grandma is dead."

Why didn't she say it that way when she told me? We called my dad's mother "Oma" and my mom's mother "Grandma." If she had told me "Grandma is dead," it would have made all the difference.

My brother cried and said, "Oh, no! No more kisses from Grandma!"

He threw his head into my mother's lap, and she petted his head.

I cried extra loud at the funeral, but that didn't get me off the hook. I really did love my Grandma, and I really was sad that she was dead, but my first reaction was not what it ought to have been, and that was unforgivable.

For the next few weeks I was wracked with guilt, and it wasn't just because I hadn't shown appropriate grief. I felt bad because I said a bad word and I hadn't been punished. I got in trouble at school at a time when my mother had her own troubles. In the midst of her own concerns, my mother had forgotten to ask the principal why she was calling our house. If I had been any kind of a decent person I would have confessed to my crime, but I didn't, and I felt guilty about that, too.

With so much grief and guilt floating around, it did not seem appropriate to ask why Negroes lived in a different part of the city. It was starting to look like getting an answer to my questions was one of those things that was never going to happen. I was never going to get my batteries, I was never going to visit the Call of the Wild Museum, and I was never going to find out why Negroes lived in a different part of the city.

CHAPTER 11

I did what I could to avoid my mom, and I especially tried to avoid talking to her. I suppose I was waiting for her to come to me and say something like, "Oh, I know you loved your Grandma. You were just caught off guard."

It didn't happen. My mother and I were talking all of the time, or maybe I should say that she was talking all of the time. Maybe she knew she'd gone overboard when she called me mean-spirited and selfish, but she couldn't apologize because then she'd have to admit that she was wrong. Instead, she took the indirect approach. She became philosophical, and spent a lot of time talking about death, mostly her own death. To her amazement, this topic did not lift my spirits.

"Do you know how I want to die?" she asked me.

"What?" I was stunned. I was pretty sure that you usually didn't get a choice in the matter, unless maybe you were facing the death penalty and you had to choose between the gas chamber and a firing squad. "What kind of a question is that?"

"Your grandmother had it easy. She died of a heart attack in her sleep. She never knew what hit her."

I wasn't in any kind of a mood to talk about death, especially not Grandma's. Maybe my mother was able to pretend that she hadn't said those things to me, but I wasn't ready to let myself off the hook.

"How is dying in your sleep any better than being murdered in your sleep?" I demanded. "If somebody came into my bedroom tonight and blew my brains out, I wouldn't know what hit me."

"Detlef, how can you say such things?" She phrased it like a question, but she said it like she was scolding. "Dying of a heart attack is a blessing," she went on to say, "but being murdered, well, that's a sin."

"But it wouldn't be my sin, would it? Don't I go to Heaven even if I'm murdered?"

"That's not the point!" she snapped. Then she pretended to see a spot on the counter and picked up a rag and wiped it away, as much as you can wipe away something that wasn't there in the first place. Of course, what she was saying didn't make much sense, either. I thought whether or not you went to Heaven was the whole point of everything, the ultimate test of how you spent your life.

"Then what is the point?"

"The point is that if I die of a heart attack, I don't want you to be sad, because that's the way I want to go. Especially if it happens while I'm asleep."

That night, while I was saying my prayers, I taunted my mother.

"And if I die before I wake, don't worry, because that's the way I wanted to go, especially if I die of a heart attack. Amen."

My mother was furious. "Detlef! Where did you get that saucy mouth?"

"What? I'm just saying the same things you said this afternoon. I thought dying in your sleep was a blessing."

She slammed the door, stormed into the kitchen, and then I heard my parents fighting. They tried to be quiet, but even when they were whispering it sounded like yelling.

"I thought you were going to talk to him!" my mother hissed.

"I can't get him to open up." My father was trying to be patient, but he had a tone to his voice that said he was getting ready to blow his top.

"In the meantime he's saying the most morbid things. And he's sassy."

"What do you want me to do? I can't take him down to the station and beat him with a rubber hose until he talks!" By this point my father was just as angry as my mom.

"Can't we have him tested?"

"For what?"

"To see why he's so... different."

Different? What did she mean by that? I never got a chance to find out, because they stopped talking, and after a while I got tired of waiting for them to start back up and I fell asleep.

My mother didn't know that I heard her talking to my dad, so the next day both she and I pretended like nothing had happened. She just picked up her creepy conversation right where it left off.

"Some people achieve a certain nobility through death. Like soldiers, or sailors, or firemen who are killed in the line of duty."

"And policemen," I added. "Sometimes policemen are killed in the line of duty."

"Yes, that's true, but I don't like to think about that. It's not always an easy death, being burned alive while fighting a fire, or having a bullet in your chest, but it's a noble death. It reminds me of a story that I read in the Free Press."

I knew I should let the conversation die, but she had aroused my curiosity. I liked stories, although I didn't know you could find them in newspapers.
"What story?" I asked, knowing that I was willingly walking into a web.

"Where is that newspaper?" She scurried to the living room, and came back a couple of minutes later, newspaper in hand.

"Here it is. It's a story about a mother and her children. They were trapped in a burning building. The firemen had a net, but the woman wouldn't jump because she didn't want to leave her children."

She called it a story, but it didn't sound like any kind of story I had ever heard. A story has three bears or three pigs and it ends happily. I could tell my mom's story would not have a happy ending.

"So what happened?"

"Nothing. She stayed in the building and burned to death. The people on the sidewalk could hear her scream. What a horrible way to die."

It was horrible, and I was thankful we had a boring family and nothing like that would ever happen to us. Somehow, my mom must have sensed that I was a little too peaceful, because she had to add one last zinger.

"I would do that for you. I would stay in a burning building and die just so you wouldn't have to die alone."

"Geez, Mom! Why did you have to go and say that? Don't you think I have enough guilt as it is?"

"Guilt? What guilt?"

She looked genuinely interested, and I realized that I had unintentionally given her an important clue.

"Nothing," I replied. "I didn't mean anything at all."

"Well, like I say, it just goes to show that life is precious. Any one of us could be taken at any time."

That brought about another wave of panic.

"Ma, what happened to the kids?" I demanded.

"They burned to death. The firemen found their burned bodies in the bedroom closet. They think the kids were trying to hide from the fire," she said with a smug tone.

Dead mother. Dead children. What kind of newspaper was this? Why did she read it? Why did she tell me? What made her think I needed to know this?

Did she think that it would bring me comfort? Didn't it occur to her that, if it actually happened, I would first suffer the horror of watching my mother burn to death, and that I would be witnessing not only the loss of my mother but the circumstances of the death I would be suffering?

Once my mother had planted the thought of her death in my mind, I could not make it go away—not that she would let that happen. There were many small reminders of her willingness to die for her children. About a week after telling her fire story, she found some cottage cheese in the refrigerator. She sniffed it and made a face.

"I'm not sure if this is any good."

I expected her to throw it in the trash, but she opened the silverware drawer and extracted a spoon. I grew nervous. What was she going to do? Was she going to eat it? She scooped a small sample onto the spoon, then held it up to her lips and touched it with her tongue.

"Seems okay," she said, and popped the spoon in her mouth. I watched her for a few seconds, and when she didn't drop dead I relaxed.

"Can I have some?" I asked.

"No, I'm not sure it's safe," she said, and then she ate some more. Within a minute or two, she had eaten the little bit that was left and threw the container in the garbage.

"Maybe I shouldn't have eaten that," she mused. Then she added, without a trace of humor in her voice, "If I die, you'll know it was the cottage cheese."

For my mother it was a passing thought, gone from her head a minute after she said it. It never occurred to her that she should get back to me just to let me know that she was okay.

I fretted for a few hours, wondering if she was going to die, but then she didn't. I knew that food poisoning can take a while, so for the next couple of days I was pretty jittery.

I stayed jittery, too, because even after I figured out that cottage cheese wasn't going to get her, she kept finding new ways to rattle my cage. Anytime anybody died, my mother would rate the death according to its degree of gruesomeness and horror.

"I just read the most interesting magazine article about winter weather. You really have to be careful in the winter. A whole family was wiped out in a blizzard when their car got stuck in the snow. Three kids. What a shame. They found the two-year-old still in her mother's arms. They tried to walk to safety but only managed to get about thirty feet from the car. Horrible way to die.

"Did you know that a guy fell into the cement while they were building the Mackinac Bridge? Well, it was horrible, but at least it was quick.

"Ach. Here's why you shouldn't smoke. A woman from Lansing was busy with her cigarette and wasn't paying attention to the road and she wrapped her car around a phone pole. The lit end of the cigarette went into her nose, but she couldn't move and it just burned and burned. Well, it could have been worse. Wait, it's continued on the next page. Oh, look at that. She died two days later."

That was Mom's new outlook on life. People die, and it's always bad. Unless you die of a heart attack—in your sleep.

CHAPTER 12

I made up my mind to set things right with my mom. If she died before we patched things up I'd have to live with the guilt forever. Since talking things over hadn't worked out very well, I took the indirect approach and did what I could to be a better son.

I wasn't sure what I could do. I had heard stories of kids who worked in factories or coal mines to help their families, but most of those stories took place before I was born, and I was pretty sure that those opportunities were no longer available to elementary school students.

After a great deal of thought, the only thing I could come up with was making my own bed. I had never made my bed, at least, not by myself, so it was somewhat of a struggle, but I hung in there and eventually did a passable job, and I was very proud. It was a statement, a beacon that said to the world, "I am a good son. I made my own bed, without being asked."

I was a bit late for breakfast, and my mom scowled a little. I thought about telling her what I had done, but that's what a little boy would have done. I was getting older now, and I could wait until she found out for herself.

The school day passed slowly. I tried to be interested in my work, but all I could think about was how proud my mother would be when I got home.

She wasn't waiting for me at the door as I had hoped, so I shouted, "Mom! I'm home!"

She came scurrying up from the basement, carrying a jar of home-canned peaches. "Here's my wonderful boy," she announced, and this was followed by many kisses. Very good. When my dad got home, she told him what I had done, and he shook my hand. Also good.

I was finally off the hook, and all I'd had to do was make my bed one time. This was going to be my secret weapon. Any time I messed up, I would make my own bed, and all would be forgiven.

Things had worked out so well that I decided to put a few bed-makings in the bank. I would make my own bed for a week or so, and the next time I got in trouble I'd say, "Remember that time when I made my own bed for a whole week?" My mother's anger would melt away, and I would be smothered in kisses.

So, the next morning, I made my bed again, but when I got home my mother casually commented, "Thanks for making your bed, Hon," and immediately went back to her housework. By the third day she was saying nothing at all, but I continued for the rest of the week. I figured that every day she didn't give me any praise was just that much more affection I was putting in the bank.

I was glad when the week was over. Making my bed was boring, and even after a week of practice it wasn't nearly as crisp as when my mother made it. Besides, all of that work was cutting into time that could be better spent playing with my Lincoln Logs or reading Mad magazine. So, exactly one week after I began, I went to school with an unmade bed and a renewed sense of freedom.

That afternoon, my mom was waiting for me, and it wasn't because she wanted to catch me up on the backlog of kisses she owed me. She was very crabby, and gave me a stern lecture about responsibility and some other stuff that I made it a point not to hear. I thought it was a load of crap. Had I made a promise to make my bed? No, I had not! Was I told that once I started making my bed I would have to make it forever? No, I was not! Was my mother yelling at me because I wasn't listening to her? Yes, she was.

I knew that in the Court of Mom there would be no justice, so I didn't even try to plead my case. This was going to be a matter of will. If I went upstairs and made my bed she would stop yelling, but only until tomorrow. If I stopped making my bed once and for all, she would keep yelling at me for a week or so until she grew weary of saying the same thing over and over. Then she'd declare that I was a lost cause and things would go back like they were before.

I learned a great lesson about responsibility. It must be avoided at all costs. One day of kisses was not enough payment for a lifetime of hard labor. I resolved that, from this day hence, I would clean my room only with great reluctance. If I had to rake leaves, I would do a lousy job, and then I would put the rake back in the wrong spot. It was the perfect plan because it was what I had been doing all along, except that now I would do it with a greater sense of determination.

The next morning, when I got to class, Miss Houk was talking to the principal, Miss Klingenschmidt. Miss Houk was whispering, but it was a loud whisper that sounded harsh and judgmental, so I didn't have any trouble hearing her.

"He's been acting like that ever since his grandmother died."

"Hello," I said, and then it got very quiet.

"Detlef," Miss Klingenschmidt said, "how nice to see you."

Miss Houk smiled at me, which was just a big act because the principal was in the room. On any other day I would have been about as welcome as a wart.

"You look a little down," Miss Klingenschmidt continued. "Is something on your mind?"

111

"Just the usual stuff."

"The usual stuff?"

"Yeah. Death. Stuff like that."

Miss Klingenschmidt's eyes got big. "Oh, do you mean your grandmother's death?"

"No, not really," I said, and then I caught myself. I had already been in trouble for not being appropriately concerned about her death in the first place, and I wasn't going to make that mistake again. "I mean, yes, that's a big part of it, but all kinds of death. People dying in car accidents and mothers being burned alive in buildings."

"I suppose you're very upset about the war, too," Miss Houk added.

"The war!" I exclaimed. "You mean the United States is at war?"

The women looked at each other, and Miss Houk began talking very fast. "I thought he knew."

"Knew what?" I demanded.

"Well, I'm going to have to tell him now," Miss Houk stated.

"Susan, I don't think any of this is helping," Miss Klingenschmidt scolded, and Miss Houk's face softened just a little.

By this time all of the other students had arrived, and before anybody could say anything else the bell rang.

"I know you'll handle this with tact," Miss Klingenschmidt said. "Detlef, if you need to talk to me, I'll be in my office after school."

"Okay," I said, wondering what she meant. Being sent to the principal was bad enough, and I certainly wasn't going to go down there voluntarily. I didn't need her suddenly remembering that I called another student a jackass.

After Miss Klingenschmidt left, Miss Houk put a very serious look on her face, cleared her throat, and addressed the class.

"You're growing older, and it's time you knew the truth. I'm going to tell you something that I couldn't have told you a year ago, but since you're older, I know you're ready to hear it."

I knew I wasn't ready, and even if I was, I didn't want to hear what she was going to say. I could tell it was going to be bad, and I was already dealing with enough bad stuff. Nevertheless, I paid attention with gruesome curiosity, because even though what she was going to say was too horrible to hear, it would also be too good to miss.

"There is a disease that is spreading around the world. It's not a disease that spreads from person to person, but a disease that spreads from country to country. The disease is called Communism."

The McCarthy era might have been over for the rest of America, but it was still going strong in Miss Houk's room.

"Communism," she explained, "is the sharing of everything, but it's not a good kind of sharing. If you have a house with extra space, the government will move extra people into your house. Maybe it will be just a person or two, but if times get tough, they might move a whole family into your spare bedroom. Sometimes, when things are really bad, they'll split families apart. They'll put a few in this house and a few more in that house."

Miss Houk picked up her globe. "Remember all of those things I told you about Russia? The reason Russia has so many problems is that it's a communist country."

Miss Houk let her head drop down, and thought very hard for a moment, as if she was trying to decide if we were ready to hear the next bit of terrible news. Then, in the grimmest of tones, she made her announcement.

"In Russia, people are so poor that both men and women have to go to work."

There was an audible groan from the classroom as we imagined the horror of men and women working side-by-side. It seemed so primitive. Men and women working together.

Lynn Spiro raised her hand. "Are we at war with Russia?"

"Not really."

Not really? What kind of an answer was that? Maybe the United States was at war and nobody had told me about it.

"We are at war, but the war is in Viet Nam."

My mind was filled with questions. Viet Nam? Why didn't anybody have the goodness to tell me about this sooner? And where is Viet Nam, anyhow?

Miss Houk, anticipating our questions, picked up her globe and pointed to a little brown squiggle.

"This is Viet Nam."

She explained that there were two Viet Nams, a good one and a bad one. She explained that just as the United States had been divided into North and South, the same thing was true in Viet Nam.

It seemed that there were two of everything. There was regular Superman and his evil and imperfect duplicate, Bizarro Superman. There were two Germanys. And now there were two Viet Nams.

To hear Miss Houk tell it, East Germany was like Bizarro Germany, the Confederacy was the Bizarro States of America, and now Communists had moved in and created Bizarro Viet Nam.

"Of course, Russia is only half the problem. The Red Chinese are involved, too."

"Is Red China communist, too?" I asked.

"Of course," Miss Houk snapped. "That's why it's called Red China. Anything communist is considered red."

I felt dizzy for a second, and then my stomach began to hurt. Not only had the Communists taken over half of the world, but they had also managed to appropriate the color red. When did all of this happen?

Miss Houk seemed especially pleased with herself when she delivered the final blow.

"Both Red China and Russia are backing North Viet Nam. The United States is backing South Viet Nam. If this thing gets just a little bigger, we'll be fighting both Red China and Russia, and do you know what that means? World War Three!"

She paused for a few seconds, and then her lips curled into a tiny smile.

"Of course, we aren't fighting World War Three just yet. We're just involved in Viet Nam. If we can win this thing quickly, maybe things won't escalate."

Miss Houk kept on talking, but I was finished listening for the day. Every now and then I tuned in long enough to hear her say something like "noun" or "sentence," but none of that seemed very important. I put my head down on my desk, and I expected her to scold me, but she just left me alone.

That afternoon I was waiting for my dad when he came home. He went through his usual routine, hanging up his hat and emptying the bullets from his gun.

"You don't like carrying a gun, do you?"

"I hate it."

"If I was in the Army, I'd have to carry a gun, wouldn't I?"

"Probably."

"And I'd have to make my bed every day, right?"

"Son, what is all of this about?" he asked.

"Is America fighting a war in Viet Nam?"

My dad laughed. "Is that what's got you so worried?"

"You didn't answer my question!"

"Well, there's fighting, and yes, I guess you'd call it a war."

My dad didn't seem worried, and maybe that should have comforted me, but it didn't. I watched him as he sat down in his living room chair and packed his pipe with tobacco, hoping that he would explain about the war, but he just pulled a copy of *Look* out of the magazine rack and began reading.

My mom hadn't even started to set the table, so I knew it would be a while before dinner was ready. I went for a walk around the block.

Francis LaGrone was sitting on his porch playing the guitar. Francis was a teenager, but not the kind of teenager that my mother warned me about. He didn't smoke cigarettes or kick over trash cans, and he never picked on little kids. I could tell by the way he was playing guitar that he was a nice kid. He played a regular wooden guitar, not an electric one, and he wasn't playing any wild Beatles or Elvis Presley-type music. He was just strumming and singing words which I couldn't quite hear.

He smiled as I walked past and I took that as an invitation, so I sat down on his porch steps and listened. He was just finishing up his song.

"For the times they are a-changin'," he sang, and beat out a few last chords on his guitar.

"You're that German kid, aren't you?" he asked.

"I guess so," I mumbled. I wondered why he didn't know my name. I knew his. Maybe it was because he was in high school and had a few more years to build up a reputation in the neighborhood. "What kind of a song was that?" I asked.

"What do you mean?"

"You said, 'The times they are a-changin'. Shouldn't that be 'The times are changing?'"

"You don't get it, kid. This is a folk song."

"Is that why you sing through your nose?"

"It's not nose singing. It's how Bob Dylan sings."

"Did you know that there's a war in Viet Nam?"

"Sure. Why do you think I'm out here playing guitar? It's time to let the world know." It didn't seem like the world was listening, but he began playing again. I

116

stopped him before he could remind me that the times were changing. I already had enough change.

"I don't like it," I said, and I was almost ready to cry.

"Hey, kid, what's wrong?" Francis asked, tugging at my shirt. "Don't you like music?"

"Not this kind. Don't you know any good songs, like 'Pop Goes the Weasel' or 'Turkey in the Straw'?"

He wrinkled his nose. "Actually, the only other song I know is 'Tom Dooley'." He began to sing. "Hang down your head, Tom Dooley, hang down your head and die…"

I decided that was enough music for one evening, and I headed home. "See ya, kid," he called, "and come back some time. I'm working on 'Where Have All the Flowers Gone?' You might like that one better."

I could tell by the title that I wouldn't like it at all, but just to be polite I waved goodbye and tried to smile.

I didn't want the flowers to be gone, I didn't want the times to change, and I didn't want Tom Dooley to hang his head and die. I didn't want to be known as "that German kid" either. Francis seemed like a nice guy, but he was confused. He didn't seem to like the war any more than I did, but all he did was sing about where the flowers have gone and some crazy Bob Dylan songs. What did that have to do with the war?

When I got home my mother was getting out the dinner plates.

"Wash your hands and help me set the table."

I didn't think my hands were particularly dirty, but I did a good job of scrubbing them and then I got right to work. I had always wondered why forks went on the left even though most people are right-handed, and today I would correct that problem. I couldn't stop the Communists or the war or the folk singers, but at least I could fix this one small problem. Unfortunately, my mother did not share my vision.

117

"Detlef! What have you done!" she shrieked.

"It's better this way," I protested. "Like Bob Dylan says, 'The times they are a-changin'.'"

"Bob Dylan's mother might not care how he sets the table, but in this house, the forks go on the left! And stop talking through your nose."

I could hear my father laughing all the way from the next room, and I hoped he read something funny in his magazine, but I was pretty sure he was laughing at me.

"Now switch those forks back the way they were!"

"Don't you think we can let the boy try this just this one time?" my father said. He was standing in the doorway, still puffing on his pipe.

"You know that I don't allow that thing in the kitchen," my mother scolded.

My father took a step backwards into the living room. "The world isn't going to come to an end if the forks are on the other side," he said.

"Just this once," she conceded. "And after dinner you're going right up to your room and making your bed."

As soon as we were done with dinner, I went right up to build a tower with my Lincoln Logs. My mother might remember to check up on me if I went downstairs and watched television, but if I kept out of her way, she'd forget that she told me to make my bed. She was already back in the habit of making it for me most days, and today she must have run out of time.

I had only started when I heard my father thumping up the stairs. He didn't tell me to make my bed or lecture me about responsibility, but just watched me play. Long before I ran out of Lincoln Logs, the tower began to list, and I figured it was time to stop.

"Dad, if you build things up high enough, they're going to fall, aren't they?"

"Maybe. I'm not sure what you mean."

"It's like everything falls apart just when you think you're starting to make progress."

"Son, you have created one mighty powerful metaphor."

"What's a metaphor?" I asked. I was a little suspicious, because a couple of days before he had tricked me into asking "What's a hen weigh?" and it sounded like this was the same kind of joke.

"A metaphor, well, it's like an example. So that's what you're worried about? Everything falling apart?"

"Something like that. You know, Dad, the times they are a-changin'."

"Well, don't worry about it, Son. There's always an answer."

"Really?" I asked, accidentally allowing a little bit of hope to creep into my voice. "What is the answer?"

"The answer, my friend, is blowin' in the wind," he said, speaking through his nose. "Now let's put your metaphor back into the box before your mother comes up and finds out you've been playing instead of making your bed."

CHAPTER 13

If I was going to find some kind of peace or order in the world, I wasn't going to find it in the adult world. For the next several weeks, I retreated into the world of children's entertainment.

Popeye *always* beat Bluto. Superman *always* defeated Lex Luthor.

I was already too old for Romper Room and Captain Kangaroo, but Detroit had plenty of other kids' show hosts who offered a combination of sketches, sight gags, and cartoons. In addition to Detroit's most famous kids' show host, Soupy Sales, there was Milky the Clown, Captain Detroit, Johnny Ginger, Bozo the Clown, Captain Jolly, and Jerry Booth.

Jerry Booth commanded a special loyalty from the children of Detroit. Most of us were too young to understand that he was only a local celebrity, not a national celebrity like Captain Kangaroo. I noticed that Jerry talked about Detroit almost every day, but I thought it was because we were his chosen people.

Jerry first appeared as Jingles the Clown, the Court Jester of Boofland, a fictional kingdom which was an intentional mispronunciation of "Boothland," named for Jerry Booth. There was even a "Boofland Loyalty Song," and every day viewers at home faithfully sang the song to their unlistening television sets. You could actually go to Windsor, Ontario and visit Boofland. Our family did that, and I met Captain Jolly, the host of another local show. It was a great time, and I hoped to go back one day, but Boofland burned down and Jingles the Clown went off the air.

Jerry Booth came back a few years later with "Jerry Booth's Fun House." Like Boofland, you could actually visit the Fun House, but unlike Boofland, it was portable and came to various shopping malls in the Detroit area.

That was my dream: to visit Jerry Booth's Fun House and enter the drawing and win the Sinbad the Sailor Magic Belt. According to the Sinbad cartoon, the belt possessed magic powers that gave Sinbad incredible strength. I needed those powers and I needed that belt, because if I had those powers I could really show those bastards a thing or two. Of course, "showing those bastards" was my real dream, and visiting Jerry Booth's Fun House was just a means to an end.

I seriously doubted that a belt that was being raffled off at a shopping mall would give me incredible strength, and yet, even in the midst of my own doubts, I desperately wanted it. And so, when Jerry Booth actually did come to a mall near us, and when my mom and Mrs. Hedgecock planned to take us, I took it as sign from God.

That was not a figurative expression. My understanding was that if you did the right thing, God would reward you, and apparently I had earned enough points. I wasn't sure why my brother and Mark were going along, since they got into a lot of mischief, but I had heard that the Lord moves in mysterious ways, and I supposed this was the kind of thing they were talking about.

It was not an act of God. I later found out that Mark Hedgecock, who was my brother's age and lived right next door, conspired with my brother to keeping nagging both of our mothers until they gave in just to get them to shut the hell up.

When the big day finally arrived, my mother gave me one rule.

"No matter what, stay with your brother. Mrs. Hedgecock and I are going to do a little shopping. We'll be back to get you later. In the meantime, stay with your brother."

Now I understood. It was a test. God would be watching to see if I stayed with my brother. God wanted to see if I was going to obey His commandment to honor my mother and father. Of course. I congratulated myself for being so clever, and I thanked God for giving me such an easy test. All I had to do was stand next to my brother while we stood in line. How hard was that?

The line to see Jerry Booth was very long, and at first it didn't seem like it was moving at all, but as we got near the front, it zipped right along. Up ahead I could see a kid on crutches, and he wasn't able to keep up. People were stepping around him as if he were an inanimate obstacle, and my stomach churned. What would happen when we got up there? Would we cut in front of him?

He wasn't a kid with a broken leg; he was crippled. One of his legs was shorter than the other, and he had a special shoe that was built up to make up the difference. There were velvet ropes and metal stands that guided us, and the line wound back and forth, so at one point I was nearly face-to-face with the kid on crutches. He looked dark and handsome and sad, and I was resolved that I did not want to take cuts in front of him.

I tried to talk to my brother, but he and Mark had their own conversation, and before I was able to butt in we had caught up with the kid on crutches. My brother and Mark went around him, but I stayed back. That got their attention.

"I don't want to take cuts!"

"Remember what Mom said? You have to stay with me."

"Then come back here."

"I'm going ahead, and if you don't come with me, I'm telling Mom."

So this was it, my test. I hadn't heard of a "Thou shalt not take cuts" commandment, so I was pretty sure that I should stick with my brother. The kid looked very sad, and I didn't want to take cuts, but I had to honor my mother and follow her instructions.

As I walked around the kid on crutches, I tried to establish some kind of connection. I hoped he would give me a little look or a nod of the head that said, "Hey, kid, thanks for trying. I know you had to stick with your brother." But the kid on crutches didn't react at all. To him I was just another guy taking cuts in front of him.

Jerry Booth was a big letdown. The reason the line moved so fast is they rushed you through. Jerry himself looked very red and very hot, and he pinched my hand when he shook it. After that, some guy from the mall handed us each a ticket and then moved us on our way.

The tickets, of course, were for the big drawing. There were several prizes, but the only one that interested me was the Sinbad Magic Belt. It would be just my luck that our mothers would take us away before the drawing, but they didn't and we were actually there when they drew numbers.

The tickets were numbered sequentially, with six digits on each one. I can't remember the first three digits, but Mark's ticket ended in 001, my brother's ended in 002, and mine ended in 003.

I waited through as they drew for the first few prizes, and none of our numbers were even close, but I really wasn't paying any attention. When they announced the numbers for the Sinbad Belt, however, I was very focused.

The first three numbers matched, but I knew that a thousand kids had matched the first three numbers. It was the last three numbers that caught my attention.

"Zero," called the announcer, and my heart quickened.

"Zero," he said again. I had matched five of the six numbers. My brother and Mark Hedgecock were still in the drawing too, but I had a feeling this was my moment.

"Four."

Four? My number was three! At first I thought there must be some kind of a mistake, because I had passed the test. I stayed with my brother. I waited for the announcer to say that he had made a mistake, but it didn't happen, and another kid excitedly claimed my prize.

I knew that God must be punishing me, but I couldn't think of anything I had done, at least, not anything bad enough to earn this kind of punishment. I sometimes hid my brother's shoes so he'd be late getting ready for school, but I did it out of revenge for the many times he picked on me, and I thought God would understand that he just got what he deserved.

I ran through the Ten Commandments in my mind, or at least as many of them as I could remember. I hadn't worshipped any false gods or carved any graven images. I didn't bear false witness against my neighbor. I hadn't committed adultery or stolen anything or killed anybody.

Then it occurred to me. I cut in front of a crippled kid. No wonder God was punishing me. Maybe it wasn't exactly against the Ten Commandments, but it certainly violated the "Do unto others…" statute.

I didn't want to finish the thought because I could see where things were headed, but it's pretty hard to stop your brain once it's decided where it wants to go. If I hadn't cut in front of the crippled kid, I would have had the winning ticket.

I sulked around for the rest of the afternoon, hoping that my brother would ask me about it. Maybe he'd say, "What's wrong?" and then I'd tell him what happened, and then he'd say, "It wasn't your fault. You were just following orders. If anybody should be blamed it should be me."

He didn't seem to notice, and when it was almost time for us to meet our mothers, I threw things into high gear. I sat on the floor, right there in the mall, and I hung my head. Certainly he would notice something was wrong, and then he'd *have* to ask me about it. And, sure enough, I got a reaction.

"What are you doing? Are you some kind of a retard?"

"I'm just sad," I said.

"Well, get moving! Man, I am getting so tired of this!"

"What do you mean by that?"

"When we were standing in line! You were acting like a retard then, too. Maybe we should send you and that crippled kid to some special ed room!"

"Shut up!" I shouted.

My brother slugged me in the arm and grabbed my elbow. "Now get moving!" he commanded. I thought about resisting, but I couldn't take another shot to the arm, so I got up and glumly followed along.

That afternoon, when I was home, I did some more thinking. I figured that "Do unto others" must outrank the other commandments. That was my problem; I still didn't know the Order of Things.

I wanted to wait until my father came home and confess what I had done, but I was too embarrassed. After

125

a great deal of thought, I decided that my best bet would be to run away from home and start over somewhere else.

I thought that I should tie up all of my possessions in a bandana and hang them from a stick, but I didn't have a bandana, or a stick, or much stuff to take with me. I had a backpack that we used when we played Army, and I thought that might come in handy in case I found any stuff along the way.

I made it all the way to end of the block, almost to Collingham, and that's when I ran into Mrs. Ballenger, who was carrying in a load of groceries.

"Detlef, what are you doing here? Are you playing Army?"

"I'm running away from home."

"How wonderful! Kids today are growing up so fast. When I was a girl, nobody ran away until they were in the eighth grade. So, what is your plan?"

"Plan?"

"Sure, where are you going? If I were you, I'd change my name and move to New Zealand. Of course, that's just me."

"I don't have a plan."

"Well, that's a problem, isn't it? Why don't you come into my house, and maybe we can come up with a plan together? Now, you be a good little gentleman and open the door for me so I can manage these groceries."

I opened the door for her, and then followed her into the kitchen.

"Have a seat. Maybe we can discuss this over a cup of coffee," she said, while calmly putting her groceries away.

"I don't drink coffee! I'm only eight!"

"Well, let's see what else I have. Maybe you'd like a glass of whiskey. Don't tell anybody, though, because I could be arrested for aiding to the delinquency of a minor."

She got a tall glass tumbler out of the cupboard and set it in front of me. "I'm giving you a big glass because it looks like you could really use a drink." Before I could react she disappeared into her pantry, and when she emerged she had a round tin box. "I'm fresh out of whiskey. The best I can do is milk and Oreo cookies. Would that be okay?"

"Sure."

"Now, it seems we need a map. I have a map of Michigan in my car, but that won't get you very far. You have to get out of Michigan or your parents will find you and drag you back home."

"Okay," I said, and I noticed a little tremble in my voice.

"I have a globe. Let's start with that. It's in the living room. Why don't you fetch it?"

"What about my food?"

"It will be waiting for you when you come back."

I took the globe from its big wooden stand and brought it to the kitchen. Mrs. Ballenger took the globe from me and immediately began examining it.

"You could move to the South Pole," she suggested. Do you like penguins?"

"Sort of. Where else could I go?"

"Well, there's China, but I don't suppose you speak Chinese, do you?"

"No, not really."

"Then I think we're back to New Zealand. Or maybe Australia. Possibly England, but I don't know how much of it has been rebuilt since it was bombed by the Germans."

"What about Canada?"

"If you were any other boy on the block, that might work, but your father is a policeman and unless you leave the continent entirely, he'll track you down."

Mrs. Ballenger put the globe on the chair next to her. "I hope you don't mind me asking, but what are you running away from?"

"I messed up real bad."

"What could you have done that was so bad that you have to run away from home?"

"I took cuts in front of a crippled kid."

Mrs. Ballenger's face fell, and I could see that, for the first time, she really was disappointed in me. "My Lord, Detlef, why on earth would you do a thing like that?"

"My brother made me."

I looked for a glint of understanding in her eye, but there was none, so I kept talking.

"My mother told me that I had to stay with my brother, no matter what, and then he took cuts and then I…" My mouth kept moving, but no sound came out, and then all of a sudden I started to cry. I didn't want to, because Mrs. Ballenger had treated me like a grownup, but it just came out.

"You didn't want to take cuts, but you felt you had to stay with your brother because your mother told you to?" she asked.

I nodded my head. "And now God hates me!" I managed to blurt out, just before I was hit with another wave of tears.

"Well, I'm sure God can look past this."

"That isn't all…" I managed to say.

"There's more?" she asked.

I nodded my head.

"More stuff like this?"

I wanted to tell her what a rotten kid I was, and how horribly I had acted when my mother told me that Grandma had died, but all I could was nod.

"You didn't murder anybody did you?"

"No," I managed to say.

"Hmm. Joseph's brothers sold him into slavery. Did you do anything that bad?"

"No!"

"Well then, I don't think you need to go all the way to New Zealand. Would you like to stay here for a while?"

"Okay. I mean— that would be great."

"Uh-oh," she said, knitting her eyebrows.

"What?"

"What about your parents? We don't want them worrying. Besides, with you living so close they're bound to find out where you are."

"Maybe you could call them and tell them where I am."

"What a wonderful idea! What's your number?"

"DR1-1443."

She wrote it down on a notepad that she kept by the phone. "When you're done with your milk and cookies you can take a nap in the guest bedroom. How does that sound?"

I was pretty tired, and it sounded great, but I could feel myself getting ready to cry again, so I didn't dare answer. I weakly nodded my head, and on the last nod I kept it down, just in case I started crying again.

I helped Mrs. Ballenger clear the table, and then I went to the spare room. I could hear Mrs. Ballenger dialing the phone, and I tried to listen to what she was saying, but I fell asleep and missed most if it.

I don't know how long I slept, but when Mrs. Ballenger woke me up it was already dark.

"Detlef, your parents are here. Would you like to see them?"

I hadn't been gone that long, and I was asleep most of the time, but for some reason I really missed my parents as much as if I had been gone a month. If I hadn't been so embarrassed, I would have rushed out to see them.

"Did you tell them what I told you?"

"No, I didn't. But I was hoping maybe you would. Do you think that you could talk to your mother?"

I shook my head.

"How about your dad?"

"Would I have to tell him right now or could I wait until later?"

"I'm sure he'd be willing to wait."

"Okay."

"Why don't you put your shoes and socks on, and I'll tell your parents you're ready to see them."

I could hear Mrs. Ballenger talking to my parents, but they were pretty quiet and I couldn't hear much. My dad said something about a guy named Tommy DiPaolo, somebody he knew from when he worked at the Youth Bureau, but other than that, I wasn't able to make much out. Just about the time I was finished tying my shoes, Mrs. Ballenger came in to get me.

My parents seemed glad to see me, but the whole thing was pretty awkward. I ran over to my dad, and he picked me up.

"Sounds like you've had a long day. Want to go home?"

"Okay," I said, pretending to be interested in a loose button on my shirt.

My parents didn't yell at me or really say much of anything on the way home. Under normal circumstances I would have heard a long and spirited lecture about how worried they were and how inconsiderate I had been. Maybe they thought that I was on the edge of a breakdown and the slightest thing would send me over the edge. Maybe they thought I already had gone over the edge. I wasn't going to ask.

As soon as we got home, I got myself ready for bed. I couldn't talk to my mother, I wasn't sure what to tell my father, and sleeping seemed like the only way out. I was able to shut off the lights and get under the covers before anybody talked to me, but I knew this wasn't over.

CHAPTER 14

"Detlef, this is Mr. DiPaolo."

Mr. DiPaolo was shorter than my dad, and maybe five or ten years younger. What remained of his hair was curly and black and looked it hadn't been combed since his eighteenth birthday. On the table next to him were a briefcase and a red Thermos bottle.

"Hey, Detlef, nice to meet you," he said, shaking my hand. He looked across the table at my father. "I'd like to give him the Stanford-Binet, but I don't have the time. I'll just talk to him for a while."

"Should we wait in the living room?" my mother asked.

"Sure. Just watch TV or whatever you normally do," Mr. DiPaolo advised.

"What's the Stanford-Binet? Is that some kind of a test to see if I'm crazy?"

"You're half right. It's a test, but it's an intelligence test."

"To see if I'm retarded?" I said, glumly.

"I can already tell you that you're not retarded." He didn't even bother looking up at me, but opened his briefcase and began removing stacks of papers. Just then I heard the television click on.

"That makes me feel better," I said.

"How come?" He glanced up from his stack of papers, but then began tapping his pockets for a pen.

"Because if they're listening to the television, they can't hear us."

"Do you ever wonder what's inside of a television?" Mr. DiPaolo stared right at me, like he really wanted to know the answer to this question, but I couldn't understand why. I was pretty sure my parents didn't invite him over so we could chat about what makes a TV work.

"Sure."

"What do you think you'd find inside of a TV? All of the little people you see on the screen?" He smiled, but it was one of those fake smiles that adults use when they know you're retarded but don't want you to feel stupid.

"Of course not. It's filled with tubes, but I'm not sure what most of them do. The big one is the picture tube, but other than that…"

"It sounds like you've got a good idea about how a television works," he said and went back to his stack of papers.

"Not really. I know that a gun shoots electrons onto the screen, but when the guy came to fix the TV last month I looked for the gun and I couldn't find it. Maybe it's inside of the picture tube."

Mr. DiPaolo stopped shuffling papers and was completely still for a couple of seconds. "Wait, you're telling me that a gun shoots electrons—"

"Yeah, everybody knows that. Except in a color TV, because they need three guns. One for red, one for green, and another for blue. Those are the primary colors of light."

"I thought the primary colors were red, yellow, and blue." Mr. DiPaolo's tone of voice sounded like he wasn't quite sure, and I wondered if he was testing me.

"Those are the subtractive primaries—the ones you use when you're mixing paint," I explained. "Red, green, and blue are the additive primaries, the ones that make up white light."

"How come the additive primaries are different from the subtractive primaries?" he asked, using a tone of voice like he really didn't know.

"I don't know," I snapped. "I read it on a poster in the art room, but I really don't understand what it means."

"How does that make you feel?"

"Like a retard."

"You feel like a retard because you don't understand the difference between the additive and subtractive primaries?"

"Yes."

"Can you name three teams in the American League?"

"No. The only team I know is the Detroit Tigers. I think they're in the American League."

"But you're not sure."

"No," I said, crossing my arms. "I'm telling you, I'm borderline retarded."

"Who are the Big Three automakers?"

"I don't know." I was really getting irritated and I started looking at him more carefully, trying to find things I didn't like.

"What does it mean to double dribble?" He leaned back, and I noticed that the hair in his nose needed trimming. In fact, some of the hair in his nose wasn't exactly in his nose, and it was creeping out of the corners.

"I don't know!" I said angrily. "Look, you've made your point. I don't know anything. I'm stupid, okay? That's why everybody thinks—" I stopped talking. This guy knew how to push my buttons, and I didn't want to let him.

"What is it? What does everybody think?" he asked, leaning forward.

"I don't know. Why don't you ask them?"

"So that upsets you? What everybody thinks?"

"Kind of, I guess."

"Hey, Wally!" Mr. DiPaolo called. "Come in here for a minute."

My dad popped through the doorway. "What's up?"

"Did you ever take this kid to a ball game?" Just like that, Mr. DiPaolo was off my back and on my father's, and just like that I decided he wasn't so bad.

"We saw the Tigers play last year."

"How did that go?"

"I had a great time," I said. "I had a hot dog with mustard and onions, and—"

"That's great, Detlef, but I want your father's thoughts. Wally, how did your son like the game?"

"He wasn't focused on the game. I bought him a program, and he spent the whole time drawing pictures in the margin."

"Pictures of what?"

"Robots!" I shouted. "I like to build robots with my Erector Set. Would you like to see one?"

"Sure."

I ran up to my room and got a robot I had been building with my Erector Set. It wasn't quite finished, so I was a little embarrassed, but Mr. DiPaolo didn't seem to mind. He just asked me how the claws worked and then he played with it for a while.

"Do you ever worry that robots are going to take over the world?"

"No, that isn't how the world is going to end," I stated.

"So you know how the world is going to end." I couldn't tell if he didn't know, or if he was testing me again.

"Sure. Everybody does." I tried to put a tone of finality in my voice so he'd know that I was done with the topic, but he was not going to let it go.

134

"Why don't you fill me in?"

I rolled my eyes to let him know that I was tired of answering obvious questions. "There are rules that everybody has to follow, and as long as we follow all of the rules everything will be fine. The problem is that some people don't follow the rules..."

"Like who?"

"Hitler, the Russians, East Germans, Lee Harvey Oswald..."

"Yeah, I get the picture."

"Anyhow, if they don't follow the rules, then anything can happen."

"Like what?"

"Well, a hundred years ago there was the Civil War, which was just our country. And then things got worse and we had a World War, and that didn't solve anything so we had another World War. But now we've got The Bomb, so the next time something happens it's going to be the end of everything."

"So how do you fit into the picture?"

"Well, I think the problem is that I'm German."

"Really?" he replied, taking a sip of coffee.

"Yeah. Germans aren't very good at following rules."

Mr. DiPaolo laughed, and coffee shot out of his nose.

"Excuse me," he said, and then he started coughing. It was a deep, hacking cough, and coffee kept coming out of his nose. My parents must have heard it, because they came rushing in from the next room.

"Is everything okay in here?" my dad asked.

"Yeah, we're fine." Mr. DiPaolo said. "Give us another couple of minutes."

My mother got a clean dish towel from the drawer and gave it to Mr. DiPaolo. He wasn't sure what to do with it and just looked at it for a second, but then he wiped up the coffee from the table and, finally, from his face.

135

"Let me have that," my mother said," taking the towel.   She turned away and then, unable to control herself, turned back and wiped one last coffee smudge from Mr. DiPaolo's face. My dad pulled the towel from her hands, threw it into the sink, and led her into the living room.

"What makes you think that Germans can't follow rules?" Mr. DiPaolo tried to be serious, but the corners of his mouth kept curling up into a smile.

I told him about how I took cuts in front of the crippled kid, and how God punished me.

"So God punished you because you took cuts?"

"Yes."

"And that's why you didn't win the magic belt?"

"Yes."

"Okay, then who did?"

"I don't know. Some other kid. Whoever was behind me in line."

"This other kid—the one who won. Did he take cuts in front of the crippled kid?"

I thought back. I was neither the first nor the last to take cuts. All of a sudden it was hard to breathe.

"He must have taken cuts, just like me! But then why did God…"

"Did you ever think that maybe God doesn't care about who wins a Sinbad the Sailor Magic Belt? Maybe He's busy dealing with earthquakes and floods. Maybe He's more of a Big Picture Guy."

"Is that what you think?" I asked.

"Me? I don't think about things like that."

"But that doesn't make sense!"

"Lots of things don't make sense. But I'm not going to beat myself up until the world makes sense."

"That's it? That's your answer?"

"Who said I had answers?"

"But I thought you were a—"

"What? Psychologist?"

136

"Yes!" I said accusingly.

"Maybe I am. What does that have to do with anything? Look kid, you've made up your mind that you're not going to be happy until the whole world makes sense. I can't change the whole world for you."

"But..."

"Sorry kid, that's all I got. If I figure anything else out, I'll give you a call."

"You don't understand. There is an order to things!"

"Really? Why don't you tell me about it?"

"I can't. It keeps changing. It's like things used to make sense, but now it's like..."

"Like somebody shuffled the deck?"

"Yes!"

"And this new order. It seems random and unjust."

"Yes!"

"Oh, so maybe if we could put things back the way they used to be..."

"Yes!"

"Sorry kid. It ain't gonna happen. The Magic Belt is going to go to whoever is holding the lucky ticket, and it might not be the person who deserves it."

"No, that isn't how it works! There are always two groups!"

"Two groups?"

"Sure, like during the Civil War. You had Yankees and Rebs. Or North and South Viet Nam. Or in Germany, you've got the good West Germans and the evil East Germans..."

"So you think all of the good Germans live in West Germany, and East Germany is filled with war criminals and ax murderers?"

"Something like that."

"And in this line, there were two kinds of people. Ones who took cuts and ones who didn't?"

"Yes!"

He called to the next room. "Wally! Come in here. I think I've found out what I need to know."

I heard the TV shut off, and then my mother scurried into the room, followed by my dad.

"What do you think? Did you find out what's wrong with him?" my mother asked. Mr. DiPaolo and my father exchanged a glance.

"There's nothing wrong with your son, Mrs. Niebaum."

My mom made a funny face, like it wasn't the answer she wanted to hear.

"We had a nice talk and a change of plans. Like I said, I didn't have time to give him the Stanford-Binet, but just from talking to him I can tell that he's a very bright young man."

"Okay," my father said.

"He's just a little nervous. He's picked up a little information here, some other stuff there, and when he connected the dots it wasn't a pretty picture. He thinks the world is a very dangerous place. And he worries about it. A lot."

"What are you so worried about?" my mother asked, sounding a bit too concerned.

"I don't know."

"He's afraid that he's offended God, and that the entire world is on the brink of nuclear destruction. Not the usual childhood fears."

"Where would he get such ideas?" my mother demanded.

"Who knows? He sees his father carrying a gun. Maybe that tells him that the world is a dangerous place."

"I don't think that's it," I offered.

"Be quiet and let the man speak!" my mother snapped.

"Is there anything we can do to make him less...nervous?" my father asked.

"Spend some time with him. Take him around. Show him the world isn't such a scary place."

"Okay," my dad said. He sure seemed quiet.

"But don't take him to Disneyland. Take him where the action is. Downtown, maybe."

"Downtown!" my mother exclaimed. "It isn't safe Downtown!"

Mr. DiPaolo looked at her. "Exactly. But your son will be fine. People go Downtown every day, and most of them come back alive."

"But—"

Mr. DiPaolo cut her off. "Don't worry. He'll be with his father."

My mother still seemed skeptical. "Will any of this do any good?"

Mr. DiPaolo started shuffling some papers, and for a second I wasn't sure he even heard what my mother had said. Finally he answered. "It took him his whole life to get this way. Don't expect him to change tomorrow."

"Okay, then," my dad said.

"Just one more thing," Mr. DiPaolo asked, "where did you get that robot kit? I've got a six-year-old and I think he'd love it."

"It's an Erector Set!" I exclaimed.

"Yeah, well if it's all the same to you, I'll stick with robot kit. That other name has too many Freudian connotations."

"Huh?"

"Never mind. So where do I find this kit?"

"You get it at any toy store."

"Thanks." He tossed the few remaining papers into his briefcase and snapped the lid shut.

For the next couple of days, nothing seemed any different. My dad was still busy reading books, and my mother still treated me like I was from another planet. But a few days later, on Saturday, my dad got me out of bed early in the morning.

"Come on," my dad announced. "You're going to help me fix up your old bike so we can give it to the Salvation Army."

I knew my bike was pretty crappy. It had first belonged to a neighbor and then to my brother, and by the time I got it the paint was chipped and there was a light layer of rust on the handlebars, but I didn't realize it was so bad that we had to fix it up before we could give it away. "

"What's wrong with my bike? And why are we giving it away?"

"It's too small for you. You need a bigger bike."

"Am I getting a new bike?"

"Not a brand new bike, but one that's new to you."

"When do I get it?"

"That depends on how fast we can get your old bike ready for the Salvation Army. Now get dressed and meet me in the garage."

By the time I got out to the garage my father had already started. I expected him to be painting it or maybe even decorating it with decals, but instead he was cutting it apart with a hack saw.

"What are you doing?" I shouted.

"What?" he asked, laughing.

"Look what you're doing to my bike! You're wrecking it!"

"I'm just taking off the top bar. This used to be a girl's bike, and I'm changing it back."

"What?"

"Mr. McCallen bought it for Linda, and when she outgrew it he welded this bar on and gave it to Bobby."

"I've been riding around on a girl's bike?" A lot of kids had been teasing me and calling me a sissy, and I wondered if my dad caught wind of it and decided to get me a boy's bike so he could be somewhat less ashamed of me.

"Howard gave me an old bike that he picked up at the police auction. He was going to fix it up and give it to Alex, but Howard never got around to it and now Alex is driving a car," he explained.

"Where is it?" I looked around the garage, and I didn't see any place a bike could be hiding.

"It needs a lot of work," my father warned.

"I don't care!"

"And we've got to fix up your old bike first."

"Fine! Just tell me where it is!"

My dad scratched his head. "Let me see if I can remember…"

"Dad!"

"It's in the trunk of the car. Catch!" He threw me his keys. I stuck out my hand like I was going to catch them, but as soon as they got close I could see that he had thrown them too hard and I moved out of the way and curled into a standing fetal position. The keys clanged against the garage door, and my father sighed in a sad way.

I ignored my father's advice not to get my hopes up, and I hoped for the best, so when I laid my eyes on the bike for the first time I was very disappointed.

Both tires were flat. The front wheel was bent out of shape. I'd heard that you could straighten a bent rim by adjusting the spokes, but this one was bent in half and it looked like a banana. I was pretty sure that no amount of spoke adjusting would fix it. It had been black, but a lot of the paint was chipped off.

I struggled to get it out of the trunk, and then I dragged it into the garage.

"What do you think?" he asked.

"I think it needs a lot of work."

"Yeah, well, we'll get a new wheel, some chrome fenders, a coat of paint…"

Chrome fenders! That would be cool.

"But first we have to finish your old bike."

141

I tried to be interested in my old bike, but there wasn't much for me to do. My dad was stripping it down to the frame so he could paint it, but I was pretty bored and my thoughts wandered.

"Is Mom going to Heaven?"

My question caught my dad off guard. He was trying to take the front wheel off the bike, but the nut was stuck, and I asked my question just as it was about to break loose. For half a second my dad was caught between two worlds. His head was thinking about what I had said, but his hands were still pushing on the wrench. All of a sudden the nut finally let go. My dad's hand shot forward, he dropped the wrench, and his knuckles scraped against the spokes. He lost a pretty good chunk of skin, and blood welled up in the hole where the skin had been.

"Son, you have a unique sense of timing," he said, trying not to lose his temper. "Of course she's going to Heaven. Why would you even ask?"

"Well, she's so afraid of dying that I thought she might be going to Hell."

"That's not the problem. It's a funny thing about Heaven. Everybody wants to go to Heaven, but nobody wants to die to get there."

"Oh."

My dad picked up the rag he used when he checked the oil in the car. He looked for a clean spot, which of course didn't exist, then he tore off a piece of rag and tied it around his hand.

After that we didn't talk too much. We painted my old bike that afternoon, and by evening it was dry enough to get it back together.

Over the next couple of weekends we worked on my bike, not all of the time, but a couple hours here and a couple hours there. I didn't want my dad to bust another knuckle, so I was careful not to ask too many questions or to talk about anything that might upset him. Every now and then he asked a question, and I did my best to answer

142

without saying too much, and then he'd just breathe heavily and go back to work.

By the end of the third weekend the bike was almost finished. It had fresh paint, chrome fenders, butterfly handlebars, and a banana seat. You could tell that it wasn't new, but it still looked sharp.

"Son, I'm going to be pretty busy for a while, so this might be the last chance we have to talk."

I looked at the floor. I thought my dad was cool and we weren't going to have this conversation, at least not until I was ready, but maybe he was running out of patience.

"There are going to be some changes around here." I stiffened and prepared for the bad news. "You know how I've been to going to night school, right?"

"Sure."

"Do you know what I've been studying?"

"Not really."

"I've been studying Christian Education, so that maybe when I retired from the force in eight years I could…" His voice trailed off and he thought for a few seconds. "You know, none of that shit matters anymore."

"Huh?"

"The bishop and the district superintendent have been talking, and they think that I should be a church pastor."

"Like Reverend Hotchkiss?"

"Yeah."

I looked at my dad and I couldn't see it. There was a big smudge of grease across his forehead, and he had once again patched up a cut on his hand with that same greasy rag. Revered Hotchkiss was always clean and well-dressed, and moved gently, like he never touched a wrench or even mowed his own lawn. My dad was tall and gangly, and when he moved he looked like some kind of Disney cartoon. He never looked scholarly or thoughtful. I thought back to earlier that week, when I'd

143

seen him reading a book. He was sitting at the kitchen table, with one knee propped against the edge of the table and the book delicately balanced on his knee so he could use both hands to peel a banana. I thought he looked like a monkey, and a minister was supposed to look, well, I wasn't exactly sure how a minister was supposed to look, but it wasn't like a monkey.

"You can't be a minister!" I blurted out.

"That's what I tried to say. But they looked at my transcripts and they say I've got enough classes in theology and Bible studies…" My dad stopped talking and his eyes narrowed to slits. "Oh, you think I can't be a minister because I'm a big galoot who goes hunting and plays baseball…"

"Something like that."

He looked down at his crudely bandaged hand and laughed. "Yeah, I don't exactly fit the mold, do I?"

"I guess not," I said, and then I laughed, and then we both got to laughing so hard we couldn't even talk.

"Son, the Fort Street Church doesn't have a minister. The gentleman that was there passed away, and they need somebody."

"So it's like you're in the Legion of Substitute Heroes."

"What?"

"The Legion of Substitute Heroes," I explained. "There's a group of super-powered crime-fighting teenagers in the Thirtieth Century, and they're called the Legion of Super Heroes. But sometimes they're busy fighting crime deep in space, and that leaves the Earth unprotected, and that's when the Legion of Substitute Heroes takes over."

"Oh, I understand," he said in a voice that told me he didn't understand at all.

"You're in the Legion of Substitute Ministers. And as soon as there is an opening, you can move up to the Legion of Regular Ministers."

"That's actually pretty close to the truth," he mused.

"Are you still going to be a policeman?" I wondered aloud.

"Sure. This is just part-time. And it's just until June. They'll have new appointments and new graduates by then, but…" His voice trailed off.

"But what?"

"But it probably doesn't matter because it looks like I'm going to be the last minister this church ever has."

"Are they closing the church?"

"Well, they're merging it with another church, but it amounts to the same thing."

"What happens then?"

"Well, I guess this congregation will attend—"

"No, I mean, what will happen to us? Are you going to still be a minister?"

"I don't know. I'm just going to accept this one appointment, and we'll take it from there. Maybe I'll stick with the police force, or maybe I'll continue my studies and become a minister. You know, full time—in the Legion."

While we were talking he had taken his electric drill out of the toolbox and installed a bit. He held the bit next to the fender.

"What are you doing?" I yelped.

"I'm going to drill a hole in your fender for the reflector."

"You can't do that. The drill bit will go right through the fender and punch a hole in the tire."

"I'll be careful."

"Why don't we take off the wheel, just to be safe?" I pleaded.

My dad was finished with the conversation, so instead of saying anything he just drilled. And, just like I predicted, the drill shot through the fender and punctured the tire.

"I told you so! Now what are we going to do?"

"Relax. I can fix the tire."

"This is just the kind of thing I was talking about. You can't be like this when you're a minister!"

"Like what?"

"Like drilling holes in tires and wearing a greasy flannel shirt," I said, trying to be calm.

"I suppose I'll have to make a few changes, you know, to make sure I'm setting the right example, but I think the greasy flannel shirt is here to stay. Now, let's patch that tire."

My dad had a kit, a little cardboard container with a metal lid, and he got it out whenever he had to patch a hole in our bike tires or galoshes. In no time at all he had the hole patched, and I felt a little better.

"Okay, before we put it back on your bike, let's check it for leaks."

He got out the pump and began inflating the tire.

"You know, son, I've been waiting a long time for you to talk about whatever it is that's bothering you. In a couple of weeks I won't have this kind of time, so if you've got something on your mind…"

"No, I'm fine."

"Okay," my dad said, and he kept on pumping up the inner tube.

"Maybe you should stop pumping so we can listen for leaks," I suggested, but he just kept on going, even though it looked like the inner tube was plenty full. I wasn't sure if he heard me, because his head was down and his eyes were focused on the tire, and there was no visible reaction.

"I think that's good," I said. Still no reaction. Then, suddenly, part of the tire bulged to about twice the usual size, and even though my dad's eyes were fixed on the inner tube he just kept on pumping.

"Stop!" I shouted. Calmly, like he was waking from a peaceful sleep, my dad picked up his head and looked at me.

"What?"

"Take a look at the tire!"

"What? The bulge? I don't think we need to worry about that," and then he started to pump again.

"What's wrong with you?" I shouted.

"I don't see what you're so worried about. If it breaks we'll just patch it."

"You patch a hole. You can't patch a blowout!"

"Oh, so by time there's a blowout it's too late?"

"Yes!"

"So what should we do?"

"Undo the thing!"

"What?"

"Release some of the pressure!"

"Oh, the thing," my dad said, pointing to the valve stem.

My dad unscrewed the tire pump from the valve, pressed his thumbnail against the stem and released some of the air. "How do you feel now?" he asked.

"A lot better. What were you thinking?" I demanded.

"What do you think I was thinking?"

He was unusually calm and quiet. I thought about waiting him out, but he could be pretty stubborn. He was probably trying to teach me some kind of lesson, but I couldn't figure out what it could be.

"That wasn't about the bicycle at all, was it?"

"No, it wasn't," he confessed. He tapped the side of his head.

"Are you saying that my head is like the inner tube, and if I let the pressure build up it's going to blow?"

"Something like that. Now, are you sure there isn't something you want to tell me?"

I told him everything, and I mean everything. I told him that I was embarrassed about being German, and how everybody thought that I was a retard, and that I was so lousy at sports that I shouldn't even be allowed to watch a game, and I even included the stuff about how I was an ungrateful bastard who didn't appreciate his own grandma.

"How long have you been thinking about this?"

"Since Kindergarten."

"And how often do these thoughts go through your head?"

"Most of the time. Why, is that weird?"

"Son, you can't let the pressure get to you. Everybody is under pressure."

"Even you?"

"Sure. I'm supposed to be this font of wisdom, and I'm going to have to write a sermon every week."

"That doesn't sound so bad."

"Son, there are over fifty weeks in the year, and if I go into the ministry for twenty years that's a thousand sermons. I'm not sure I have a thousand ideas in me."

"So what do you do about it?"

"Nuthin'. I've got enough ideas to get me through the first few weeks, and after that I'm sure I'll think of something."

"But what if you don't?"

"Then I guess I'll just stand in the pulpit with my mouth shut for fifteen minutes."

"But..."

"But nuthin'. You know, if we stop talking and get to work your bike can be ready in about ten minutes. So, what do you want to do, keep talking about sermons or finish the bike?"

I was pretty sure that we could do both and that this was just a trick to distract me, but I really wanted that bike so I was ready to agree to just about anything.

"Let's finish the bike!"

"Okay then. Did you see what happened to that half-inch wrench?"

CHAPTER 15

It was difficult to convince my classmates that, in addition to being a police officer, a clown, and a magician, my father was now a Methodist minister. To put it another way, everybody thought I was full of crap.

I didn't even see the church until the Sunday when my father first conducted services. We got there early, which gave me plenty of time to look around. Since it was ready to close I expected it to be in pretty rough shape, but it was in surprisingly good condition. The paint looked fresh, the glass was clean, and there was not a speck of dust to be found anywhere. The metal folding chairs in the Fellowship Hall were unscratched, almost like they were brand new. In the church office I found a box of key chains. I pulled one out, and it had a little red tag that was embossed with the words "Fort Street Methodist Parsonage: I Bought a Brick." None of these things seemed consistent with a church that was ready to close.

Clearly there had been some kind of an error at the district office, and closing this church would be a crime. No, it would be a sin. I knew my father was busy and I was told not to bother him unless it was important, but it seemed like this was the kind of thing he needed to know. I found him in the church office, reading through some papers.

"They can't close this church! It's in great shape!"

"It's not the church," he explained. "It's the neighborhood. It's…changing."

"How is it changing?"

"It's just different. It isn't as safe as it once was. Maybe we can talk about this later. I need to take one more look at my sermon."

I left his office and went out to the sanctuary to kill time. About half an hour before church started, people began showing up. My favorite was Mrs. Clark, who introduced herself not only to my parents but also to the kids. "My name is Mrs. Clark, and you'll never forget it because I'm Mrs. Clark from Lincoln Park." By the time church began the small sanctuary was nearly filled.

I was still pretty worried about my father's ability to act like a minister, but he emerged from the church office wearing a black robe, and he looked like another man. My doubts as to whether or not the old man could really pull it off were finally squashed when he began the Pastoral Prayer: "Almighty and Most Merciful Father, we humbly beseech Thee…"

I wondered where he had learned to talk like that. I'd grown used to his ability to come up with previously unheard of obscene words and phrases, but his eloquent language shocked me. It was easy enough to imagine my father picking up foul language at some loading dock or back alley, but I could not conceive of a place where scholars and ministers stood in a circle tossing around flowery phrases. Yet "bestow upon us Thy tender mercies" was falling from his lips as easily as "this son-of-a-bitch is trying to take his half of the road out of the middle" had spouted forth on the drive to church earlier that same morning.

After church he stood by the door and shook hands with the people as they left. Everybody milled around outside, and nobody seemed to be worried that the neighborhood was unsafe, not even the old ladies. I didn't hear any gunshots or see any criminals, and I really thought that everybody was worried about a bunch of nothing.

After nearly everybody left, my dad went back into the church office to change out of his robe. A couple of men, probably members of the administrative board, were still lingering around.

Because the church was within the city limits, my father had to wear his gun. I had grown used to it, but when he removed his robe and the men from the church saw it, they were goggle-eyed.

"What's that?" asked an old guy in a gray suit.

"What?" my father answered. "Oh, that. That's my service revolver. I've got to carry it even when I'm off duty."

My dad dismissed the thought and began brushing lint off his robe, but the church men looked at each other and smiled.

"Well, I guess we don't have to worry about anybody walking off with the collection," commented the old guy in the gray suit.

After that we all got in the car, but instead of going straight home my dad made an announcement.

"If you promise not to eat like barbarians, we'll swing by the Red Barn for hamburgers on the way home. But first we have to take a look at the parsonage." Parsonage. There was that word again.

"Dad, what's a parsonage?"

"It's a home that the church provides for the minister's family."

"Are we going to live there?" I excitedly asked.

"We can't," my mother answered. "It's not a safe neighborhood."

By that time my father was already pulling into the driveway.

"Hey look, there's a bike on the lawn!" my brother shouted. "Can I have it?"

"It's probably stolen," my father answered.

Stealing a bike was a pretty big crime as far as I was concerned, on the same level as stealing a cowboy's horse. I thought my dad would take out his badge and his gun and I'd finally get to see him act like a cop, but he didn't seem concerned.

The lock on the front door of the parsonage didn't work very well, but my dad managed to get it open with a minimum amount of swearing. Once inside, it was just an empty house, no better than ours, except that it had a fireplace.

"It's a shame we can't live here," my mother clucked. "It's such a beautiful house."

"The phone works," my dad announced.

"What are you doing?" I wondered.

"Phoning the police to tell them about the bike," he hurriedly replied. Then he put his finger to his lips and talked into the receiver. "This is Walter Niebaum, I'm an off-duty policeman, and I found what I think is a stolen bicycle."

That was it? That was how my father solved crimes? By making phone calls?

I needed answers, so as soon as he hung up I unleashed my curiosity. "Are they going to send detectives? Will they take fingerprints? Do you think the kid is going to get his bike back?"

"They're going to send out a squad car, and the officers will take the bike back to the station. The boy who lost it can come down to the police station and claim it."

"What if he doesn't claim it? Then can I have it?" my brother asked.

"If it was a lost item, like a wallet, you could, but since this is a stolen item it will go in the property room until it is claimed or sold at the annual auction."

153

The next Sunday when we got to church, a photographer from the Detroit Free Press was waiting for us. He took a picture of my dad changing into his black robe, but I couldn't understand why. A few days later, I saw the article. You could clearly see my dad's gun, and the words "Pistol Packin' Preacher" were in big letters below the photo. I still didn't get it. What was the point of a policeman changing into a ministerial robe? It was like watching Superman change back into Clark Kent. They should have taken a picture of my dad ripping his robe open and revealing his gun.

Except for the time when he was in the pulpit, my dad was still the same guy he had always been. After that first Sunday in church I thought he might say things like, "Wilt thou kindly pass me the salt," and then go into some kind of speech about how Jesus called His followers the salt of earth, but he just said, "Hand me that salt shaker when you're done with it."

Other people treated him differently. His police buddies still dropped by, but they didn't swear as much, and the rude sexual jokes were completely gone. I was at the perfect age, when I was old enough to understand some of the remarks, but still young enough that my dad's friends could convince themselves that everything was going over my head.

He was making a real effort to spend more time with me and often dragged me along when he had to run errands or do work at his office. On those days, he'd take me to the library first so I'd have something to read and maybe stay out of his way. On one particular day, I found a great magic book that had always been checked out on our previous trips to the library.

"Hey, Dad! Here's a good trick. It's called Red Hot Ball. You have this little brass ball, and it mysteriously becomes so hot that you can't even touch it. All I need is quicklime and sulfuric acid."

My father sighed. "Aren't there any rope tricks in your book? People like rope tricks."

I took that to mean that eight-year-olds weren't supposed to play with quicklime and sulfuric acid. I wanted to argue, but someone was knocking on the open door.

"Excuse me, Revrund, I hope you don't mind, but the outside door was open, so I let myself in." Standing in the doorway was a little man who kind of looked like a bum, except that he was young, maybe twenty. He had thick, black hair, and not too many lines on his face, but other than that he looked like every other bum I'd ever seen. He was wearing an overcoat and a stocking cap, and it looked like he hadn't shaved in a couple of days.

"Can we talk to you?"

My dad buttoned his suit coat, a habit he had acquired since becoming a minister. He didn't want to lean forward and flash his gun. "Sure. Come on in."

The little man stepped out of view for a second, and when he reappeared he had with him a woman he introduced as his wife. At first glance, Mrs. Bum looked a little too good for her husband. She was shabbily dressed, but I thought that even though she was shabbily dressed she was kind of pretty, but when she smiled and shook my father's hand I could see a crescent-shaped void in one of her front teeth, and what remained of her tooth was black at the edges. I did my best not to look at her teeth, but before I forced myself to look away I noticed that a lot of her teeth had either rotted away or were in the process of doing so.

In her arms was a baby, who looked like every other baby. I expected that the baby of poor people would be crying all of the time, but he gurgled and cooed and made the usual baby noises.

"To be honest with you, Revrund, I am having some financial problems. I came here from Texas because I heard there were jobs, but it hasn't worked out so good for me. Now me and my wife got a little one, and we don't know what to do."

My father looked extraordinarily sympathetic. "I've got a friend at the Ford Foundry," he said, writing a name on the paper. Give this guy a call, mention my name, and he can probably get you in." My father handed the paper to the man, but the guy didn't even look at it.

"To be honest with you, Revrund," he explained, "my baby is hungry today. I mean, I'll give the guy a call, you know, but in the meantime he's gotta eat."

My father looked at the baby, and then his brows knitted, like he was thinking very hard. He almost looked cross for a second, but then his face softened.

"The church has an emergency pantry, groceries that we keep in case somebody has a house fire or something like that. This sounds like it qualifies as an emergency."

We went down to the church pantry, and my father began loading groceries into a paper bag. "This is enough to get you through until tomorrow. I'll make some calls to some other agencies who can help you out until you get a steady paycheck. Come back here tomorrow at the same time and I'll tell you where you can go."

My father led us upstairs, past what would have been the easiest door for the couple to exit, to the front doors of the church, where he let them out.

"Good luck, and God bless," my father called as the couple walked off.

"Thanks," the woman called back, acting just a little sad.

My father dashed back to his office, and when I caught up with him he was sitting at his desk, leaning on one elbow, staring out the window, and I noticed that his coat was unbuttoned. "I don't care if they keep the groceries, just so long as they don't..." He leaned forward and put his hands on the arms of his chair.

"Oh, crap!" he shouted. He lurched forward and stood up, but when he did so his belt buckle got snagged on the partially open drawer of his desk. He grabbed the desk by the top, rocked it on two legs, and then attempted to push it away. Instead of simply moving forward, the desk tipped over and landed on its front side. The phone and Rolodex spilled onto the floor, but my father just left them there and ran out of the office.

I stood on the seat and looked out the window. The young bum from Texas was selling the groceries to some other guy I hadn't seen before. I slid the window open so I could hear what was going on, and just about then my dad showed up.

"Give me the groceries," my father commanded, hardly out of breath.

The woman hung her head down, but the two men seemed to have an in-your-face attitude. "Hey, I thought those were mine to keep," the young bum answered.

"But you didn't keep them. You tried to sell them to this guy," my dad answered. The two men looked a little startled. I guess they expected a minister to be more timid, or at least more civilized.

The new guy squared his shoulders toward my dad, like he was getting ready to hit him, but my dad snapped his head around, gave the man a mean look, and the guy wilted a little. The young bum began to talk.
"Okay, maybe I didn't need groceries. Maybe I needed money."

"For what? What's more important than food?" From the way my father asked the question, I could tell that he already knew the answer. The woman grabbed the young bum by the arm.

"Henry, I told you this was a bad idea," she moaned.

My dad just stood there, and in a couple of seconds the new guy handed him the bag of groceries. Instead of turning around and taking the groceries back to

157

the church, my father watched the people walk half a block away, get into an old car, and drive off.

Only then did he start walking back toward the church, but as soon as he did, the car spun around and drove up on the curb and headed for my father. My dad must have known they were coming, because he jumped out of the way, but not like he was scared. He didn't even drop the groceries, at least not right away.

Once the car had passed him, he reached into the bag, pulled out a can, let the bag fall to the ground, and, looking very much like a second baseman for the Detroit Tigers, threw the can at the speeding car. The can smashed through the rear window, which shattered completely.

"You can keep that one. It's on me!" he shouted.

The driver of the car gave my dad the finger as he sped away, and I could hear them shouting what I assumed were obscenities. After I was sure the car wasn't coming back, I went outside to help my dad gather up the groceries.

"What was that about?"

"That young couple was running a con game," he explained.

"I don't get it."

"Last week I had another couple come in with the same story."

"And that's how you knew they were cheating the church? You recognized the story?"

"No, I recognized the baby." He picked up a can of creamed corn, which had been slightly dented in the fall, decided it was okay, and put it into the bag. "It was a different couple, but they had the same baby."

"Then why did you give them the groceries?"

"Just to see what they would do." I started to ask a question, but my dad knew where things were going and cut me off. "They tried to sell the groceries to the guy in the car. They probably wanted cash to buy alcohol." My dad got quiet for a few seconds. "Oh, hell."

"What?"

I just busted out the back window of some poor person's car in order to protect a bag of groceries."

"Yeah, but they were stealing from the church."

"Maybe you're right. Jesus didn't like it when the money changers tried to run a scam at the temple."

By this time we had finished gathering the groceries and were on the front steps of the church.

"Do you think they'll come back?"

"I don't know. They might have looked around to see if there was anything worth stealing so they could break in later. You can never tell."

"Is there anything worth stealing?"

"I guess not. The only valuable thing we've got is the pipe organ, and they can't take that."

We walked down the hall to his office in silence. I figured he was going to lose it when he got back to his office and saw what a mess he had made, but he just seemed sad.

"You know, you flipped over the table just like…"

"No, it was nuthin' like that. I was just thinking like a police officer instead of a minister."

With one quick motion, he flipped his desk back onto its legs. The phone had come unplugged from the wall, and some of the cards had spilled out of his Rolodex, but he set those things straight.

"Are you ready to go home?"

"Can we stop by the drugstore and pick up some quicklime and sulfuric acid on the way?" I asked.

My dad's face turned a little angry, and I realized that the incident had taken more of a toll than I had thought. "I thought I told you…" He paused for a second, and then smiled. "Detlef, you're getting a sense of humor."

"Well, if you're not going to let me have sulfuric acid, then we should probably stop by the library and return this book."

"Okay, but let's take the cross and candelabras from the sanctuary and lock them in my office closet, just in case those guys return for a little after-hours shopping."

We secured things as much as we could, and then we headed out to the car. As we pulled out from the church lot, a song by the Byrds was playing on the radio.

"To everything, turn, turn, turn, there is a season…"

"I like that song," my dad said. "It says it all."

"What do you mean?"

"Turn, turn, turn. You've got to know when to turn the other cheek, and you've got to know when to turn over the tables at the temple."

"That's only two," I commented.

"What?"

"You need three. It says turn, turn, turn."

"Okay. How about sometimes you have to turn a disadvantage into an advantage?"

"But you didn't do anything like that. It doesn't fit."

"I suppose not. Okay, how about this. You could turn over a new leaf."

"That's as bad as the other one."

"This is awful. My own son has turned against me."

"Hey, Dad!"

"What?"

"Don't forget to use your turn signals."

"Keep working on that sense of humor, Son," he commented as he pulled into the library parking lot.

CHAPTER 16

The following Monday my dad came home from work early and announced that we needed a new television antenna. I couldn't understand why, because the old one seemed to work just fine, but he was particularly determined.

He had borrowed a long wooden ladder from Mr. Hedgecock. It wasn't an extension ladder, but a single ladder that could reach all of the way up to the second floor.

In an uncharacteristic and lickety-split fashion, my father unhooked the old antenna and erected the new one, with very little swearing and no injuries. Soon he was making final adjustments, shouting to my mother who was watching the television.

"How does that look?"

"Channel seven looks better, but now we've got a ghost on channel four."

"Okay, how does that look?"

"There's somebody at the door," she replied.

"Is it the guy from Hudson's?"

"No, it's somebody else."

"Oh shit," my father muttered. "I wonder who this could be."

I followed him into the house, and waiting in the living room was a middle-aged couple. Their clothes were very clean and pressed, but something seemed odd. Beneath his gray suit, the man was wearing a white shirt

161

with red spots, and the woman had an oversized handbag that was decorated with a large artificial flower.

"Reverend Niebaum? I'm John Rathbun, and this is my wife, Adele."

"Nice to meet you," my dad replied. "Sorry about the way I look. I was hooking up a new antenna."

My dad gestured toward the couch, and the Rathbuns sat down. My dad lowered himself into his chair, and I found my usual place on the floor.

"Reverend Niebaum, we're members of the Bethel Baptist Church. We've started a unique ministry, and we'd like to invite you to join in our crusade. Are you familiar with First Corinthians, Chapter Four, Verse Ten?"

"I don't know that one offhand," my father admitted.

"The Apostle Paul says, 'We are fools for Christ's sake.' Adele and I have taken that to be our mission, to be Fools for Christ, and we've started a clown ministry."

"Really?" my father said in his "maybe-we'll-go-to-the-Call-of-the-Wild-Museum-on-the-way-back" voice.

"Yes, it's very exciting. We go to nursing homes and to the Children's Hospitals and we spread the glory of God and the joy of His word. In fact, we have led several people to find Christ, all through our ministry."

"I'm sure you bring a lot of happiness to a lot of people."

"Yes, yes, we do. We have one sketch—it's a retelling of 'The Prodigal Son'—and I'm telling you, it's a hoot. But lately we find ourselves blessed with more invitations to perform than we can handle, and we hear that you're both a minister and a clown, so we were wondering if perhaps you'd be interested in joining our little crusade."

"Gee, it sounds great, but I'm having trouble keeping up with my commitments as it is," my father explained. "But maybe this is a blessing in disguise.

Maybe there's some very lonely, very talented person who is just waiting to be part of something like your ministry."

"Reverend Niebaum, are you sure you can't accept our offer? We'd love to have you."

"Yeah thanks, but I'll have to pass on this one. But good luck with your ministry, and I'm sure God will continue to bless your work."

The men shook hands, and for some reason Mrs. Rathbun hugged my father, and then he led them to the door.

"Gee, Dad, why didn't you want to be a Christian clown?"

"Are you kidding? I can't afford to get mixed up with Bibles for Bozo, especially at this point in my career."

"Huh?"

"I can't show up in church with a Bible in one hand and a bottle of seltzer water in the other. If I go down, I'm going down big. I'm not going to get caught with the clown white behind my ears."

I still couldn't quite figure out what he meant, but he seemed to be talking for his own sake, not mine. He walked out into the yard, talking to nobody in particular. Or maybe he was praying. I wasn't sure.

"What am I supposed to do? If I want to make a statement I'll go Down South and make sure that the Klan doesn't stop people who are trying to vote, or something like that."

"The Klan? Who are they?" I asked.

"Another group of clowns. They just wear different costumes. Ones with pointy hats."

I was pretty sure he wasn't giving me the whole story, but I let it go. He settled down a bit, and then explained things once again, this time for my benefit.

"If I'm going to be a minister, I've got to do it the right way, or people won't take me seriously."

He climbed up the ladder with extra energy, probably because he was trying to make up for the time he spent talking to the Rathbuns. Just as he grabbed the top rung, it snapped off in his hand.

"Uh-oh!" he yelled. He fell forward, just a bit, but he caught himself on the next rung. Unfortunately, the shift in weight put too much pressure on the ladder, and another rung snapped clean off. "Detlef, get out of the way!" he shouted, and the rung beneath his feet broke. After that they began breaking too fast to keep track, but in a few seconds he was standing on the ground in a pile of broken rungs, and instead of a ladder leaning on the house there were just two sticks.

"Are you all right?" I yelled.

"I'm fine. I can't say the same for Mr. Hedgecock's ladder."

He laughed, and then I laughed, and then we couldn't stop. Finally, he caught his breath, and said, "Well, so much for people taking me seriously," and then we started laughing all over again.

"Wally," my mother called. "You've got a phone call."

"Okay," he replied between laughs. "It looks like we're not going to get it finished today. Detlef, pick up the rungs and put them in the trash while I take care of this phone call."

I thought that we should ask Mr. Hedgecock before throwing his ladder away, but then I thought about it some more and I was pretty sure he wouldn't want it.

It didn't make much difference, because I hardly had a chance to get started when my father came back out.

"Detlef, come in the house and get cleaned up! We're going to the hospital."

"What's going on?"

"It's Mrs. Ballenger. She fell and twisted her ankle, and she needs a ride home."

"Is she—"

"She's fine. Anyhow, I thought you'd like to go along, and I know she'd like to see you."

I changed into school clothes, but my dad went all out and put on a coat and tie. I didn't know if he was dressing up so he would look like a minister or if he was wearing the coat to cover up his gun.

Mrs. Ballenger was glad to see us.

"They say I'm going to have to walk with a cane for the next few weeks. Well, at least that will give me a weapon so I can beat off all of the young men who are always asking me out on dates."

Even with a sprained ankle, she was still Mrs. Ballenger. My dad offered her his arm, but she wouldn't take it. She held up her cane in an act of gentle defiance.

"No, I've got to get used to this thing right now. If I'm going to fall, I want to do it when you're here to pick me up. Besides, how do I know that you're not going to get fresh with me?"

It was pretty slow going, but eventually we made it to the elevator. When we got off on the main floor, two nurses were talking in panicked tones.

"He's out of control. We're going to have to do something!"

I barely paid attention and was ready to walk on and forget about it, but my dad opened his wallet and showed his badge to the nurses.

"Is there some way I can help?"

"Oh, thank God. We've got a gentleman in the lobby and he's making a scene."

"Let me see what I can do. Detlef, can you keep an eye on Mrs. Ballenger?"

"Okay," I replied.

The lobby was only a short hallway from the elevator landing, and we could hear the ruckus even before we got there.

"I just want to see my girlfriend!" the man was shouting.

"Hey, pal, what's the problem?" I heard my father ask.

"I want to see my girlfriend, but she won't let me!" the man shouted.

Mrs. Ballenger and I had just entered the lobby, and I had a clear view of everything. My father was talking to a man who looked like he was about twenty years old. He had a crew cut and a light blue jacket and looked like something from the cover of a USDA brochure on the importance of eating balanced meals and not at all like a guy who would be screaming in a hospital lobby.

"Just tell me what room she's in!' he demanded.

"Sir, I can't do that," said a nurse. She was older than the other nurses so I guessed that she was in charge.

"They said that I can't go up because I'm not a member of the family." The young man took a good look at my father. "Who are you? Did somebody call the cops?"

"My name is Walter Niebaum, and I'm a Methodist minister."

The nurses looked a little surprised, and my father shot them a look.

"Are you sure you're a minister?"

"Positive. I'm the pastor of the Fort Street Methodist Church. I was here making a hospital call."

The young man thought about it for a second. "Okay, Reverend."

"Now, you've got yourself in a situation. If you don't calm down, they are going to call the police, and then you won't be able to see your girlfriend for sure. You don't want that, do you?"

"No."

"How is your girlfriend? Is she okay?"

166

"She was in a car accident. I think she has a concussion. That's why I need to see her."

"I'm sorry, but there are no visitors unless there is a family member present," the nurse at the desk interjected. My dad scowled at her, then turned his attention back to the troubled young man.

"Listen, fella, uh what's your name?" my dad asked.

"Larry."

"Listen, Larry, you're not going to do your girlfriend any good if you get arrested. She needs you to get control of yourself, okay?"

"Okay," he answered, and dropped his head submissively.

"Larry, how do you get along with her family?" My dad put his hand on the young guy's shoulder.

"Great. They treat me like a son."

"Where are they now?"

"I was supposed to meet them here, but I couldn't get off work until a few minutes ago. I guess they went home."

"They're upset, just like you, and I'll bet they could use your support."

"But I need to see Karen."

"It sounds like the nurse's saying that Karen needs a little rest now."

"But Karen—"

"Go to her parents' house, have a meal, and then you can all come back together and see her this evening."

It was my dad's voice, well, at least sort of, and it looked like my dad, but he had never acted like this before.

"I guess I looked like an idiot, didn't I?"

"You just did what people do when they're worried about the ones they love."

"Yeah, but—"

"There's nothing wrong with being a fool for someone you love. In First Corinthians, the Apostle Paul said he was a fool for Christ's sake."

"Maybe you are a minister after all." The young man shook my father's hand. "Thanks, mister."

My dad leaned close and spoke to him in low tones. "You know, the afternoon shift is about to end, so when you come back there will be a whole new set of nurses, and they won't know anything about what happened and we can just pretend like this—"

"Yeah, I get what you're saying. Thanks again."

"I hope Karen gets better. We'll pray for her."

Mrs. Ballenger hobbled over to my father. "Wally, I'm very proud of you."

My dad blushed, not just on his face, but his whole bald head turned bright red.

"Thanks," he mumbled.

"Dad, why didn't you take out your gun and arrest him?" I asked.

Mrs. Ballenger answered for him. "You're confused. You see, your father isn't a policeman right now. He's a minister."

"Let's get you home," my father said.

"After we stop at Chick's for ice cream," Mrs. Ballenger commanded. "I want to thank you boys for coming to get me."

"Dorothy will kill me if I ruin Detlef's appetite," he pleaded.

"Don't make me use this," she said, holding up her cane.

"Okay, but you can explain it to Dorothy," my father muttered.

Mrs. Ballenger made us eat the ice cream at her house, and then she made us wait while she dug through her jewelry box and found an old lapel pin. It was a tiny gold cross, not gold like the metal but just gold like the color. Part of the plating had chipped off, and it was spotted here and there with bits of rust.

She put it in my father's hand and closed his hand around it.

"It belonged to Stanley," she said.

By the time we got home it was almost dark. My brother was in the back yard, stomping little green army guys into the ground, pausing every so often to beat his chest, but my dad pretended not to notice. He lifted me out of the car, flopped me over his shoulder, then bounced through the side door into the kitchen.

"Let me down, "I complained.

"Not yet. Dorothy, did the guy come?"

"Yes."

"And everything is okay?"

"He got it all set up and everything works. Should I get..."

"No, he's outside playing Godzilla."

My father lifted me off his shoulder and held me against his body, facing out.

"Okay, close your eyes."

I did as he asked.

"No peeking!" he commanded, and held his hand over my face.

"I'm not peeking and I can't breathe!" I shouted, pushing his hand off my nose.

"He's just a little tired. We've had a big day," my father explained.

He clomped into the living room, and when he moved his hand I found myself looking at the television.

Except it wasn't our TV. It was a new TV, one with a bigger screen and a fancy wooden cabinet.

My dad reached for the switch and my mom scolded him. "Wally, you don't know what you're doing. The man said..."

"Relax. The salesman at Hudson's showed me how to use it." My dad pulled a little gold knob, and there was a click and a tiny circle of light.

"What does the salesman know?"

"He must know something. I mean, when you buy a car…"

The circle of light expanded into a picture.

"It's color!" I shouted.

At that moment my parents became very quiet.

I knew I was supposed to be excited, but as soon as the picture appeared I became tense. Everything looked wrong. We were watching the Andy Griffith show, and Andy's uniform was khaki, but it was a vivid shade of khaki that seemed didn't exist in our own universe, and yet there it was.

I could have lived with that, but for some reason, just about everything else was green. The walls, the trim, and the woodwork in the courthouse, which I had always imagined to be the color of a well-worn wooden church pew, were a disturbing shade of lime green. Even the gun rack was green.

I tried to work it out in my mind. Maybe the courthouse looked dingy and the city fathers decided to paint it, but lime green? That would never happen, and certainly not in Mayberry. I could imagine an episode where Goober or Gomer would accidentally paint the courthouse lime green and Andy would say something folksy and then it would be restored back to its original color and everything would be as it always had been, but clearly that was not what had happened. I started breathing hard, and I tried to catch my breath, but that just made me breathe harder.

The scene changed to Andy's house, and I hoped that I'd seen the last of the lime green, but it was there, too. The walls, the chairs, the curtains, everything was green, and what wasn't green had a green caste. Andy and Opie and Aunt Bea were walking around like they didn't even notice. For a second I thought maybe they only could see themselves in black and white, but that didn't make any sense. If I could see it in color, it actually had to be in color.

"I don't like it!" I shouted.

"How can you not like color television?" my mother demanded.

"What's wrong, son?" my father asked.

"It's green!"

"What's green?"

"Everything! The walls, the woodwork! It's all fake."

"Of course it's fake. It's television!" my mother snapped.

My father shot her a look and she stopped talking, but I could see that she hadn't changed her mind.

"Let me see," my father muttered. He gave my mother a look that said "Don't say a word," and then turned a little flat dial with his thumb.

The color became less intense and eventually faded to black and white and the show looked just like it always had.

"Is that better?" my dad asked.

"Not really," I answered.

"Why not?"

"Because I know it's green. Once you know the ways things are, it's just never the same."

My father took a quick breath and looked like he was going to argue with me, but then relaxed and said, "Maybe it's time for bed."

He took me upstairs and helped me changed into my pajamas, and then tucked me in. He always tucked the blankets too tight, but tonight it felt good. He kissed me on the forehead and shut off the lights.

It was dark, but not dark enough. I could still see the shapes of things in the room, and in the dim light it looked like everything was monochromatic, but I knew that things were not black and white and never had been.

CHAPTER 17

Fort Street Methodist closed in June, right on schedule. There were tears, but the congregation merged with another church, so it was supposed to be a success, even though I couldn't understand how closing a church could be anything except a failure.

After Fort Street closed, my father was appointed to the Bethlehem church. Bethlehem was located in a much worse neighborhood, and was everything that I feared Fort Street would be.

"What smells like pee?" my brother asked as we ascended the church steps for the first time.

"I'm guessing that some wino pissed on the steps," my father bluntly stated.

"What kind of a guy pees on the steps of a church?" I asked.

"Son, that guy was probably so drunk that he didn't have any idea this was a church."

There was a broken vodka bottle at the bottom of the stairs, and I wondered if it had been left there by the Phantom Pisser.

"I don't want you boys going outside, not even for a minute, not even if you're together."

Ernie Craddock, the church custodian, was waiting for us inside of the building.

"I'm sorry you had to see the building in this condition," he said. "I get it clean on Sundays or when we have programs during the week."

Mr. Craddock was neither tall nor beefy, and had to be at least sixty-five years old, but when he shook my hand it felt like he was made of iron. I could tell from his accent that he was English, but he didn't seem fancy enough to be a nobleman. He seemed more like a chimney sweep.

He led us into the sanctuary, which was in need of a coat of paint, but in all other ways was quite impressive. Unlike the quaint and homey atmosphere of Fort Street, Bethlehem was stately, almost majestic.

"Is that a pipe organ?" my father asked.

"It sure is," Mr. Craddock answered. "Want to hear it?"

He threw a switch and the old pipe organ grudgingly heaved to life. He pulled out one of the stops and then played a couple of notes.

"Very impressive," my father said, and then he copied Mr. Craddock and pulled one of the wooden knobs, which came off in his hand. "Uh-oh," my father gulped.

"I should have warned you about that," Mr. Craddock said. "A lot of the things around here aren't in the best shape. We do what we can, but we're short on money. Most of what we raise we spend on coal for the furnace."

"Mr. Craddock, are you from England?" I asked.

"I'm from Cornwall, and yes, that's in England."

"And you came all the way to America to be a church janitor?"

"Listen here, young man, I am not a janitor, I'm a custodian, and you would do well to learn the difference." There wasn't the slightest trace of meanness in his voice, and I didn't feel like he was scolding me at all.

"I don't get it," I said.

"A janitor cleans buildings. A custodian cares for them. And no, I didn't come from England to be a custodian. I was a machinist with the Ford Motor Company. This is just my retirement job."

"So you get paid for doing this?"

"Actually, I don't. That's the best part."

"Really?"

"Sure. I choose my own reward. Every time I sweep a broken whiskey bottle off the front steps, it's like they lose and I win. Do you see?"

"I think so," I lied.

"Well, wait until Sunday morning," he said. "It might make more sense to you then."

The people who came to the Sunday service were even older than the people at Fort Street. There were a few Negroes, and some of those people were young, but most of the parishioners were very white and very old.

"You know, a lot of these people drive past two or three other Methodist churches just to get here," Mr. Craddock said.

"Then why—"

"Because this is their church. It's where they were married, and where their children were baptized."

"And that's why you clean the front steps?"

"I knew you were a bright young man," he said, rubbing my head with his knuckles.

Mr. and Mrs. Craddock were the only white couple who still lived in the neighborhood. Hattie, who owned a hat shop and didn't seem to have a real name, lived in a store across the street from the church, and a few old ladies lived in apartment buildings that weren't too far away, but only the Craddocks actually lived in a house.

That afternoon we ate dinner with the Craddocks. Mrs. Craddock was a wonderful cook. She made soft bread dinner rolls that broke apart in delicate translucent layers, a pot roast that didn't seem to have any fat or gristle, mashed potatoes, two kinds of vegetables, and apple pie. This was served on a fine tablecloth with their best china, which they had brought with them from England.

175

What I liked best was their clock. It was a wind-up clock, and every quarter of an hour it played a few notes. Then, at the top of the hour, it played a whole tune and chimed the hour.

"Do you know what that is?" Mr. Craddock asked. And then, without waiting for a reply, he answered his own question. "That's the Westminster Chimes. Did you know that it has words? Not many Americans do." And then he began to sing. "'Oh Lord Our God, be Thou our guide, and by thy power, no foot shall slide.' Back in England, Big Ben has been ringing those notes since 1859."

"Why do you live here?" I asked him.

"Live where? In the United States?" he asked back.

"In the ghetto," I sheepishly answered.

"Young man, I do not live in the ghetto. The ghetto might surround my house, and people from the ghetto might throw trash on my lawn, but this piece of property will not be a part of the ghetto unless I let it turn into the ghetto."

Mr. Craddock had a complex Sunday morning routine. While the rest of us were still asleep, Mr. Craddock was picking up broken glass or scrubbing the church's urine-soaked steps. He did not do it happily, but he did it with love. Once the church was in an acceptable condition he'd go back home, clean himself up, and then go out again to pick up Mrs. Henderson, an old white lady that lived in some run-down apartments near the church. She lived within what would have been walking distance, but she was pretty feeble, and even the walk from Mr. Craddock's car to the church door challenged her. And, after all of that, Mr. Craddock still got to church with enough time to pass out the bulletins.

I tried to be inspired by his attitude, but mostly I was sad. The church was old, and so was Mr. Craddock, and I wondered how much longer either of them would be

176

around, and whether either one could survive without the other.

My father had been told that the church was scheduled to close next June, but I think he secretly hoped to turn things around. He was always planning special events to attract the people who lived in the neighborhood around the church. He brought in a folk singer, and then a Jazz quartet, but few of the people who lived near the church attended. Most of the people who came were the same ones who attended the potluck dinners and the white elephant auctions, and they probably would have been a lot happier just singing some old hymns.

For the first few months, nothing seemed to bother my father. He kept planning special events, and advertising them on a homemade plywood sign he posted on the side of the building. And, after each attempt failed to attract those living closest to the church, my father would paint the sign white, then stencil black letters announcing his latest scheme.

The church members seemed as unaware as my father. In October, they had an evening of sketch comedy to raise coal money, and spirits couldn't have been higher. One couple did a comedic rendition of "There's a Hole in My Bucket," complete with hillbilly costumes and blacked out teeth. Mrs. McKee read a poem that she had written just for the occasion. The Women's Society parodied television commercials.

I found the whole thing macabre and depressing. It felt like the hangman was warming up the crowd with a few jokes just to get them into the swing of things. But, since everybody else was having such a great time, I kept my thoughts to myself.

The only time my father let his frustration show was when he discovered the church had been broken into. If it only happened once or twice he probably would have let it go, but there were many break-ins, and they wore him down. Nothing was stolen because anything worth stealing had long since been taken, but there was usually a big mess and always some broken glass.

One Saturday I went with my father and Mr. Craddock to clean up after a break-in, and my father finally cracked.

"I don't know what's wrong with the people in this neighborhood! I can't get them in here on Sunday, and during the rest of the week I can't keep them out!"

The December fundraiser was a Christmas tree sale. There wasn't much point in trying to sell trees to people in the neighborhood, like we did at the Messiah church, but the Bethlehem church could at least sell trees to its members. The Methodist Men arranged to have the trees delivered so they'd be in the church parking lot on the first Sunday in December. Families would buy the trees right after church, the men would tie them on top of the cars, and the whole sale would be over in a single afternoon.

My father chose to use the Christmas tree as an illustration in his sermon.

"In December, when everything is cold and dead, we bring the evergreen into our homes to remind ourselves that there is life and there is hope. December is the month of the Winter Solstice, the darkest day of the year, and on that day the evergreen brings us hope. I know things look pretty dark right now, and some people don't have a lot of hope for this church, but—"

"Reverend Niebaum, Reverend Niebaum!" came a voice from the rear. It was Hattie, and she was pretty upset.

"You'd better get out there," she shouted. "You gotta get out quick!"

She always was a character, so nobody seemed too concerned. Hattie lived in her hat shop with eleven dogs that she treated like children, and most people thought that her grip on reality was tenuous at best, so there wasn't a great reaction when she came in yelling and waving her arms.

"Reverend Niebaum!   You'd better get out there. They're stealing the trees! They're stealing the trees!"

With no further instructions, the men of the church got out of their seats and headed for the parking lot.   Those who were young enough ran, and the rest walked as fast as they could. I got up to join them, but right from the pulpit, my father spoke directly to me.

"Detlef, stay where you are."

It's a sin to dishonor your parents under any circumstances, but that doesn't stop kids from getting into mischief. However, when your father is wearing a clerical robe and speaks to you from the pulpit, you do what he says, so I froze in my seat.

My father tried to go on with his sermon, but there wasn't much point. A few minutes later, when the men returned, my dad just said the Benediction and we all went home.

About three weeks later, during the Christmas Eve candlelight service, burglars broke into the Craddock's home and stole all of the presents, and the Craddocks put their house up for sale.

After that there was a feeling of resignation. There were no more comedic sketches or Jazz ensembles. People still came to church, and they still stood up to sing hymns and sat down to listen to the sermon, but we were all just going through the motions.

One Wednesday night, when Mr. Craddock went to Mrs. Henderson's apartment just to see how she was doing, there was no answer. Mr. Craddock had a key to her apartment, just in case, and when he went in he found her dead body. Her apartment had been robbed, and she had been beaten to death. Death was not a stranger to an old congregation like the Bethlehem church. There were no weddings, no baptisms, but plenty of funerals. This was one different, though.

179

The administrative board met and decided that there wouldn't be any more mid-week activities at the church. Mr. Ernie Craddock lowered the asking price for his house and it sold within a week. My father began talking more and more about resigning from the police department so he could accept a full-time appointment at a different church.

CHAPTER 18

Just as Bethlehem was in its final days, Pulaski, my elementary school, went through a big change.

Miss Houk said she had an important announcement. Miss Houk tried to add an air of importance to everything she said, and by now I wasn't taking her very seriously. Most of the other kids were into it, though, so I feigned a little interest in a halfhearted attempt to fit in.

"Next year we're going to get some new students. There's another school in Detroit that has so many students that it's bursting at the seams, and we have plenty of extra room, so they'll be coming here."

I was shocked. The old bird actually did have something to say.

It went on like that for a couple of minutes, with Miss Houk talking in circles, and then she mentioned that, oh yes, by the way, these new students happened to be Negroes.

Everyone was abuzz with excitement and I, as usual, was out of step.

New students? About time. We needed some fresh blood, some new kids who might treat me a little better. That they were Negroes was unimportant. The white kids hadn't exactly been standing in line to make friends with me, and I got along pretty well with the colored kids that came to Sunday School at Bethlehem, so maybe this would be an okay deal.

This also appealed to my sense of justice. Negroes didn't seem happiest among their own kind. A lot of them didn't seem very happy at all, and I heard that part of the reason was that they didn't have the same educational opportunities. Hell, let them come to Pulaski. I wasn't sure what we had to offer—we really didn't have much of anything, just the usual desks and chalkboards— but they were welcome to it.

Maybe there was going to be some order after all. From what I could gather, the world was a chess set. Each piece had its place, and some pieces were valued more highly than others. Now, the world was changing, and it was going to be more like checkers. All the pieces had the same value. Sure, some made it to the other side of the board and became kings, but those were the ones that persevered. That was America. We were all equal, and we all had a chance to better ourselves.

My feeling lasted about two hours. On the way home from school, I heard my schoolmates saying things they had not said before.

"You're going to hafta to go to school with Negroes."

It was Matthew Swales, a sixth grader who lived a couple of blocks away. "At least I won't be here to see it," he smugly stated. "I'll be at Von Steuben." Von Steuben was the name of the junior high.

"So what?" I replied, pretending like it was no big deal, while secretly suspecting that it was.

"You'll see."

What would I see? What experience did he have with colored people? Matt was usually pretty levelheaded, but apparently he had some kind of hang-up about Negroes. I told myself that he was ignorant, and yeah, some of the other kids might be ignorant too, but you're bound to get some of that, especially from kids.

Surely the adults would not act so foolishly. Still, I thought I should notify my dad and once again I was waiting for him when he got home.

"Dad, did you know that there are going to be a lot of colored kids coming to Pulaski?"

"Yep."

He didn't seem concerned. He had already put his hat in the closet, and was emptying the bullets out of his gun. It was just like any other afternoon.

"But Dad, some of the kids…"

"Don't worry about the kids. This is a big bunch of nothing. What do you think is going to happen?"

"I don't know."

"In September, when school starts, the people in the neighborhood are going to see that Negro kids aren't all that different from white kids, and that will be the end of it."

"But everybody's saying—"

"I know. But people are always saying stuff. Believe me, nothing is going to change. Have you ever known one person in this neighborhood who actually got off his ass and tried to change anything?"

But things did change, and we didn't have to wait until September. Adults who never seemed to have anything against colored people were now freely using the word "nigger." These were Northerners, good Christians who went to the Methodist or Catholic church.

I began to sort out who said "nigger" and who did not. The Fords, the Hendersons, the Chapps, and the Hedgecocks did not use any racist language. They were a little worried about what might happen, but clearly had no ill will toward Negroes. In fact, they seemed more concerned about what the white people might do.

Ed Lorraine was a racist, but we had known that for a long time. Other than Ed Lorraine, the rest of the neighborhood racists seemed to be incredible cowards.

They were like jackals, brave enough when they were in the pack, but skulking and cowardly when caught alone.

Some of the kids were racists, too. Craig Bartel wore his hatred for Negroes like a badge of honor, and he became my tool for rooting out the adult racists.

Craig always looked around, suspiciously, no matter where we were, before making a racist comment. It didn't matter if we were in a public place or alone in my garage fixing a flat tire on my bike, he looked around, but I couldn't understand why. I supposed he was looking for Negroes, even though there weren't any in our neighborhood. At that point of my life I did not yet understand that paranoia knows no logic. Only after he was satisfied that we were alone would he share his thoughts.

"Do you know what Mr. Clark said?"

"What?"

"Negroes is colored people. Niggers is when they're jammin' down my throat."

I didn't know how to react. First, he had used the wrong verb, and if you're going to take a position of superiority, it's always best to use correct grammar. Since I couldn't think of anything to say, I just rolled my eyes, which was the highest level of disapproval I could give to a friend. Had he been someone I didn't care for in the first place, I could have called him ignorant, but his parents and my parents went way back.

I wandered home and found my dad in the garage. He had taken the lawn mower apart and was cleaning some of the parts with a gasoline-soaked rag. He wasn't swearing or holding some broken part in his hand, so I figured it would be a good time to tell him what I had heard.

"Why would Mr. Clark say something like that?" I asked.

"Why do you think?" he asked back.

"Because he's a jackass?"

184

I think my father had forgotten that I'd picked up the word from him in the first place, and he laughed pretty hard. "Yeah, he's a jackass."

"Like Mr. Lorraine?"

"No, not like Mr. Lorraine. I guess Mr. Lorraine is a jackass, and Mr. Clark is more like an asshole."

"But why did he say something that was so wrong?"

"Because he's a bully. It's like I told you—bullies are cowards. That's why you have to stand up to them."

"But…" I protested. I wanted to tell him that bullies only pick on smaller kids, ones who can't stand up to them, but I could see from his expression that he wouldn't have believed me.

"What?" he asked.

"Never mind," I muttered.

"If you let bullies have their way there's no telling how far they'll go. Down South they had all kinds of crazy laws, like Black people had to use separate drinking fountains and attend their own schools, and in order to make that work they resorted to lynchings and bombing churches, and they even dragged one young man to death just for looking at a White girl—"

"You mean back during the Civil War?" I asked, reminding my father that such events were in the distant past.

"No, I mean like ten years ago."

"But it's all changed now, right?" I regretted my question as soon as I had asked it, because I wasn't prepared for the likely answer.

"It's better than it was, but that's not saying a whole lot."

"But that was Down South. Nothing like that could happen here?" I could hear the desperation in my voice. My father massaged his face with his hand, unsure of what to say, and my stomach began digesting itself. I

185

waited for him to say something, but he just picked up the rag and the box of matches, and headed for the barbecue pit in the back yard. He told me to stand back, and he set the rag on fire. He stared into the blaze and began to speak.

"Back when I was working undercover, I had a partner named Albert."

"Is he a Negro?"

"Yes, he is. How did you know?"

"I think that you've talked about him before."

"Well, Albert and I were having lunch at a restaurant, just like we did every day, and I got up to go to the bathroom, and I guess a couple of guys must have followed me in there. I went to the urinal, and I was doing my business, when I heard somebody say 'nigger lover.' It really didn't register, but then I heard it again, and I realized that they were talking to me."

"Holy shit!" I replied. My father gave me a hard look, and I could tell that even though it was okay for me to hear that word, I wasn't allowed to use it.

"Anyhow, I reached into my coat, and pulled out my revolver. I turned around, with my pecker in one hand and my gun in the other, and that was the last I saw of those guys." By now the rag was pretty much gone, and my dad poked at its ashes to make sure that the fire had really burned itself out.

"What happened next?"

"I don't know; I guess I just finished going to the bathroom. Anyhow, that must be what those kind of people do. They think you're a nigger lover, but they're only willing to say it if they've got you outnumbered or you're at a disadvantage."

"But they didn't have you at a disadvantage, did they."

He laughed. "No, I guess they didn't."

I wanted to tell my dad that I could stand up to bullies if I had a gun, but I was pretty sure he wouldn't let me have one.

Not more than a week later, Mr. and Mrs. Johnson, a Black couple that we had known from the Bethlehem church, came to visit us in our home. Mr. Johnson was a teacher in the Detroit public schools, and seemed to have little in common with the other residents of the Bethlehem neighborhood. He was younger than most of the teachers at Pulaski, and he seemed like one of those teachers you see on television shows, the ones that make learning fun. Mrs. Johnson was very pretty, but never seemed to say much of anything. Mr. Johnson talked almost as much as my dad, and when the two of them got together, nobody had much of a chance to say anything.

Not too long after they arrived, my dad told me that I might want to play outside, which was his way of saying that they were going to be involved in adult talk and I should give them some privacy.

I didn't mind because I thought this would be a good chance to practice jumping off the porch. I was working on my leap-off-the-porch-land-and-do-a-somersault stunt, and every time I was making decent progress my mother would come out and tell me to stop before I broke my neck. She was busy serving coffee to the guests, so I saw this as my chance to finally perfect my stunt. However, just when I was getting started I heard somebody calling my name.

"Detlef!"

It was Mr. Clark.

"Detlef! Who are those people?"

"What people?"

"The, you know…" and then he looked around before he continued "…the colored people."

"I don't know," I lied.

"Are they here about your house?"

Our house? Why would they care about our house? Then it occurred to me. Mr. Clark wanted to know if we were selling our house or, more specifically, if we were selling our house to Negroes.

"What do you think you're doing? Stop that right now!" The voice was piercing and harsh, and oddly familiar, but I couldn't connect it to a person. "Children aren't supposed to discuss adult business!"

It was Mrs. Ballenger. She was standing on the sidewalk, in front of our house, and she must have been walking by and heard Mr. Clark and I talking. She had never raised her voice to me before, and I knew that whatever I had done must have been awful. I was too embarrassed to look at her, so I hung my head and dug my toe into the ground.

"Don't think you're too old for me to turn you over my knee!"

I froze, and Mrs. Ballenger scurried across the lawn.

"William Clark, how dare you pump this boy for information!"

The color disappeared from Mr. Clark's face, and he just stood there with his mouth open for a few seconds. He might have kept quiet, but some of the neighbors came out on their porches to catch the action, and I think he felt like he had to put on a show.

"Did you know that Wally has a couple of Negroes in his house?" he announced in an attempt to gain support for his cause.

"William, you are an embarrassment to our neighborhood. Now stop carrying on before Reverend Niebaum's guests think we're a bunch of... well, I'm afraid what they might think."

Mr. Clark started to say something, but Mrs. Ballenger gave him a look and he kept quiet. "Now, go on home, and if you have any questions for Reverend

188

Niebaum, you can come over later and ask him like a gentleman."

Mr. Clark hung his head and skulked off like a disobedient dog that had been caught digging up the neighbor's flower garden.   Mrs. Ballenger turned her attention to me.

"And, you, young man, I thought you were more of a gentleman."   She was smiling, so I knew she wasn't scolding me for real.   "My ankle is bothering me again, I don't have my cane, and you haven't offered to walk me home."   She took me by the arm and led me down the street.   "Of course, manners dictate that I'll have to invite you in for a snack."   She pretended to hobble for a few feet, but then dropped the act, still holding onto my arm. "Now, when you grow up, I want you to be gentleman, not a bully and coward like that William Clark."

She kissed me on top of my head, and I waited for the flush of embarrassment, but it never came.   "Of course, I shouldn't invite you into my house without a chaperone, but I think I can rely on your honor just this once."

CHAPTER 19

Change came quickly.

Just before school was out my dad told me he was leaving the police force and we were moving to Chicago, not forever, but just for the summer so he could finish his classes. A week later we were packing up our stuff. I learned that he was not just in college; he was in seminary, a special school for ministers. Then, when we got back, he'd start work at his new church, wherever that was going to be.

The Bethlehem church died hard. During World War II churches in Europe had been bombed. This was sad, but it was a quick death, like a heart attack. Bethlehem went piece by piece, like cancer. After all she had been through, I thought the old girl deserved better.

I told everybody at Pulaski that I was moving away. They were a whole lot nicer to me once they found out I was going away and never coming back, and for my part, I was willing to give up my dream of showing those bastards once and for all, provided I never had to see any of them again.

I wanted to take my bike, but my dad said there wasn't room, and that seemed to be the end of it, but on the day we left it was tied to the top of the car. I didn't ask, but I assumed that he thought I was on the verge of a major breakdown and my bicycle was the only thing holding me together. Other than that, I couldn't take much stuff. I had my GI Joe, my walkie-talkies, a small box of Lego blocks, one issue of *MAD* magazine, and a few comic books.

The summer started out great. We had passes that got us onto the Northwestern University beaches and went swimming every day. We went to museums and to the Shedd Aquarium and to the Baha'i Gardens. Apartment life suited my mother. With fewer things to manage she became calmer, and even insightful.

"I like living in an apartment. It reminds me of when I lived in Esther Hall."

"What was that?"

"It was a dormitory for girls, young ladies, really, and it was run by the Methodist Church. I had a room, and it didn't have a stove, but I had a hot plate and I could, oh, boil an egg, or something like that. It's where I lived when I first moved out of my mother's house."

For many years after, my mother would talk about our time in Chicago as an orderly time, when the toys were always put away and the dishes were always washed.

For me there was a new kind of peace; my brother was gone almost all of the time. He had just turned twelve, and that was the age at which you were allowed to go off on your own provided you were back home before the street lights came on.

That temporary peace didn't last long, not even for the duration of our stay in Chicago. On the evening of Sunday, July 23, our family had finished dinner. My dad was in the bedroom reading, and my mom had just finished the dishes. She wandered into the living room and switched on the portable black-and-white television we brought from Detroit.

Up until that point she had only a passing interest in the evening news, and of course I had none at all, so it had all the earmarks of a major non-event. I, on the other hand, had turned my GI Joe into the ultimate fighting machine by encasing his hands in Lego blocks.

"Hey, mom, look what I did!"

"Shh! I need to see this," she answered. She didn't even bother to glare at me, but gazed intently at the television for a while, and then shouted, "Walter, you'd better get in here! Detroit is on fire!"

"What? Like a warehouse or something?"

"No, I think it's a riot!"

My father came thundering into the room and stared at the television. "Holy crap."

I watched, too, but I had trouble figuring out what was going on. From what I could gather, the riot had been started by some angry Negroes.

I couldn't imagine that they'd burn down their own neighborhood, and imagined that they were headed north. Our house, which was empty, seemed like an easy target.

"Do you think they're coming to our house?"

"No, the riots are in the area where the Black people live," my father said.

"Why would they burn their own neighborhood?"

"Well, they're upset," my father answered.

"About what?"

"I don't know," he said. "But it probably will simmer down once it gets dark and the temperature drops. I'll bet this whole thing will be over by morning."

It didn't simmer down by the next morning, or the morning after that. And so, by Tuesday, when the news came on, I had seen enough. I was tired of burning buildings and broken glass and blocks of burned out buildings.

The first looters I saw seemed like thugs, and were running into buildings and leaving with armloads of whatever they could grab, but later they looked more casual, almost like shoppers. I saw a pretty woman wearing shorts and a nice button down shirt carrying an armload of groceries. She looked like any other mom doing the grocery shopping, except that she exited the store by stepping through a broken-out window.

192

My own mother stockpiled groceries in anticipation of just this sort of event, but I supposed that most people had not, I wondered if this lady was forced into a position where she had to steal or starve.

The atmosphere in our apartment was pretty tense, too. My parents demanded absolute silence during the news, and once it came on I knew I had to get out. I leafed through my stack of comic books looking for one I hadn't read too often, and took extra care to leave the *MAD* magazine carefully hidden on the bottom of the stack.

I had picked *Adventure Comics* 359, "The Outlawed Legionnaires," a story about how the world had given way to mob mentality. On page seven, a confused Duo Damsel asked her father what was happening, but her father hushed her up because it was time for the 3-D Tele-News. Apparently things were no different in the year 2967.

I left the courtyard of our apartment building and went for a walk around the block. I found a fairly clean newspaper in a garbage can, and since I didn't see any other trash on top of it, I fished it out.

According to an article in the paper, the riots got started when a group of police known as "The Big Four" arrested some guys who were drinking in an after hours night club. Since my dad had been on the Liquor License Bureau, I knew that drinking after hours was against the law, but I couldn't figure out the business about "The Big Four."

This wasn't the right time for questions. If I went back to the apartment and asked, my dad would tell me to be quiet and my then my mom's face would turn red and she'd be mad at me for the rest of the evening. I tried to puzzle it out for myself. It didn't seem possible that an entire riot could be started by four cops.

The next morning my mom was in the bathroom and my dad was rooting around the refrigerator for food in a guilty sort of "Yogi-Bear-digging-through-a-picnic-basket" fashion. He found some strawberries that we were only allowed to eat with cereal, but he dug right in and popped three of them into his mouth. When he realized I was watching he popped one in my mouth so I couldn't squeal without implicating myself.

"Dad, who are the Big Four? I asked.

My dad looked upset, and for a second I thought he was mad at me, but then he just rolled his eyes and smiled.

"The Big Four is a nickname. It's the name the Negroes gave the Tactical Squad. Those are the guys who ride around in cruisers."

"Cruisers?"

"Yeah. Every precinct has a cruiser, a black Buick with four big policemen. Those are the guys we called when we needed some muscle, like if there was an armed robbery or something. Those guys are so big that the Buick rides low to the ground."

"You mean they're so heavy that they weigh the car down?"

"Right, but they're not fat—just beefy."

"So why are people upset with them?"

He took a bag of apples from the refrigerator, tossed one to me, and took out another for himself.

"Cause they're all bullies and Bozos. Back when I was a rookie at the Hunt Street station I would ride with them once in a while, like maybe if a guy had to make a court appearance and they needed somebody to fill in. At first I thought it was exciting, and I was impressed by all of the muscle and firepower, but it didn't take too long to see that they were a bunch of badge-heavy half-wits."

"Why would you say that?"

"Oh, a lot reasons. Like one time, we got called out on a run, I think it was an armed robbery, and we ended up chasing after another car. The boss, his name was Harry Kreg, always sat in the passenger seat in the

194

front, and on this day he had a cherry pie in his lap. We had gone to the bakery earlier in the day and he was going to put it in his own car before we got back to the station. Well, we never made it back to the station because we got this call about the armed robbery.

"As it turns out, we saw the car we were looking for going one way while we were going the other, so the driver, who was the only uniformed cop in the car, spun around and we chased after him.

"Now Harry stuck his head out of the window and began shooting at the other car. The guy sitting behind Harry, they used to call him Ass Kicking Slim, well, he stuck his head out of the window every now and then, too, just to see what was going on, but he couldn't shoot because he didn't want to hit Harry.

"Harry was having a hell of a time with that pie, and just to get it out of the way he threw it out the window. At the same time, Slim stuck his head out and got hit with the pie.

"Slim didn't know what was happening, and he shouted, 'I've been shot! I've been shot!'

"I looked over and saw that his face was all red from cherry filling, and I thought he was shot, too."

"That's why the Negroes rioted? Because the Big Four are oafs and clowns?" I asked.

You could tell that he hoped that explanation would have satisfied me, and I watched the cogs in his cranium crank around while he tried to think of another explanation.

"No, it's more like that they're trigger happy clowns. When you get all that muscle and firepower in a car, guys are going to use it whether they need to or not.

"Back when I was still walking the beat, a steer got loose from the Eastern Market and was running all over Mount Elliott cemetery. The cruiser was called in, and the four Tac guys tracked down the steer."

"How hard was it to find a steer in a cemetery?"

"Not hard at all. Anyhow, these guys got out their guns—handguns, the shotgun, whatever they had, and all at once, they blasted the cow until it was hamburger. After that it wasn't any good, and the guy who owned the steer was madder than hell because he couldn't use any of the meat."

I tried to picture it in my mind, but it seemed like a cartoon, or maybe a comedy sketch from the Field Day. I imagined the Big Four wearing Keystone Kop outfits and firing shotguns with split barrels.

It almost made sense. The police acted too much like cops during the Field Day, and too much like clowns when they were on the street.

But that didn't explain everything, and my father could tell that I still had questions, and he finally cracked and got ready to tell me whatever it was that he had been avoiding.

"Those guys are mean. The people in the neighborhood used to call the boss 'Chew Tobacco' because when he was talking to people he'd chew tobacco and spit the juice right on them."

"How often did he do that?" I asked.

"Often enough that people called him 'Chew Tobacco.'

"Anyhow, one time I was riding along, and we pulled up alongside of a guy—you know, a Black guy—and the boss began questioning him, and I guess he didn't get the answers he wanted, because he grabbed the guy's tie, pulled it right into the cruiser, then rolled up the window.

"Now, the driver of the car, he drives away, kind of slow but not that slow, so the guy has to run alongside of the cruiser. Finally, they stopped, and talked, and I guess the boss got whatever answer he wanted because they let him go and we drove off."

Once again, it seemed like a cartoon, and for a second it was almost funny, but my dad wasn't laughing, and the cartoon faded into a black-and-white image, like an episode of Dragnet. I imagined an evil Joe Friday grabbing a young Black professional by his tie and rolling it up in the car window.

"But couldn't they have broken his neck or something?"

It reminded me of the picture I had seen in the April issue of *MAD* magazine, and even though my dad had been pretty honest with me, I thought it was best to keep my mouth shut about what I'd seen.

When I first got the April issue I read all of the usual stuff—"Spy vs. Spy" and the usual cartoons by Don Martin and Dave Berg— but I had skipped the political satire. One article feature, which was titled "The Preamble Revisited," promised to be especially boring so I skipped over it, and it wasn't until we were on the long drive from Detroit to Chicago that I took a good look at it.

It was the preamble to the Constitution of the United States, separated into phrases, and next to each phrase was a photo. I guess it was supposed to be poignant or shocking, but it just looked like a bunch of boring black-and-white photos and I almost turned the page once again when, next to the words "establish justice", I spotted a photograph of a Negro man hanging from a tree. It was not a staged photograph, but an actual picture of an actual dead guy, a naked dead guy, hanging by his neck. Next to him was a very smug white man who seemed to be hamming it up for the camera.

I hunched over, both to get a closer look at the photo and to block my brother's view of the magazine. I didn't need him squealing to my mom that I was looking at pictures of naked Negroes, and the fact that the Negro was both dead and a man would be just that much harder to explain.

The more I looked at it, the more the picture disturbed me. Why was the picture in my comedy magazine? Did somebody think this was funny? Who

197

was this Negro? Who killed him? Why was he naked? What had they done to him before they killed him? Why did the White man allow himself to be photographed? Why didn't the FBI use this photo to arrest him? Out of the whole FBI, there must be at least one person that reads *MAD* magazine.

My dad's voice jolted me back to reality. "Is something wrong?"

I must have looked a little too pensive, and I forced myself to think about what my dad had been saying. "What did you do, Dad?"

"I didn't know what to do. It caught me off guard. I guess I just finished out my shift and luckily nothing like that ever happened again."

"But didn't you do anything about it?"

"Nope. The next time I just rode along like nothing happened."

"But..."

"Yeah, I know. I've been reading about this guy, Nietzsche, and, uh, oh hell, I don't what to say."

Just then my mom popped her head out of the bathroom. "Well, the National Guard is on the scene, and those rioters are going to find out a thing or two before this is all over."

My father looked at me and rolled his eyes.

"More Bozos?" I asked.

He nodded his head.

The next night there was a phone call, and I answered.

"Detlef, this is Clarence Johnson from Bethlehem church. Is Reverend Niebaum available?"

I didn't think I knew a Clarence Johnson, but he knew my name so I guessed it must be Mr. Johnson, the nice Negro man who had visited us at our home.

"Dad, it's Mr. Johnson from Bethlehem."

My dad leaped up from the couch like he knew something was wrong.

198

I tried to listen in, but Mr. Johnson spoke quietly and my dad didn't say too much. At one point he blurted out, "Good Lord, no!" and then he didn't say anything again for a long time.

There was a little small talk, and then my dad lumbered back to the couch.

"What happened?" my mother asked.

"Clarence Johnson's uncle was shot."

My mother pointed her finger in the air and tightened her face, and for a second I thought she looked like Commandant Klink. "A sniper. I knew it. This thing is out of hand…"

"It wasn't a sniper. It was your precious National Guard."

"Well, he must have been doing something," she snipped.

"They said he was trying to run a road block," my dad said with a sarcastic tone that my mother chose to ignore.

"Well, there you have it!"

"There you have nuthin'!" my father snapped. "He was just some ordinary asshole driving his family back home. Do you think for one minute that he was going to crash a National Guard road block with his whole family in the car?"

Everything was very quiet for a few minutes. I had heard that some other families have moments in their house when no one is talking, but that never happened in our home. We were always loud, with some of us shouting over the television and others shouting over the shouters, and this silence scared me. I thought my parents had discovered a new level of anger, one that is above sarcasm and shouting.

Somebody needed to say something, so I spoke up. "Are we going back for the funeral?"

"No, they said he has his own pastor, and besides, we couldn't even…"

He began sputtering and just sort of ran out of words.

Before I was born, there had been a time of chaos. My dad and my friends' dads went to war, and they straightened everything out. But it didn't last, and whatever order had been created was gone.

CHAPTER 20

Eddie was one of those grimy white kids who, if he had been Black, racist White people would have used as an example of what was wrong with Negroes. But, since he was White, Eddie was just a kid from a "broken home." Maybe his parents had been divorced, or maybe his father drank. Nobody knew for sure and nobody bothered to find out, but labeling him as the "product of a broken home" was the excuse White people used to explain how one of their own could turn out that way.

I met Eddie at the elementary school playground. From the beginning, I could tell we were from different worlds. He kept calling the monkey bars the "jungle gym," and when he climbed to the top he climbed from the inside bars, instead of from the outside bars. I wasn't sure if this was the Chicago way of doing things, or if it was because he was from a broken home, but I found it disturbing.

Eddie wasn't a regular friend, but just a guy I hung around with when Norman Laughbaum was busy doing things with his family. Norman's dad liked to drive around downtown and look at the hippies. I didn't know what hippies were, so my dad said he'd show me some the next time we were in town. When I finally did see some hippies, they were just teenagers, and I figured that "hippie" was the Chicago term for "teenager" the same way the "jungle gym" was the Chicago word for "monkey bars."

Eddie asked a lot of crazy questions, too.

"Do you smoke?"

"I'm only eight years old!"

"That's got nuthin' to with it. I smoke." He showed me a pack of cigarettes.

"I'll bet you couldn't even get your hands on a pack of smokes."

"Why would anybody want cigarettes?"

"Geez, don't you know anything? You've got to have cigarettes or you can never get into a gang."

"What?"

"Sure. You put your arm next to another guy's arm, and then they put a lit cigarette in between. The first guy that pulls his arm away loses, and the other guy gets into the gang."

"That's crazy!"

"Try telling that to my brother. He's got a big old scar on his arm from when he was initiated. Don't they teach you anything in Detroit?"

"Not that kind of stuff."

"Detroit must be some kind of a sissy town."

"I don't think so. There's riots going on there right now."

"In your neighborhood?"

"No, not in my neighborhood."

"Then you must live in the sissy part of town. You need to live in the tough neighborhood."

"But the tough neighborhood is on fire."

"So what do you do for fun?"

"Read comic books. Ride my bike." That was my first mistake.

"You don't have a bike."

"I do, too."

"It's probably a girl's bike."

"Come on back to our apartment. I'll show it to you." That was my second mistake.

202

I kept my bike chained up in the courtyard outside of our building. My dad told me to chain it to a post or something, but I couldn't find a post so I just looped the chain through both tires and the frame of the bike.

Eddie wasn't too impressed. "What kind of a bike is that?"

"A boy's bike."

"No, I mean is it a Schwinn? Or a Huffy?"

"I don't know. It was used when I got it, and I really couldn't read the name of the bike, even before my dad painted over it."

I didn't know why, but Eddie got upset when I talked about my dad painting my bike. He made like it didn't bother him, but you could see that it did.

"Well, it looks like a hunk of crap to me, and I'd rather have no bike than a hunk of crap." Eddie walked away in a huff and I was glad to see him go. From that point on I stayed away from the playground, hoping never to see him again.

We were going home in a couple of days, so Norman and I were trying to read as many of each other's comic books as we could. As usual, my mom had thrown us out of the apartment and told us to get some exercise, and as usual, we just headed down to the courtyard and loafed around.

I had just finished a pretty good story about Superman coming into contact with red kryptonite when I noticed Eddie. He wasn't saying anything, just standing on the sidewalk, watching us read.

I guess he knew that I had been avoiding him, and when he saw me with Norman he must have felt like I was choosing Norm over him. That really wasn't far from the truth and I felt a little guilty. Sure, Eddie brought it on himself, what with his bragging about smoking and gang initiation, but he looked pitiful just standing there watching us read. I glanced over, expecting him to look tough, but he was just sad.

"Hi, Eddie," I forced myself to say.

He didn't say anything, but just narrowed his eyes.

"Do you want to read comic books?" I offered, and Eddie's eyes grew hard.

"Screw you," he snarled, and slowly walked away.

"Fine," I thought to myself. "I won't be seeing that guy after a couple of days anyhow." I picked up another comic book, thinking that was the end of it.

The next morning, when I went out to the courtyard, my bicycle was gone. It could have been anybody, but my gut told me that it was Eddie. I didn't know exactly where he lived, but I had a pretty good idea. I took a walk over to his neighborhood, hoping to figure out which house was his. It wasn't too hard, because Eddie was sitting on his front steps. He was smiling, but it wasn't a happy smile. It was a mean smile, the kind a big guy makes just before he slugs you.

His house was kind of small, just like our house in Detroit, but other than that it didn't look anything like it. Most of the houses in our neighborhood were brick or had aluminum siding, but his house was just painted wood. At least, it had been painted at one time, but most of the paint was gone and now it was mostly covered with bare wood.

"Hey, kid, want to see my new bike?" He pointed at the garage and I could see my bike. The lock and the chain were gone, but it was my bike.

"That's my—"

"I liked your bike so much I had my old man make me one just like it. Do you want to take it for a ride?'

I thought for a second. If I could get a head start I could ride off with it and he wouldn't be able to catch me until I got back to the courtyard, and then he'd have to deal with my dad.

"Yeah, I'll take it for a spin."

"Maybe that's not such a good idea. You might steal it. I hear there's a lot of theft in this neighborhood."

"That's my bike!" I shouted.

"So, you are trying to steal my bike."

"Give me my bike!"

"I'll give you something," he said, getting up from the porch, making a fist.

I ran as fast and as far as I could, but I don't think he was chasing me because by the time I turned around I couldn't even see him.

It was Saturday, so my dad didn't have class, and I told him the whole story. He gave me a pretty intense lecture about how I should have kept it chained to a post. I wanted to tell him that there weren't any posts in the courtyard, but I could tell he was angry, and I wanted him to deal with Eddie while he was still good and mad.

He might have, too, but just as we were leaving the courtyard we ran into Norman and his dad, and Mr. Laughbaum decided he would go with us. Mr. Laughbaum seemed to have a calming effect on my father, and I didn't like it.

Eddie was no longer sitting on the steps by the time we reached his house. The garage door was open, and I wanted to grab the bike and run, but my dad said we needed to do this the right way. I wasn't sure what that meant. What was wrong with taking back my own bike?

My dad knocked on the door and a grubby little man answered. He was at least six inches shorter than my dad, and even though he had twig arms and bony shoulders, he wasn't what you'd call skinny because he had a pot belly. He had a full head of black hair, but his face was lined and leathery, so I couldn't really tell how old he was.

"What can I do for you?"

"Are you Eddie's father?"

"I am."

"I think we need to sit down and talk things over," my dad said, in the calmest of tones.

"I don't let strangers in my house," he stated, taking a puff from his unfiltered cigarette.

"Okay, we can talk right here. It seems your son has my boy's bike."

"Are you calling my boy a thief?" Eddie's dad stepped forward, almost all the way out onto the porch, but still with one foot inside of the door.

"I don't know what happened. I think the best thing for everybody concerned is if we give the bike back to my son and forget this ever happened."

"You'd like that, wouldn't you? My son doesn't have much, but it seems like you don't want him to have anything." Eddie's dad flicked an ash from his cigarette, and ground it into the porch with his foot.

My father didn't say anything. He didn't make an angry face, and his head didn't turn red. He just stood there, waiting.

"Can you prove that bicycle is yours?" the little man asked. Instead of looking at my dad, he was peering over my dad's shoulder. I turned around to see what he looking at, and there was a police car. I looked back at the little man, but instead of being scared, he smiled, and then I got scared.

A very bored policeman got out of the patrol car and waddled his way to the front door. Before my dad had a chance to say anything, the little man started to talk.

"Officer, this is the kid I called about. The one who is trying to steal my son's bicycle. Now he's brought his father, and I need some protection."

The policeman took out a pad of paper and asked what happened. He looked up every now and then, and once in a while he stopped writing to wipe his brow, but mostly he just took notes and acted bored.

Eddie's father spoke first. To hear him tell it, I had been coming around for days trying to steal the bike and he finally had enough and called the police. He threw in a few details about how he and his son had fixed up the bike together, and by the time he was finished even I was halfway convinced.

Then it was my dad's turn. He introduced himself as a former Detroit police officer, but the cop looked skeptical and it went downhill from there.

"Can you prove the bicycle is yours?" the cop asked.

"It's licensed in my son's name."

"Is it an Evanston license?"

"No, it's a Detroit license. Walk on over and see for yourself." My dad pointed at the bike.

"That don't mean nuthin'" the little man squawked. "I got the bike from my wife's sister, and she lives in Detroit."

The cop frowned, and for a second it seemed like he was on our side. He sidled up to Eddie's dad. "Mister, how would this kid's dad happen to know that your son's bike has a Detroit license?"

"My kid's been riding that bike all over town. This boy probably seen the license. That's how these people do. They get one little bit of information and use it against you."

The cop sighed and looked to my father for help. "Do you have a copy of the original registration?"

"No, they keep that in the Hall of Records in Detroit."

"Maybe you could write a letter and get a copy."

"We're going to back to Detroit in a couple of days."

"Don't you know anybody on the force who could help you out?"

"I know lots of people, but they've got their hands full mopping up after the riot, and they're not going to drop everything to take care of a stolen bicycle." I knew my dad was right. Nothing happened when we found that

207

stolen bike on the Fort Street parsonage lawn, and nothing was going to happen now.

"Listen, fella, I'd like to help you, but I need some kind of proof before I can take a bike out of this guy's garage and give it to you."

"So that's it?"

"I can file a report, but I don't have to tell you what that means."

For the first time my dad's head started to turn red. The policeman headed back to his patrol car, and Eddie's father just stood there on his porch, with the same mean smile I'd seen on his son's face earlier that morning.

As we walked home, Mr. Laughbaum tried to be encouraging.

"Well, maybe this is God's way of providing that family with a bicycle."

My dad gave him a skeptical look.

"Then again, maybe not," Mr. Laughbaum added.

For the first time I started to cry, not just a few tears, but actual sobbing. I knew we were going to go back to Detroit and my bicycle was going to stay in Illinois.

"This isn't right. Why can't we just go back and take my bike?"

"I wish it was that simple," my dad said.

"But you chased after those guys when they took the groceries from the church…"

"Yeah, and I'm not sure I should be doing those things anymore. Maybe I need to turn the other cheek."

"But you're not turning your cheek. You're turning mine."

My dad stopped, and for a second I thought he was going to go back and get my bike, but then he just kept on walking.

"Son, this really stinks, but we're going to have to let this go. I'll see if I can find another bike we can fix up."

"Can we get another bike as soon as we get back?"

"Not right away, but maybe in a few weeks."

This was sounding like The Call of the Wild Museum all over again.

"But what will I do for a bike until then?"

"You could ride your brother's bicycle."

"He won't let me. Besides, it's too big. I can't even reach the pedals."

"Well, you could ride your old bike."

"But that's a girl's bike!"

"Yeah, it is. But give me some time. I'll think of something."

"You promise?"

"I promise."

"And the new bike can have chrome fenders and a reflector on the back?"

"It will be every bit as good as the old one."

Dad had never let me pin him down like this before. He was always pretty cagey, and avoided promises, especially if they were that specific. Maybe this time he meant it.

"Dad?"

"What?"

"There aren't any posts in the courtyard."

"What?"

"That's why I didn't lock it to a post."

"Oh, that? After meeting that asshole, I think he would have found a way to steal your bike if was locked in the basement of the police station."

"What do you mean?"

"He feels cheated by life, like everybody has more than he does. When he takes something, he doesn't consider it stealing. He just thinks he's evening the score."

"But he isn't right, is he?"

"Of course not."

"Then why can't we—"

"Go back and punch him in the nose and take the bicycle?"

Finally my dad seemed to be getting it. "Yeah!"

"Because then I'd go to jail, the police would take the bike and give it back to him, and you'd have no father and no bicycle."

"This stinks!"

"Yes it does, but we have to let this let go. Now, this is where the conversation started, so before we go through the whole thing again, we've got to let it go and move on to the next thing."

"What is the next thing?"

"Well, what do we usually do on Saturday mornings?" He looked at me and winked. I was confused for a couple of seconds, but then he winked again. "What do we usually do on Saturday mornings?"

I didn't know what he was talking about. We didn't usually do anything on Saturday mornings. But he just kept staring at me, and I finally got his meaning. He wanted me to make something up.

"On Saturday mornings, you and I usually walk down to the store and you buy me a comic book," I lied.

"Okay, let's get going."

"And then we usually go out for ice cream."

"I don't remember that part."

"No, usually after we buy a comic book I go for a ride on my bike. Of course, I can't do that today, but maybe some ice cream would make me feel better." I hung my head and tried to look very sad.

"Nice try, Son, but you'll have to settle for a comic book."

CHAPTER 21

On our last day in Chicago, we drove past the beach. The beach was covered with the decaying bodies of alewives, an invasive species that had found its way into Lake Michigan, and there was the stench of rotting fish.

"This place stinks," my dad said. "It's time to go back to Michigan."

We didn't come home to the same house we left. It smelled musty, and even after we opened the windows it still seemed smaller and darker than I remembered.

True to his word, my dad found another old bicycle. It was in better shape than the one that had been stolen, and maybe when it was all finished it would have been better, but every time he asked if I wanted to work on it I just told him we could get to it later. After a while my dad got wise to what I was doing, so he confronted me.

"Detlef, why don't you want to work on the bike?"

"Because it might get stolen. Why do I want to spend all of that time getting it fixed up just to have it stolen?"

"You can't think like that, Son."

"Sure I can. I mean, that's how I feel."

"Well, if you change your mind, let me know."

That was the last time he mentioned it.

Even though the riots hadn't taken place in our neighborhood, the kids in our neighborhood demonstrated a sense of personal violation, as if their own homes had been broken into. A couple of days after we got back, a bunch of guys came over to play War, but instead of getting into the game they just stood around and complained about Black people. Craig Bartel, as usual, led the conversation.

"During the riots, the colored people looted all of the stores, and now they're living like kings. If you go into any of their houses, they all have three or four color televisions."

The other kids nodded in agreement, and Craig smiled. I hated his smile. It seemed too familiar. Maybe it was like the smile of the racist guy in *MAD* magazine, or maybe it reminded me of Eddie's father. The more he smiled the madder I got, and all of a sudden I found myself shouting at him.

"How on Earth would you know that?" I demanded. "Have you ever been to their houses?"

"What makes you an expert, Detlef? Have you ever been in a colored person's house?"

"As a matter of fact, I have!"

Everybody got very quiet for about twenty seconds and just stared at me. I had no idea what they were thinking or what I should say. Finally, Mark Hedgecock asked a sincere question.

"What was it like?"

"Well, I've been in a lot of them, and they're all different. But mostly they seemed pretty sad, like they don't have much money."

Craig wasn't buying it. "Yeah, but that was before the riots! Now they've all got color televisions!"

"What difference could that make? Even if you brought a color TV into a poor person's house, he'd still be poor. He'd just be a poor person with a color TV."

"Well, screw you," he barked, and then walked off.

After that nobody was interested in playing War, so all of the other kids went home. Maybe White people weren't that different from Black people. Maybe, back before the riots began, the Negro version of Craig Bartel was standing around with a group of his friends, complaining and saying that White people all have color televisions, and maybe they used that as justification for the looting.

I stormed into the house. I wanted to talk with my father, but he was on the phone, so I just clomped my feet as hard as I could when I walked past.

I thought I'd cleared him by a safe distance, but he grabbed me by the back of my collar and gave me a look that said I needed to be quiet until he was finished talking.

"Well, I've got to get going," he said into the phone. "I'll call you back on Monday. Bye." He turned his attention to me. "Okay, Sport, what's the problem?"

"I hate this city and I hate this neighborhood. I can't wait to move."

"Funny you should mention that. I was just talking with the district superintendent on the phone."

"Did he tell you where we're moving?"

"Actually, I've known for a little while. We're going to the Sterling Heights United Methodist Church."

"Thank God. I couldn't handle another year at Pulaski."

"Yeah, about that. I'll be starting a new church in Sterling Heights, and until things get going, we'll be living here."

"What?"

My father got quiet. "You'll be at Pulaski for another year."

"I can't go back to Pulaski! I already told everybody that I was moving!"

"Well, I guess you'll have to un-tell them."

He didn't get it. I'd already told everybody I was moving, and if I came back they'd assume that I was lying, the same way they assumed I was lying when I said my father was a policeman, a clown, and a minister.

"Why can't we move right now?"

"Son, there isn't anywhere to move to. There isn't a church building or a parsonage. Hell, there isn't even a Sterling Heights. It's still Sterling Township."

"How can they do that? Don't they need a building or something?"

"Well, they've got some property where they're going to put a building, but right now all it has is an old farmhouse, a run-down barn, and a chicken coop."

"Can't we move into the farmhouse?"

"We need to use it as an office until the church gets going."

"Why are they using it as an office? What does that leave for us? A run-down barn and a chicken coop? I need to get away from Pulaski, and all they've got is a run-down barn and a chicken coop?"

My father was gone most days and many evenings. He was "canvassing the neighborhood," which is a police term for going door-to-door and talking to people, inviting them to his so-far-non-existent church.

I couldn't see how his plan was going to work. For one thing, he was going to hold services in the gymnasium of an elementary school. Going to church was bad enough, and going to school was worse, so who would want to go to church and school at the same time?

Going back to school was exactly as bad as I thought it would be. The librarian, Mrs. McCain, was shocked to see me and said, "Detlef Niebaum, what are you doing here? I thought you moved." It sounded like an accusation.

I wasn't the only person who got the cold shoulder. There was a lot of fear and suspicion when the

214

Black students arrived. There weren't any fistfights or shouting matches, but the White kids ignored the Black kids as much as possible. For all of their big talk, the racists were pretty quiet once the Black kids actually showed up. Neither the students nor their parents said much of anything.

The new students arrived in yellow school busses. I had never actually seen a school bus, and up until then I thought everybody walked to school. My parents and teachers tried to make me feel sorry for the Black kids because they had to go on a long bus ride every morning, but I had to walk to school through rain and snow. A twenty-minute bus ride seemed a lot better than a fifteen-minute walk.

For the first couple of days, the neighborhood kids stood and watched the new kids as they got off the bus. The neighborhood kids didn't say anything like "Welcome to Pulaski," and the new kids didn't say, "Glad to be here." The neighborhood kids just watched, without saying anything, as the new kids left the buses, talking only to each other.

After those first couple days, most of us lost interest, but there still was a core group of kids who watched the daily procession. Then, maybe a week later, a strange thing happened. The neighborhood kids began booing at the new kids. At first it was just a few kids, but the crowd got bigger every day, and after a week it was part of the morning routine. You walked to school, you waited outside for the busses to come, and you booed at the new kids.

At the time, it didn't seem that weird. The booing the new kids received was nothing compared to the jeers I got when I went to bat for my Greenbriar softball team. The insults hurled at me were personal, and generally came from my own teammates. "Detlef, you stink! Do us all a favor and quit the team!"

Booing at kids from another school just seemed like a rivalry to me, like University of Michigan versus Ohio State. From what I could gather, students at competing schools stole each others' mascots, chanted about how they would destroy and kill each other, and smashed into each other on the football field. There were limits—you couldn't hit them with your fists or shoot them or stuff like that, but you could run after them and tackle them to the ground. And, of course, you booed.

In that context, I didn't think twice about booing at the busses as they pulled into the school lot. Hell, I didn't think once. I wanted to show my Pulaski school spirit, so at some point I joined the mob and booed at the new kids. It felt good, and I could hardly wait until the next day so I could do it again, but that never happened. At the end of the day, after the buses pulled out, Miss Klingenschmidt called all of the remaining students down to the auditorium.

"I cannot believe that the young ladies and gentlemen of Pulaski would act in such an impolite fashion. Booing at the school buses…"
She lowered her head and pinched the bridge of her nose with her forefinger and thumb. I thought she was making it out to be more than what it was.

"Do you have any idea of how it makes the other students feel, being booed as they enter a new school? How would you feel?"

I gave her another look, and I could see her jaw muscles tighten and I knew that there had to be even more to it. All of a sudden I got it. I was a White person, in a group of White people, booing at a busload of Black people. Oh, crap. What was I thinking?

The more I thought about it, the worse it got. I could replay the incident in my mind, and I could see the faces of my classmates. Jeff? He was joking around, like he always did. He booed, too, but he didn't seem to mean it any more than I did. Lewis Gerard? He was taunting,

216

and standing shoulder-to-shoulder with Jim Matheson, who was waving his fist. Those were the mean boys, opportunists who took every chance to be hurtful. Craig Bartel was booing with excessive enthusiasm. And there I was, aligning myself with the worst our school had to offer.

My ears felt hot, and I had trouble sitting still. Had any of the Black students seen me? Did they recognize me? Did they think I hated Black people?

"These students are our guests, and you have made them feel very unwelcome."

The next day, when the Black students came back, they treated me the same as they always had. They were nice enough, and the ones who had been friendly to me were just as friendly as before. I guess they hadn't noticed me, or they hadn't given the event much thought. Even so, I didn't feel much better. Once you're sprayed with the stink of racism, it's hard to clean it off.

I still hadn't given up on my dream of making new friends, and before too long some of the Black kids were pretty friendly, but my interests went beyond socializing with the boys. Secretly, I found some of the Black girls very attractive. I was attracted to them not because they were Black, but because they were girls and they were pretty. I tried to keep my feelings from everybody, especially my mother, but she seemed to know. Perhaps by coincidence, but most likely not, she went into a crazed oration one night as we drove back from my Oma's house.

"What do you think happens when Black people marry White people?" she asked.

I was pretty sure I knew. Stephon Johnson, one of my new friends, was mixed. He had curly hair, and his lips and nose more-or-less resembled those of the black students, but his skin was really pretty light, and he had freckles. Even so, I didn't try to answer my mother's question. It was an obvious trap, and she was going to go into her spiel no matter what I said, so I said nothing.

"I'll tell you what happens. When Blacks and Whites marry, they have speckled children."

"Speckled children?" I said, unable to hide my disbelief.

"Well, actually, it looks more like spots. Sometimes you see them when you go Downtown. They're dark like colored people, and they have colored features, but they've got white spots."

One of the boys at school, Marshall Day, had the same condition, except it was just a couple of white spots on his hand, and he told me all about it. He said that there were a couple of places where he didn't have any skin pigment and it was no big deal. My gut told me I should change the topic and forget about what she was saying, but this was too weird, and I wasn't going to let my mom off the hook.

"Spotted? Like a cow?" I said that just to tease her, to make her explain again. I glanced at my brother, and we exchanged grins.

"Yes, like a cow," she said, and her tone suggested that she was glad we finally understood. Then I heard a laugh, a big, loud laugh. It could only have come from my father.

"Spotted children? Like a cow?" He was laughing so hard it was hard for him to keep control of the car.

That was it. I couldn't keep it in, and I laughed, too, and then so did my brother.

"Like a lucky gumball," my father said, between laughs.

My mother became haughty and adjusted her clothes, as if that would show us.

"What's a lucky gumball?" I asked.

"They used to have speckled gumballs in the gum machine, and if you got one you could trade it in for a prize."

My mother wasn't going to give up. "I don't care what you say, I've seen them." There was an air of superiority in her voice.

"Mom, those are people who have pigmentation loss," I explained. "It's called vitiligo."

My father decided it was time to be more serious. "Dorothy, Detlef is right. Mixed children don't turn out sp-sp—" he again began to laugh, "—speckled." He managed to finish his sentence before bursting into laughter.

From then on, this became a running gag in our family. Spotted cows, spotted shirts, Neapolitan ice cream—anything where colors were mixed—now became an opportunity to revisit the topic.

My mother chose to revisit the topic on her own terms. One evening, when my dad wasn't around, she made it a point to tell me that mixed couples had it bad because they couldn't live in the White neighborhood, and they couldn't live in the Black neighborhood.

"And what about the children? They're neither Black nor White. Where are they supposed to live?"

What about the children? Stephon Johnson didn't seem to have any trouble. Hell, the other students accepted him better than they accepted me, but then again, he was a pretty good shortstop and could safely hit any pitch that was even close to the strike zone.

So my mother's warning did not have much of an effect. Some of the Black girls at our school were very pretty, and I was going to be attracted to them no matter what my mom said.

One girl, Clarissa, was tall and willowy, and always carried two or three library books. She didn't say a lot, but from her few words I could tell that she was intelligent and well-spoken. She would raise her hand

219

only as a last resort, only when the teacher had asked a question that no one else could answer. Quietly, with eloquence, she would answer the question with not a hint of boastfulness. She never looked at me or noticed me or talked to me, but, then again, she never seemed to look at anybody else, either. She was in a world of her own, and that only made her more attractive.

About once a week, Clarissa wore a pink fleece dress with white and yellow flowers. It was a pretty dress, and it made her seem even taller, more slender, more graceful. Since she wore it so often, I supposed it was her favorite dress, but after a while I noticed that it was threadbare, almost to the point of being shabby, and I wondered if her family had much money.

Weekends were spent in Sterling Township, getting things ready for the new church, but it wasn't until the day of our first church service that I actually visited the elementary school which was to temporarily house our church and would most likely be the school I attended once we moved to Sterling Township.

It was nothing like Pulaski. Pulaski's playground was just a gravel lot, but the new school had swings and teeter-totters and monkey bars. The building was a light brown brick. Every classroom had a door to the outside, but there were no doors on the lockers or the classrooms, and except for the gymnasium, all of the rooms were centered around the library, which they called the Resource Center.

Just like Pulaski, the gymnasium could be converted into a lunchroom, but in Sterling Township it also served as a makeshift auditorium. There was a stage that ran the length of the room, and it had a piano, an American flag, a low table, and a lectern.

It occurred to me that having church in a gymnasium might be fun, and I was going to make the best of it.

"Detlef! Slow down!" my father commanded.

220

In the Bethlehem church, my father forbade us from running around the church because we were, in his words, "in a sanctuary, not a gymnasium." This time I would catch him in his own logic.

"But this is a gymnasium, not a sanctuary!" I protested.

"Not this morning. This morning it is a sanctuary."

I was going to argue, but I seemed to remember Jesus saying something about a church being any place where a couple of people are gathered in His name, so I guess my dad had me on a technicality.

My dad did his best to cobble a sanctuary out of a few relics left over from the Bethlehem church. He threw an altar cloth over a table he borrowed from the resource center, followed by a cross, two candles in brass holders, and a couple of collection plates.

I helped the janitor set up folding chairs, and after that we put hymnals, also left over from the Bethlehem church, on each of the chairs.

My dad joked with the janitor. He said that he didn't know if anybody was going to show up, and it was a good thing he was wearing a robe because it would hide his knocking knees.

About a hundred people, mostly young couples, did show up. Except for being in a gymnasium, it seemed just like the church services at Fort Street or Bethlehem, and for the first time I thought this church might work out after all.

So that's how our life went. Weekends at one school in Sterling Township, and weekdays in another school in Detroit. Miss Stinson was my new homeroom teacher. She was younger and prettier than Miss Houk, but still seemed to preach the party line.

"I've noticed that many of you haven't taken the time to make new friends this year. I think it's wonderful that you treasure your old friends, and I certainly can't tell you what to do when you're outside of the classroom, but I've made a new seating chart and I'm going to mix things up a bit."

Some of the kids rolled their eyes, and some of us froze in terror. A new seating chart was almost always a form of punishment, and it usually meant...

"And since there is a little too much socialization in the classroom, I'll be seating you boy-girl-boy-girl."

I pretended to be upset but hoped for the best. Leslie Shane ended up in front of me. She was kind of cute, but had never taken notice of me and wouldn't take the time to turn around and look at me unless I was on fire. But by a great stroke of luck, Clarissa ended up behind me.

Sitting in front of a girl that you like is a dicey situation. If you turn around to talk to her it's almost like admitting that you like her, so for the first few days I pretended like she wasn't there. It probably would have stayed like that, but I got an itch in my back that I just couldn't reach, and Clarissa must have known it because I felt her long nails rubbing against my shirt.

"Did I get it?" she asked.

I turned around and she was smiling. "I think so," I said, and then instantly regretted it. I should have told her that it still itched so she'd keep scratching.

The next day I got to class before she did, and instead of just walking past me she smiled and said "hello." After that we became friends, and even sat by each other when the whole school went down to the auditorium to see a magician. I expected the other kids to tease us or to call me a "nigger lover," but nobody said anything. Nobody teased me or hinted that Clarissa might be my girlfriend.

The only person who seemed to notice was Miss Klingenschmidt. During the assembly, I pretended to know how the magic tricks worked, and Clarissa pretended to believe my explanations. Miss

222

Klingenschmidt normally responded to talkers by making them sit apart or at least telling them to be quiet, but she just smiled.

"You know, I can do some magic tricks, too," I bragged as we left the auditorium. I did my "disappearing penny" trick, and she seemed to like it, although she was not overwhelmed to the point where she confessed her undying love, as I hoped she might.

By now my family was going to Sterling Township at least twice a week. Thursday night was choir practice, but we always went early so my dad could check on the new house that was being built for us on Charwood Street, not too far from the elementary school where the church was meeting.

Choir practice was held in the old farmhouse. My dad dragged along the old black and white television that had accompanied us to Chicago, and on a good night we could get a clear picture and watch Batman, but on that Thursday night all three stations just had a bunch of newsmen, and I knew something was wrong.

I thought maybe the president had been shot, but it turned out to be a Black guy whose name I didn't recognize. Still, it was on all three channels, and he was a minister, so I thought I'd better interrupt choir practice and tell my dad.

"Dad, some Martin King guy has been killed."

My dad was rattled. I didn't expect that. I thought he might be mad, or not care at all, or maybe something in between.

The next day at school I wasn't sure what to say to Clarissa. It seemed strange to say something, but it also seemed strange to say nothing. I thought maybe she would say something, but she didn't, and we never spoke about it.

That afternoon in homeroom, Miss Stinson talked about Dr. King. Like cancer and polio and Viet Nam, it seemed that everybody else except me knew all about him.

She told us all about how he won the Nobel Prize and acted like anybody who hadn't heard of him was either a moron or had been living in cave.

I didn't buy it. Weeks earlier, when we had to write reports on famous Americans, she gave us a list of names, and it was people like Davy Crockett and Thomas Edison. Up until this point, she had never indicated that there had been any famous or important Negroes, and I wondered how many others there were who had been just as important but who hadn't been shot.

When I got home, my dad was in the basement sorting through boxes of junk. We were going to be moving in a few months, and he was trying to get a head start on the packing.

"Dad, how come my teachers didn't tell me anything about Dr. King until he was dead?"

"I don't know. They probably should have."

"And it seems like a lot of the good guys get killed."

"Like who?"

"Like everybody. Abraham Lincoln, Jesus, President Kennedy…"

"And now Dr. King."

"Yes."

"So what are you saying?"

"It's like my bicycle. Any time you get your hopes up, some asshole comes along and messes things up."

"I think I've got something for you."

He snatched me up and tossed me over his shoulder. I thought I was getting too big for that, but he didn't seem to have trouble carrying me up the stairs. He carried me into his bedroom, dropped me onto the bed, and then went over to his dresser.

On his dresser was a little cloth-covered box that held cuff links and tie clips. He pawed through the box for a few seconds, mumbling and possibly swearing, then finally called out, "Aha! Here it is!"

"Okay, close your eyes and open your hand," he commanded. When I did as I was told, he placed something very small and very light into the palm of my hand.

"Okay, open your eyes."

In the middle of my hand was a rectangular tin lapel pin. It wasn't one of the nice ones which actually had a pin on the back, but a cheap one that had a tab that folded over. It was white, and had red letters that spelled a single word: Kennedy. My heart sank.

"But he's dead," I moaned.

"Not President Kennedy. Senator Kennedy. Do you know who he is?"

"You mean Bobby Kennedy?"

"That's right. And before that he was Attorney General for the United States. And now he's running for president."

"What's the Attorney General?"

"That's kind of like the nation's top policeman."

"Did he arrest any bad guys?"

"Well, he prosecuted a lot of union leaders and racketeers."

"You mean like gangsters?"

"Yup."

"But wasn't he afraid?"

"He sure didn't seem to be. He was like a bulldog. They called him 'Ruthlesss Robert,' but I think he was more like 'Relentless Robert.' And now you've got a hero who isn't dead. How do you like that?"

"But what if somebody shoots him?"

"Nobody's gonna shoot Bobby Kennedy. If they were going to, they would have done it when he was going after Jimmy Hoffa."

I thought about it for a while. "Okay."

"Let me put this on your pocket."

"No! I'll lose it! Put it on my sport coat."

"Okay, go get it."

I ran upstairs to my bedroom and got my Sunday sport coat. When I got back, my dad attached the pin to the hole in the lapel of my sport coat.

"I'm pressing it down real hard so it won't fall out."

"Did Robert Kennedy win the Nobel Peace Prize?"

"No, but he has some of the same beliefs as Dr. King. When somebody dies or gets killed, usually there's another person to carry on where he left off."

The following week, my dad accompanied my mom to parent-teacher conferences. I loved having the day off, especially since I was able to spend it with Mrs. Ballenger. She knew how to have a good time. Other adults might have tried to get me to play board games or play catch or something horrible like that, but Mrs. Ballenger let me help her paint the hall closet. She didn't want me to get any paint on my clothes, even though they were play clothes, so she found one of her husband's old shirts and had me put it on backwards and then buttoned it up the back.

When I was finished she cleaned me up and sent me home. As I neared our house, I could see my dad's new car, a blue Ford Galaxy 500, parked in front of our house, and I knew my parents were home.

Even before I opened the side door I could hear them arguing, so I carefully turned the knob and slipped in as quietly as I could, closing the door behind me. I peeked around the corner and saw them fighting in the dining room.

"She called him a little ambassador," my father shouted. "What's wrong with that?"

"I don't care if he gets along with the colored boys," my mother shouted back. "I just don't want any speckled grandchildren."

226

"Good God, they're in fifth grade. What do you think is going to happen?"

"It's the first step on the wrong road."

"So what are you going to do about it? You know what Tom DiPaolo said. If we keep pressuring the kid he's going to end up as a basket case."

I heard enough and I started to leave, but I was in too much of a hurry and my dad noticed the sudden movement.

"Hey, Sport, I didn't see you come in," my father said in the calmest voice he could conjure up.

"This is about me, isn't it?"

"I warned you to stay away from colored girls," my mother reprimanded.

"Dorothy, don't make this about him!" my father commanded. "No, Son, your mother and I don't see eye-to-eye, but you haven't done anything wrong." He glared at my mother. "He hasn't. Now there's nothing wrong about having friends of any kind, and there's nothing wrong with looking at a pretty girl."

My mother huffed, but my dad wouldn't back down. "Isn't that right, Dorothy?"

"I guess so. Take that Diana Ross. She's very attractive for a colored girl, so I guess I can see…" That was all my mom could spit out, and if it was supposed to make me feel better, it didn't. Why did she have to be attractive "for a colored girl?" Why couldn't she just be attractive?

The next day, when I went to school, Clarissa acted strange. I wasn't sure if it was my imagination or if her parents had given her a good talkin' to, but even though she was polite to me and said "hello" once in a while, she never scratched my back or voluntarily sat next to me again. In gym class, when the girls had to pick partners for square dancing, she chose a kid from her old school.

On June fifth, my brother woke up early and turned on the television, just like he wasn't supposed to. When the portable television wasn't in Chicago or at choir practice, we were allowed to keep it in our room under the condition that we wouldn't abuse the privilege. That was the official explanation, but my mom didn't really care when we watched television as long as it kept us occupied and out of her way. I could hear it click on, but I didn't pay attention. Unlike my brother, I preferred a few additional minutes of sleep.

There was no sleeping in this morning. My brother grabbed my shoulder and shook me.

"Detlef! Wake up. Kennedy's been shot!"

"That was four years ago. Let me sleep!"

"No, Bobby Kennedy's been shot."

I bolted up in bed. "Dad! Mom! Come here!"

My brother punched me in the arm. "Good going, asshole. Now I'm going to get in trouble for watching TV."

I was still rubbing my arm when my parents came in the room.

"What's wrong?" my father asked. I was afraid he'd be mad for violating our agreement that I wouldn't wake him with my irrational fears, but he didn't seem too upset.

"Bobby Kennedy's been shot!" my brother announced. He seemed especially pleased with himself, as if he enjoyed spreading bad news.

"Was he killed?" my dad asked.

I hadn't thought of that. Maybe they only winged him.

"No, but it doesn't look too good. He got shot in the brain, and even if he lives he's going to be a retard." My brother had a gift for making bad news sound even worse. "They caught the guy that did it," he added.

"What difference does that make?" I demanded.

My father was wise enough not to give me some phony answer, but he had to say something. "Not much, but I suppose it would have been worse if he got away."

I was in no mood to be comforted, so I pushed past my father and went downstairs to the living room. Once I got there I wasn't sure what to do, so I started plinking out the Westminster Chimes tune on the piano. "Oh Lord Our God, Be Thou our guide…"

My father crept down the stairs, but I pretended not to see him.

"Hey, Sport, are you okay?" he asked.

"I'm fine." I replied, and kept on playing. "And by Thy power, no foot shall slide."

"Mr. Craddock told me that the Westminster Abbey celebrated its nine hundredth anniversary last year. Of course, the current building wasn't there back then. They didn't start work on that until the thirteenth century."

My father seemed confused.

"That's not how we do it in America," I explained. "We think churches are like flashlight batteries. You use 'em for a little while and you throw 'em away."

"You mean like the Bethlehem church?" he asked.

"And Fort Street," I added. "But it isn't just the churches. It's whole parts of town. If we don't like it we just burn it down or move away."

"Son, you saw what happened when Mr. Craddock tried to stay."

"And it's the people, too. If you don't like somebody, just throw 'em away. Shoot 'em in the head and toss them out."

"It's okay to be upset. I'm upset, too."

My mother broke in. "Well, your teachers are going to be upset if you're late for school. It's time for you to eat your breakfast."

I looked to my dad for support, but he gave me a look that said, "You might as well do what she says."

For the next couple of days it was all anybody could talk about. Senator Kennedy died the next day. My teachers said it was all for the best, that he would have been a vegetable even if he had lived, but I wasn't sure how that was supposed to make me feel any better.

Clarissa looked at me like she wanted to say something, but she didn't. I wondered which bothered her more, the death of Dr. King or the death of Bobby Kennedy. Even if we had been on talking terms, it wasn't the kind of thing you could ask.

On Saturday, the same day they buried Bobby Kennedy, they caught the guy who killed Dr. King. I wondered where he was from. If it turned out to be that he was a Southerner my teachers would say that was why he killed Dr. King. If it turned out to be that he was from the North they'd come up with some other line of crap, like he was from a broken home or something like that.

The next day was Sunday, and as I was getting ready for church, I noticed the little tin tag on my coat.

"Dad, can I still wear this, or do I have to take it off?"

"You can leave it on."

"But he's dead."

"You can wear it in his memory."

I left it on, but only because it would have seemed disrespectful to take it off.

"A lot of people were killed during World War II, like it was a dying time, but then it seems like there was a time when a lot of people were born,"

"That's right. They called it the Baby Boom."

"Well, now it seems like a lot of people are dying, but maybe it will end soon. Maybe when we get to Sterling Heights we'll be around younger people, and there won't be so much death."

"Maybe."

"You know Dad, it seems like there's a time when people are born, and then a time when people die, and then maybe the whole thing starts over. What do you think?"

"I think that's very Ecclesiastical, Son."

I wasn't sure what that meant, but I hoped it meant that we could enjoy Sterling Heights while its batteries were still fresh.

CHAPTER 22

After school got out for the summer, packing up boxes was our main focus. The attic was full of junk and my mom and dad spent a lot of time going through old stuff. I liked it a lot because the entrance to the attic was a doorway right off my bedroom and I got to watch all of the action. Sometimes my dad would find something that he thought I'd like and give it to me. I got a couple of little magic tricks, a set of teeth that clacked when you wound them up, and some old coins that he brought back from the Philippines.

My mother was pretty good at finding things for me too, but they were always boring, like an old itchy wool sweater that she thought I might grow into. Mostly she was working in the kitchen, packing things so they wouldn't be broken during the move. My job was to ball up newspaper to take up the extra space in the boxes, but I kept doing it wrong.

"Honey, this isn't tight enough. I've got my good CorningWare in this box. We can't afford to make a mistake."

After about an hour of that, I decided to see if my father needed help packing up the workshop.

Helping my father pack up his workshop was a lot of fun. He had a hard time staying on task, and often stopped to show me how this tool worked or tell me how he happened to pick up that one. I was more than happy to encourage his off-track behavior, and I actively led him astray every time I found an interesting tool.

"What's this for?"

"That's a spindle gouge. You use it for turning wood."

"Turning wood?"

My father stopped what he was doing and dug through his scrap box until he found a slender scrap of wood, and mounted it in his lathe. He flipped the switch and the wood started spinning.

"That's why they call it turning wood," I announced.

He moved the gouge into the block and it bounced up and down on the edge of the block.

"To everything, turn, turn, turn," I sang.

My father groaned. "Good Lord, not that again!"

He shut off the lathe. What had once been a square piece of wood was now roundish, but still didn't look like much of anything.

"That reminds me," I said. "I think I've figured out the third one."

"The third what?" my father asked warily. He threw the wood into the scrap box and rummaged through a pile of old tools.

"The third 'turn.' Remember?"

"I guess not."

"Sure you do. 'Sometimes you have to turn the other cheek, sometimes you have to turn over the tables...'"

"Oh, yeah."

"Well, I came up with the third one. 'Sometimes you have to turn tail and run.'"

My father stopped working and got very serious. "Where on Earth did you get that idea?"

"From you, Dad."

"I don't remember teaching you that."

"Sure. Like now. Things got bad in Detroit so we're running away to the suburbs."

"It's a little more complicated than that." He tried to get back to work. He spread a thick layer of oil on an old pair of pliers, and then he wiped it off with a rag.

"Or when we were in Chicago. We tried to get my bike back, but we couldn't. So we just gave up."

"Sometimes discretion is the better part of valor," he said, trying to focus on cleaning up the pliers.

"What does that mean?"

"It means that sometimes you have to use your head and accept that there are battles that aren't worth fighting." He dropped the pliers on the workbench, wiped his hands with the rag, and threw the rag in the trash.

"Oh, I get it. You have to turn the other cheek, even if you get walked on once in a while?"

"For God's sake Son, I never said that you had to let people walk on you."

"So we just let the guy have the bike because he was poor, and it would be easier for us to buy a new one?"

My father rubbed his head, and I wished that I had never brought the whole thing up.

"No, that's not it. Rich or poor really has nothing to do with it. You have to have the same rules for everybody. Let me show you something."

My dad pulled a cardboard box from a shelf underneath the stairs.

"Do you know what's in this box?"

I looked inside. It was a bunch of junk.

"I don't know. Car parts?"

"Son, this is a treasure chest. See this—it's the hubcap from the first car I ever owned. And here's the key to the apartment your mother and I rented when we were first married. This union pin belonged to my father."

I didn't get it.

"Here's what I'm looking for." He held up a rather unremarkable piece of black plastic.

234

"What's that?" I asked, using a tone that indicated I seriously doubted his hunk of plastic could convince me of anything.

"That is a trophy."

"You could have fooled me."

"A few years ago I got stuck directing traffic for the State Fair. Have you been to the fairgrounds?"

"Sure."

"Do remember the entrance? At Woodward and State Fair? You know how there's a median?"

"Yes."

"Well, you couldn't park in the median. Anyhow, this guy parks in the median, and I blow my whistle and tell him he has to move. Then some of the other guys say to me, 'That's Barry Gordy from Motown Records.' And I said, 'I don't care who he is, he's not allowed to park in the median.' So I called him to come back and move his car, but he just kept walking and ignored me. I wasn't going to give him any special privileges because he was rich, but I wasn't going to cut him any slack just because he was Black."

"So what happened?"

"Well, I couldn't chase after him, so after he left I popped open the hood of his car and I unscrewed the distributor cap, and then I threw it as far as I could."

"What's the distributor cap?"

"It sends electricity to the spark plugs, and if you remove it, the car doesn't run."

"But wasn't that wrong?"

"It sure didn't feel wrong at the time. He disrespected the law and he disrespected me as a human being, and I felt that I had to do something."

"But—"

"Anyhow, as I was walking back at the end of the shift, I found the distributor cap."

I could see where this was going. God had guided my father to the distributor cap, and my father thought better of his acts and undid his sin. I excitedly finished the story for him.

"And you felt guilty and you put the distributor cap back in the car!"

"Son, don't you know what you've got in your hand?"

I could tell by my dad's expression that I had missed the point. "This is Barry Gordy's distributor cap?"

"Yeah."

"But didn't we let those people walk on us in Chicago?"

"No. We didn't let them. We did what we could. It's just that, well, in life you don't win every battle. Anyhow, we're going to fix up the new bike, and that's going to give us another chance to spend time together."

He didn't get it. The distributor cap was special, and if it got lost or stolen you couldn't just replace it with any other. Couldn't he see it was the same way with my bike?

"Dad?"

"What?" he sighed.

I looked into his eyes, and I could see that he was out of stories. Nothing he could say was going to make me feel any better, so maybe it was my turn to do the right thing. "Thanks for making me feel better," I said, trying to make it sound like I meant it.

"Sure," he blankly replied.

CHAPTER 23

One Friday afternoon, when I got home from school, I found my mother in her bedroom packing a suitcase.

"What's going on?"

"I'm going away for a couple of days." She was in an especially good mood, and I felt cheated. If she wanted to take off for a while, she should have done it when she was in a crappy mood.

"Away?" That was strange. The only time my mother went anywhere by herself was a year ago when she took the train to Ohio for her cousin Adeline's funeral, and I was pretty sure that was a one time thing.

"Yes, to a ministers' wives' retreat."

She scurried to the bathroom to pack her medicine bag. Besides the usual toiletries, my mother always brought an assortment of pills, potions, and prescription medicine to cover virtually any medical emergency. Her most prized remedies were the unused portions of prescription medicine, which she doled out according to her vague recollections of what ailment the medicine had been prescribed to cure.

"What's a ministers' wives' retreat?" I asked.

"I really don't know. I've never been on one before. But I'm going to meet a lot of other ministers' wives and there are going to be activities and crafts and worship services."

She vainly tried to fit one last bottle of prescription pills in her box, and when it didn't fit, she opened it up and dumped its contents into another bottle.

"I'll just have to remember that the white diarrhea pills are on the top and the cold capsules are on the bottom."

I knew she would never remember, and this would just add one more layer of confusion to her alleged system. She forced the lid shut, walked back to her bedroom, and then turned back to add one more comment.

"And don't worry. You'll be fine. Your father will take care of you."

Yes he would. We always got the best food when Dad was in charge. He wasn't much of a chef, and on the few occasions when he tried to cook it never turned out well. On Mother's Day he tried to make my mom breakfast in bed and prepared scrambled eggs. Instead of being yellow and fluffy, the eggs were gray and mealy, and my brother refused to eat them because they looked like uncooked Aunt Jemima pancake batter.

But the best part about my dad's cooking was how easily he was discouraged. He might start out cooking a meal or two, but it wouldn't take him long to buckle and then we'd be eating sub sandwiches or pizza or Kentucky Fried Chicken and drinking pop right from the bottle. We wouldn't even use paper plates. Dad would just set a roll of paper towels on the table along with whatever carry-out food he'd carried in and let nature take its course. The only rule was that we had to clean up when we were finished, but since there were no plates or forks or pots or pans, cleaning up was more like throwing things in the trash.

This time my dad dispensed with any pretense of civilization and we had pizza the very first night. My mom usually ordered a fourteen-inch pizza and doled out the slices, but even though there were only three of us he ordered sixteen-incher and let us eat all we wanted. In fact, he insisted that we gorge ourselves so there wouldn't be any leftovers.

Since he'd allowed us to act like a poorly organized group of Huns during dinner, I thought for sure we'd be able to stay up late and watch television, but as soon as we were done eating, he told us to clean up and go to bed.

"This is way too early!" my brother protested.

"We've got a big day tomorrow, so we need to get off to an early start."

"Are we going somewhere?

"Yup, but it's a surprise." My dad was finished with the conversation, and was already shutting off lights. My brother, realizing that he could not win the argument, hit me in the shoulder.

"Come on. You heard what Dad said. We've got to go to bed."

It seemed like we had just fallen asleep when my father came in to wake us up. He rushed us through breakfast, which was just cereal and milk. Instead of a big box, Dad bought a Kellogg's Variety Pack of single-serving boxes. The small boxes served as disposable bowls, and since we were using plastic spoons there was, once again, nothing to wash.

"We usually get bananas with our cereal," my brother complained.

"Geez, is there anything you don't gripe about?" my father replied.

We threw our boxes in the trash and dad put the milk in the fridge, and once the table was wiped we were ready to go, at least as far as my dad was concerned. My brother was still fooling around with his shoes so my dad scooped him off the couch and threw him over his shoulder.

"You can put your shoes on in the car," he said.

I knew that it must be something special. Maybe we were going to the circus or to Greenfield Village, or maybe even to Silverstein's, but the trip turned out to be a big letdown. Instead of heading out on a highway or major road, we just wandered down the same streets we traveled every Saturday, and to my great disappointment, the car ended up parked in front of Oma's house.

"Oma's? That's where we're going?" my brother asked. My dad reached over and whacked the back of his head.

"What did I tell you about griping? Your cousins from Muskegon are going to be there. Don't you want to see Tammy and Becky and Frankie?"

Seeing the Muskegonites was pretty special, but something still seemed odd. My dad was a little too hurried, and he looked like he was thinking really hard about something else. My brother must have been suspicious, too, because he didn't let my dad off the hook.

"How are they going to get all of the way from Muskegon this early in the morning?"

"They came last night. And later today Charlotte is going to be there, and maybe even Albert and Jimmy."

My brother seemed satisfied, but I smelled a rat. "What about you?" I asked.

"I've got to take care of a little business," he mumbled.

"Isn't that what you said yesterday?" I asked, being careful not to use a tone that would get me whacked in the back of the head.

"That was Downtown Detroit business. This is other business."

My dad shuffled us out of the car in a hurry, said something in German to his mother, kissed her good-bye, and then drove off. He went about halfway down the block, turned the car around, and came back. He had barely rolled to a stop when he threw the passenger door open.

"Detlef! Get in the car!"

"I thought I was going to stay here," I said as I scrambled into the front seat.

"I changed my mind. You're coming with me. You can keep me company."

Even before I had my door fully closed, my dad was pulling away.

"Where are we going?" I dared to ask.

"You'll see when we get there."

I tried to stay awake and keep him company, but I dozed off after a couple of minutes. After what seemed like a long time, I woke up to a terrible smell, like the worst industrial pollution I had ever smelled. It seemed oddly familiar. I couldn't quite remember where I had smelled it before, but wherever it was, I figured I must be there again.

I moved a little bit and I found that my dad had put his jacket over me. I took that to mean that it was okay for me to sleep, and I dozed off again and didn't wake up for a long time.

"Detlef! Wake up. We're almost there!" My dad was pushing on my shoulder. I sat up and tried to get my bearings, but everything looked strange.

"Where are we?"

"Chicago," he said mysteriously.

"Chicago?"

"Yeah. Well, Evanston, actually."

I looked around for our apartment building, but all I could see were a bunch of houses. The car stopped.

"This is the place, right?"

I didn't see what he was talking about, but then he placed the palm of his hand on my head and turned it around. It was Eddie's house.

"I thought you might like to get your bicycle back," he said.

"But the policeman said—"

"Yeah, well, I've had a chance to think about that. Maybe he wasn't right after all."

241

"Mom isn't going to like this."

"Mom isn't going to know until it's all over, and then what can she do? Make me take it back?"

I knew this was a bad idea, even worse than the coffin trick. By now Eddie was probably attached to the bike, and he was even less likely to give it up, and we'd both be arrested for stealing.

"I don't want the bike anymore. Let's just go back to Detroit," I pleaded.

He didn't seem to hear me. "Okay, the garage door is closed, but it doesn't look like it's locked."

"But what if they call the police?"

"Let 'em."

"Because by then we'll be long gone!"

"Oh, no we won't. Wait in the car."

Waiting in the car was the only part of the plan that made sense. Yes, I decided that I was in a special category of people who best serve humanity by waiting in the car. When the policeman came to arrest my dad, I would say, "Officer, I had nothing to do with it. I was waiting in the car."

My dad bounded to the garage and threw the door open. The bike was buried under a pile of garden tools, but he noisily threw them aside and snatched the bike with one hand. He stood in front of the garage for a second, and then slammed the door shut. What was he thinking? With all of the crashing of tools and slamming of doors somebody was bound to hear us.

My dad walked over to the car, but instead of throwing the bike in the trunk and driving off, he just leaned on the door. He knocked on my window and I unrolled it.

"What do you think?" he asked. Even though he was talking to me, he kept an eye on the house.

"I think they didn't take very good care of my bike. The paint is all scratched."

242

"Who cares? We painted it once. We can paint it again. What color do you want this time?"

"How about black?"

My dad reached through the window and honked the horn. A couple of minutes later, Eddie's dad came out the front door. It was already early afternoon, but he looked like he had just crawled out of bed. Of course, that was assuming he slept in a greasy t-shirt and pair of ragged jeans, which seemed pretty likely.

"What are you doing here?" he demanded.

"I just wanted you to know that I'm taking my son's bike back," my dad said in a friendly voice. "It would be awful if you found it missing and didn't know where it was." Despite my dad's friendly tone, I could tell he was taunting Eddie's father.

"You ain't taking that bike nowhere!"

Eddie's father took a couple of steps toward my dad, but my dad glared at him, and Eddie's dad wilted.

"I'm gonna call the cops," Eddie's dad threatened.

"Go ahead," my dad said, without the least bit of concern in his voice.

"I got your license number," Eddie's father croaked, shaking his finger all the while.

"That's okay."

I got out of the car and stood next to my dad. I figured he might want some company in jail.

I thought my dad might be mad at me for disobeying his directive, but he seemed like he forgot all about telling me to stay in the car. He reached into his pocket and pulled out a rectangular package. "Hey Detlef, do you want some gum?"

In a few minutes a young policeman pulled up in a squad car. He looked like an athlete and had a brush cut, so I was pretty sure he wasn't going to cut my dad any slack.

"What's going on here?" he demanded.

"This guy stole my son's bike and I'm taking it back."

"Can you prove that it belongs to your son?"

"It's licensed to him. Take a look at this." He pulled a folded paper from his pocket and gave it to the officer.

"I don't see no license on that bike," cried Eddie's father.

I hadn't noticed, but he was right. The license had been removed. How could my dad have been so foolish?

Eddie's father had that same mean smile as last time, but my dad didn't seem worried. He took out his car keys and scratched some of the paint off the frame of the bike.

"Cut that out! That's private property!" Eddie's father yelped.

My dad pointed to the place he'd been scraping. "That's the serial number. Why don't you see if it matches the registration?"

Eddie's father stopped smiling. My father and the policeman spoke quietly. I couldn't hear most of what they were saying, but then they both laughed and started speaking in normal tones.

The policeman still seemed a little confused. "I can't believe you drove all the way from Detroit just to get this old bike. There's got to be more to this story. Truthfully, what did that guy ever do to you?"

"He took my son's bicycle."

The policeman smiled knowingly. "Do you want to press charges?"

"No, I'm just happy to get the bike."

My dad opened the trunk, and I could see what looked like the handlebars of another bike. He pulled out my other bike, the one I didn't like.

"Son, do you think we'll be needing this any more?"

"Nope!"

244

"Officer, give this bike to that guy. Tell him that he and his son can fix it up, and he can make it look just like this one."

The officer shook his head. "Mister, I don't know if you're the most forgiving guy on the planet or the most vindictive son-of-a-bitch I've ever met."

My dad smiled and threw my bike in the trunk. "I guess it all depends on how he takes it. If he thinks it's a gift, then he and his son will have a great time fixing it up. If not, then I don't want to be around to see what happens."

My dad slammed the trunk shut, shook hands with the policeman, got in the car, and drove off.

"What do you think is going to happen?" I asked.

"Don't look back, Son," he said, turning my head forward. "I don't know how I'd explain it to your mother if you turned into a pillar of salt."

EPILOGUE

The rest of the trip was great. We stopped by Colonel Sanders and bought some chicken, which we ate in a park right in downtown Chicago. For a long time after that we didn't talk at all, and then we talked about a bunch of nothing, and finally we talked about what had happened.

"Dad, I thought you were going to be a new person after you became a minister. More forgiving or something."

"I thought about that. I finally decided that being a good Christian doesn't mean you let some asshole steal your son's bicycle."

"Just because I got my bike back, it doesn't mean that everything is right with the world."

"No, but just because somebody steals your bike it doesn't mean that everything is wrong with the world. There are billions of people on this planet. What makes you think that your life is the one example of what is right or wrong with the whole planet? Spaceships aren't going to land in our yard, and God isn't going to choose Detlef Niebaum as the one definitive—"

"Yeah, yeah, I get the idea."

"And just because you've been through a rough patch doesn't mean that you get all of the wings!"

"Okay, sometimes you turn over the tables at the temple, sometimes you turn the other cheek..." I looked to my dad for help.

"And sometimes you turn back to Chicago and, uh... Ah, I got nuthin'"

"I need an answer!" I demanded.

"Yeah, but you don't need it today. You've got your whole life to figure things out."

"You're just saying that because you don't have an answer."

"Maybe. But if you can stop worrying about the Eternal Truth for a while, I'll let you have the last wing."

"Okay."

Sometimes you have to turn the other cheek. Sometimes you have to turn over the tables at the temple. And sometimes you have to stop worrying about things and settle for the last chicken wing.

16129857R00134

Made in the USA
Lexington, KY
06 July 2012